Red Diamonds

Frank Lazorishak

Red Diamonds is a work of fiction. Names, characters, places, and incidents are either the product of the author's imagination, or are used fictitiously. Any resemblance to actual persons, living or dead, or to events, or locales is entirely coincidental.

Cover by Rick Holland: MyVisionPress.com

ISBN-13: 978-1532819391
ISBN-10: 1532819390

DEDICATION

To Debbie, the love of my life, my best friend,
and my number one fan.

ACKNOWLEDGEMENTS

My heartfelt thanks go to my two beta readers, copy editors, critics -- and friends:

Amy Henderson and Barb Inserra

PROLOG

Peter Bradovich's great-grandfather, Metodyj, was one of the most renowned jewelry makers in the Russian Empire. In the winter of 1917, he was summoned to the Hermitage in Saint Petersburg.

There had been no explanation of why he had been summoned, but it really didn't matter. When summoned by the Tsar, you went.

Metodyj entered the Great Hall in the Hermitage. Tsar Nicholas and his wife Alexandra sat on the raised dais. Several Metropolitans stood nearby. He bowed deeply and was nudged forward. Tsar Nicholas and Alexandra stood. Alexandra motioned him to come forward. Nicholas slowly moved forward until he was facing her; she was awesome – beautiful - regal. Nicholas stood next to her; he had his hand on the hilt of his *shashka.* Alexandra told him to hold out his right hand, palm up. He was terrified, but he did as he was ordered. To do otherwise was to die.

Alexandra placed a huge red diamond in his hand. He was awestruck. The diamond must have weighed fifty carats; it was flawless. The diamond was the deepest red he had ever seen – it was the color of a pigeon blood ruby, but it was a diamond – a magnificent Peruzzi-cut diamond. It took his breath away. He could feel warmth it had captured from Alexandra.

Alexandra told him to hold out his left hand. He was nearly in a trance; he didn't move. She said it again and Nicholas slid the first six inches of his *shashka* from its scabbard. The sound of the *shashka* sliding from its scabbard brought him out of his trance, and he held out his left hand. Alexandra placed six smaller light red, Mazarin-cut diamonds in his left hand. He stood there dumbfounded. He didn't know what he was supposed to do. It was chilly in the Great Hall, but drops of sweat ran down his cheeks.

Alexandra smiled at him and spoke. Her orders to Metodyj: "Create for me the most magnificent necklace ever seen."

***

Metodyj was housed in a small apartment on the top floor of the Hermitage. There was a workbench and jeweler's tools better than any he had ever seen. He was given anything he needed – all he had to do was ask. Alexandra stopped in when the mood struck her. Sometimes he would see her and her pretenders several times in a day. Sometimes he would be left alone for several days. He was treated magnificently. But he was restless. He missed his family. He wished he could share the apartment with his wife.

Designing and fabricating Alexandra's necklace could take a year or more. Metodyj pleaded with Alexandra to be allowed to go home to his family. His homeland was in the middle of a war not of their making. Two foreign armies faced each other in his beloved mountains. The villages and pastures of the Carpathian Mountains were the killing fields, and his people were the cannon fodder. He could not concentrate on the necklace while his family, a thousand miles away, was in danger.

Early in 1918, Alexandra allowed Metodyj to take the diamonds and return to his family home in the village of Velykyi Bereznyi. The village, nestled on the north slopes of the Carpathian Mountains, had been his family's home for many generations. His people called themselves the Rusyn; they were a small but distinct ethnic group. Their homeland had been ruled by the Polish kings for centuries, but as Poland disintegrated in the eighteenth century, the Rusyn lands fell under the control of the Austro-Hungarian Empire. In the early days of World War One, Tsar Nicholas's armies rolled into the Carpathian Mountains, and the Rusyn found themselves a part of the rapidly expanding Russian Empire. It seemed to Metodyj that the Poles and the Austrians and the Hungarians and now the Russians had been fighting over his homeland forever. But his village, and his people, survived. He was thankful to be going home to his family.

When he traveled home, Metodyj was accompanied – and guarded – by a detachment of Nicholas's elite palace guard, the Preobrazhensky Regiment. They would stay with him until he returned the finished necklace to Alexandra.

***

On July 17, 1918, the Bolsheviks murdered Alexandra, Nicholas, and their entire family. When word of the revolution reached the village of Velykyi Bereznyi, the Preobrazhensky Regiment disappeared.

Metodyj secreted the diamonds in a carefully devised hiding place. He spent the rest of his life waiting for the Bolsheviks to appear at his doorstep and demand that he return Alexandra's red diamonds. They never did…

As the war between the Red Army and the White Russians approached his village, Metodyj realized that he might well die before the war was over. He devised a plan to put the red diamonds beyond the grasp of the Bolsheviks. Though his two sons, Oleksandr and Mitri, could never escape from the Russian Empire with the diamonds, they might escape with the location of their hiding place. After the war, and hopefully after the end of the Bolsheviks, they could return and reclaim the red diamonds. The gold he had been given to fabricate the necklace would make his family wealthy! The diamonds themselves were beyond price.

To prevent one son alone from being arrested and tortured to reveal the hiding place, Metodyj made each son memorize half of the directions to the hiding place. He sent them on their way to the United States. They were to meet at the home of their cousin, Fedor, in a city called Pueblo, in the province of Colorado, USA, and wait for peace to return to Velykyi Bereznyi. Then they could formulate a plan to bring the treasure -- and perhaps their parents -- to America.

Metodyj's plan had many uncertainties. He arranged for each son to take a different route to America. Oleksandr was to go north through Saint Petersburg, Finland, and then on to America. Mitri was to go south to Italy, England and America. Both were given instructions on what to do if they could not complete their journey. They were to write down their half of the directions, hide the directions wherever they were, and send the location of the directions to cousin Fedor.

This way, either Oleksandr and Mitri, or their halves of the directions, would be reunited in Pueblo. Should either brother fail, and should Metodyj not survive the war, the red diamonds would be lost forever, but at least they would not wind up in the hands of the Bolsheviks.

PART ONE:

THE PLAN

CHAPTER 1

Uncle John is dead. He died four days before his one hundredth birthday. I will miss Uncle John.

I loved to hear the stories from his childhood, first in Colorado, and then in Pennsylvania. I enjoyed hearing the tales of the battles between him and his stepmother. Battles that finally resulted in him leaving home at fourteen and "riding the rails" across the country. And he made sure that you knew he was a hobo, not a bum. Hobos worked for their meals and lodging – bums did not!

He could talk for hours about enlisting in the Army and fighting the Nazis in North Africa and Italy. I was never sure if his tales were fact or fiction, but it didn't really matter. They were just plain fun.

As he got older, he started to repeat himself a lot, and it was a challenge to mine for new bits of information buried in all of the repeated stuff. But it was worth it. He was the last of his generation – the oldest surviving Bradovich. He was my last connection to my ancestors. He lived a long and eventful life. He once told me, "Life doesn't just happen – you have to work at it."

He worked at it for ninety-nine years. Ninety-nine is an educated guess – he had no Birth Certificate. There were no state records in those days and all of the old Pueblo, Colorado, records were destroyed in a flood in the nineteen twenties.

Now he is gone. And I will miss him. But I do not look forward to, as the new de facto family patriarch, disposing of his personal effects. He built his own home in Clark, Pennsylvania, after the Great War. And *he* built it. He dug the foundation by hand. He made the cement blocks himself. He constructed the block walls himself. He cut the floor joists and the wall studs and the roof rafters by hand. *He* built his home. And then he proceeded to spend sixty years filling it with memorabilia.

Uncle John had no direct descendants; he had been married and widowed twice, but he never fathered any children. He had few living blood relatives. But he did leave a will.

I called Uncle John's longtime attorney, Michael Bianco, shortly after his death. He has helped me navigate through the process of dealing with what Uncle John left behind. The will was short, and very like Uncle John. It said that if my sister Beth, my brother George, or I would live in the house, we would be bequeathed the title to the property after one year. Beth is an attorney in Columbus – she's not interested in moving to western Pennsylvania. George lives about a half hour from Clark -- he might have considered living there, but his wife vetoed the idea. (And I don't blame her; Uncle John's house needs a lot of work.) I live in Ohio on the Lake Erie shore during the summer and in Key Largo during the winter – I have no desire to complicate life with a third home.

Uncle John's will went on to say that if none of us moved into his house, it and all of its contents were to be sold at auction. According to the will, my siblings and I had one month to remove any of Uncle John's possessions that we wanted to keep as mementos. I was named executor, and I was given three months from his death to have the auction. The proceeds of the auction were to be split three ways: Beth, George, and me.

It looked like I was going to be spending some time in Clark cleaning up and organizing sixty years' worth of stuff. Uncle John wasn't a hoarder like those shown on reality TV; he had traveled and hunted and fished all over the world and he had just amassed a lot of – stuff. The stuff was my problem now.

CHAPTER 2

It's a bright, cold Saturday morning, and I'm off to Clark, Pennsylvania. Clark has a population of 633. There is nowhere to stay in Clark, Pennsylvania. Well, that's not exactly true. There is an Inn called Antebellum House in Clark. It was once the home of a rather strange and rather wealthy citizen who decided to model his new residence overlooking Shenango Lake on his idea of what an antebellum plantation "big house" looked like. He didn't do a very good job – and neither did the group of investors who bought it from his estate and tried to make it into a country inn.

Our old and dear friends, Sue and Ted live in Youngstown, Ohio. I'll stay with them tonight. They are almost an hour away from Clark, so if dealing with Uncle John's stuff takes a lot of time, I may look for a motel closer to Clark. But tonight I'll make the drive to Sue and Ted's. It'll be nice to be with friends after what looks to be a very long day.

* * *

As I pull into the gravel drive, Uncle John's home looks the same as it did the last time I was here – about a year ago. And it looked the same then as it has looked for as long as I can remember. The fruit trees have gotten bigger, and the white stucco has gotten grayer, but nothing else has changed much. The house sits in the middle of a five-acre plot overlooking Shenango Lake. It's a one story home with a hip roof and an attached one car garage. It's small by today's standards; my guess is about 1200 square feet. It's not worth much, and it's not going to be easy to sell. I'm glad that Bianco has offered to find a local real estate agent to peddle it.

Bianco left the key to the front door in a lock box. I open the front door and stand there for a minute. Just looking into the dim interior. Uncle John's only been dead for a week, but the house already has an unlived in look – and smell – about it.

I go in, turn on some lights, and open some windows. It's a cool morning and the furnace is running. I find the thermostat, and turn off the furnace; I'd rather have fresh air than heat. I make a note on the yellow legal pad I brought with me to ask Bianco what to do about the utilities.

Where to start? Wow. This is more than a little daunting -- a house full of stuff. I think I need to contact an auctioneer to find out what they want me to do, to prepare for them to have a household goods auction. I wonder if Riemold Brothers from Transfer, Pa, are still doing auctions. The brothers were nearly my Dad's age – they'd be in their eighties now. Probably not them, but maybe their sons. I think I remember some sons about my age. Bianco will know – another item to add to my list.

For today, I'll just wander around, see what's what, and maybe mark a few things that I want to keep. It'll be very few, though.

The front door opens directly into the living room. No front foyer to act as a buffer between inside and outside; no closet in which to hang outer garments. I guess in the forties when Uncle John built this place, they didn't design such features into homes. I doubt that he had an architect do the plans. I wonder where he got the plans. I wonder if he even had plans...

On the wall opposite the door is his collection of fish. Stuffed trout and bass and muskies and perch and other fish I can't identify. Some are starting to show their age. I guess I'll have to take one or two to remember him by. I'm not sure what Kate will think of that; I'll find out when I get home.

The real trophies are out in his den, in the nineteen-sixties vintage outbuilding he built when his second wife wanted the trophies evicted from *her* living room. The outbuilding houses a two car garage, his office, and his den. He called it a den, but it's really more of a trophy room. There are stuffed heads of all kinds of North American animals from squirrels and weasels to deer and elk and moose. I remember my youngest son, Devin, standing there in awe when at about age five, he first saw them. I won't even ask Kate about taking one of them home. Well, maybe I will. But that's a job for another day.

As I turn my attention from the fish-wall toward the fireplace to the right, I see the big picture of the grand opening of the Western Reserve Outdoorsmen's Club Rifle Range. They named it after Uncle John in honor of his many years of service to the organization. On the other side of the fireplace is a photo of Uncle John at age ten in his Boy Scout Uniform, and next to that, a framed Boy's Life clipping, and a Lifesaving Award Certificate signed by James West, the first Chief Scout Executive in the United States. The clipping tells the story of how ten-year-old John Bradovich dived into the icy waters of the Shenango River and saved his eight-year-old brother, Peter. Peter, my father, had fallen off of a railroad bridge and crashed through the ice on the river below.

Yes, Uncle John had tales to tell.

CHAPTER 3

The rest of the main floor won't hold as many treasures as the living room.

To the left of the front door is the doorway to the dining room. The only item of interest here is the map of North America fastened to the wall. Marked on it with magic markers of various colors are the routes Uncle John took on hunting and fishing journeys. The lines cover much of the continent -- from Key West in the south, to Wyoming in the middle to Alaska in the north.

I asked Uncle John once if he ever thought about going to Africa after really big game. His answer: "Maybe when I've seen everything I want to see on this continent." I guess he just ran out of time.

Off the dining room are the other rooms in the house. There is one bedroom – sparsely decorated, and with the bed made military style. There is a single bath – last refurbished about 1947. There is a galley style kitchen – with a built-in wooden booth where he ate most of his meals. And there is the entrance to the steep staircase going down to the basement – where the real treasures lie.

Down in the basement is his workshop. Uncle John worked in the steel mills all his life. But he was also a gunsmith. He specialized in turning surplus military rifles like the German eight millimeter FN Mauser into sporting rifles. He would completely disassemble them, turn the barrels down on his lathe, remove all the extra weight, re-blue the steel parts, and hand-carve new stocks out of exotic wood. The resulting weapons were masterpieces of quality workmanship. He had customers come to him from all over the United States; and perhaps the world.

He told me that his earnings at the mill kept him and his dogs -- and his wives – housed and fed and clothed. His gunsmithing allowed him to have all the guns he wanted, and to travel the continent hunting and fishing.

* * *

As I go down the narrow staircase, I see a typically cluttered open basement area on the left, and a concrete block wall on the right. The wall has two steel doors set in it. One leads to the furnace room, and one leads to the workshop. The workshop door is closed and locked, but I am one of the few people he showed where he hid the key.

I retrieve the key, unlock the door and enter Uncle John's workshop. I've never been in here alone. To the best of my knowledge, neither has anyone else. He was very protective of his shop. The silence is almost eerie.

The workshop is about fifteen by twenty; 300 square feet crammed full of power and hand tools of all sorts, racks of bins holding all sorts of bits and pieces of hardware, and a few guns in various states of construction or repair. The shop is crowded, but neat. The customers he brought down here were always impressed by his almost fanatical neatness; everything had a place, and everything was in its place. But what was not in the shop, what few people ever saw, was Uncle John's personal collection of guns.

If you study the basement carefully, you realize that the geometry doesn't quite add up. If you go into the furnace room and turn left, you run into a wall in about two feet. If you go into the workshop and turn right, you run into a wall in about six feet. But the doors are fourteen feet apart. There's about six feet unaccounted for between furnace room and shop.

What I'm about to do reminds me of the old monster movies I watched as a kid. Uncle John has an honest-to-God secret room in his basement. In the shop, the wall that faces the furnace room is covered in brown peg board on which many of his hand tools hang. I move the drill press and pedestal grinder away from the wall. The section of peg board behind them is mostly empty, but on the right side is a row of hammers, hanging according to size. Below the hammers is one empty pegboard hook. I turn it ninety degrees counterclockwise and pull. The pegboard section swings open and reveals Uncle John's secret gun room.

The secret gun room is about six feet by twenty feet and is crammed full of guns and ammunition. Hanging on the wall opposite the secret door are dozens of long guns. There are shotguns. There are a few muzzleloaders. There are military rifles. And there are sporting rifles. Some are factory made, but many are handmade. On the wall opposite the long guns are hand guns of many different types. And there are racks of plastic bins holding ammunition of many different types. This room is a private arsenal.

I have no idea how I'm going to deal with this arsenal. I doubt that Beth or George will want anything. I may keep one or two guns to pass on to my sons, but that's all.

Uncle John's will states that his belongings are to be sold at auction, but I don't think that I can do that with his arsenal. I know that there are all sorts of state and federal regulations governing the sale of firearms. You can't just sell them on eBay! I suspect that I'll have to sell them through a dealer. But I'm way out of my depth here. My oldest son, Mike, may have some ideas on how to deal with this. Mike is a U.S. Marshal. He lives in Parker, Colorado; I'll have to give him a call.

On the six foot wall furthest from the secret door is a leather upholstered chair, a small side table, and a floor lamp. There is what looks like a very old Persian rug on the floor in front of the chair. Uncle John's little retreat? I decide to sit for a minute. As I step on the rug, I hear a hollow sound. The floor is gray painted concrete. But the rug sounds like there is a steel plate under it.

I squat down to move the rug. It doesn't want to move. I take a closer look and discover that it is attached to the floor with strips of Velcro. I peel it loose. As I suspected, underneath is a steel plate. It's about two feet square with two finger holes in the middle. I lift the plate up. And I'm looking at the door of a safe.

The safe looks old. He probably installed it when he built this house after World War Two. It doesn't look particularly fancy. The door has a dial with markings along the edge. And it has a handle that probably turns after you dial in the combination. I have no idea of what the combination might be.

CHAPTER 4

Okay. How do I open the safe? I doubt seriously that there is much of value in it, but I can't be sure. I have to look.

Question: Where would Uncle John keep the combination? Answer: He wouldn't keep the combination anywhere. He's been using this safe for sixty years. He knew the combination as well as he knew his name.

I think I need a locksmith. There's a basic-black, land-line phone in the shop and a Sharpsville phone book underneath it. I look up locksmiths in the yellow pages and find that I have a choice of three. I choose "Joe the Locksmith" because he has the biggest ad. I call and Joe answers. Joe sounds about half as old as the safe. I explain the situation and describe the safe. Joe says safes were really well built in those days, and opening it could be expensive. I ask how expensive. He says $250 if he has to drill it. I tell him I'd like to do it today, if possible, and give him the directions to Uncle John's house. Joe says he's on his way, and that he'll be here in a half hour. I close up Uncle John's Arsenal and go upstairs to wait.

* * *

Joe shows up in a well-used Chevy Astro van. Joe is even younger that he sounded on the phone – maybe mid-twenties. I ask him about his being "Licensed & Bonded" as it says on the side of his truck. He shows me his driver's license and his state license card. I don't know why, but I'm a little hesitant. Joe looks a little ill at ease, too. Then he asks if this is my house. I tell him no, and explain about Uncle John dying and me being executor of his will. He says that before he opens anything, he has to verify that I am "legal." Good point. It seems that we're at an impasse. I ask him if Clark has a police force; he says not really, and suggests that we call the Pennsylvania State Police.

I call 911, explain that this is not an emergency, and ask to be connected to the nearest State Police barracks. The operator gives me the number of the State Police barracks in Mercer. I call and get a dispatcher. I explain to him that I am the executor of my uncle's will, and that I need to have a locksmith open a safe in his home. I give him the address. He says he will send a trooper out; that he'll be here within a half hour. Joe and I sit on Uncle John's porch and wait.

* * *

The state trooper arrives in about fifteen minutes. He gets out of his cruiser, walks up to the porch, introduces himself as Sergeant Lewis, and asks to see some identification from each of us. We both give him our Driver's Licenses. He looks at them, sets them on an empty chair on the porch, photographs them with his cell phone, and hands them back to us. He asks why I requested that he come. I explain that this is my late uncle's house, that I'm the executer of his will, and that I found a safe in the basement that I need to have Joe open. The trooper asks if I have any papers that verify this; I say no, and suggest that he call Uncle John's attorney, Michael Bianco, in Sharpsville.

He goes back to his cruiser. I can see him on his radio; then his cell phone; then his radio again. He gets out of the cruiser and walks back to the porch. He looks at me and says, "Attorney Bianco verified your story and said that as executor, you have the same powers as a property owner." He turns to Joe and says, "Go crack his safe." He turns to go and I stop him. "Officer, if you don't mind, I would like you to come down to the basement with us and see the location of the safe." He looks at me, but before he can say anything I add, "I *really* would like you to come downstairs and see the room the safe is in. It's important. I think you'll understand when you see it." He shrugs and says, "Okay, let's do it."

We go into the house and down the narrow stairs. The steel door to the shop is closed, but not locked. I open the door and ask them to step into the shop. They both look a little skeptical. I explain that Uncle John was a gunsmith, and a very good one. The State Trooper looks pointedly at his watch, and says, "So where is this safe?"

I ask them to step into the shop farther. I don't say anything else. I move the drill press and pedestal grinder away from the wall. I turn the empty pegboard hook, and pull the door open. From where they are standing, they both can see the racks of rifles in the gun room. It's a true Kodak moment. They both just stand there with their mouths slightly open. I give them a moment, and then I say, "In here," and walk into the room. They follow me in without saying anything. I give them a minute to look around, and then I begin.

"As far as I know, besides the three of us, only my wife and my brother know that this room exists. This is, for lack of a better term, Uncle John's Arsenal. My late uncle, John Bradovich, has been making and selling guns like these for over fifty years. He not only made them, he used them. He has hunted for big game all over North America. He is listed in the Boone and Crockett Club annals for several trophy animals. His "den" in the outbuilding at the end of the drive has dozens of his stuffed animals, and mounted fish decorate the living room walls. He was a lifetime member and longtime supporter of the Western Reserve Conservation Club down by Shenango Lake; in fact, they named the Rifle Range in his honor.

"Before I leave tonight, I am going to take extensive photos of this room, and start a detailed inventory of the firearms. But I can't possibly remove everything tonight. I will move them to a secure location as soon as possible. The reason I asked you to come down Sergeant Lewis, is because I would like to ask the State Police to keep an eye on this property. I know that homes of deceased people are sometimes burglarized. I'm told that ambitious thieves watch the newspaper obituaries to find targets. I don't think any of us want these firearms stolen."

Joe the Locksmith is looking at the guns with great interest. I ask him what he thinks. He says, "I've been a hunter all my life. Like any sportsman, I have a few guns. But I've never seen anything like this."

"I know what you mean. My oldest son is a U.S. Marshal. I am going to ask him to come and help me with these. Uncle John's will states that all his belongings be sold at auction, but I don't think that will work with these."

When I said "U. S. Marshal," Sergeant Lewis's head snapped around. "Your son is a U. S. Marshal?"

"That is right, Sergeant. He works out of the Denver Field Office, but I am sure he will be able to fly out to help me with this."

"May I suggest that when he gets into town, he call Captain Enwright at Troop D Headquarters in Butler? I think it's important that we work together to make sure that these firearms are transferred in accordance with both federal and state regulations."

"I will be sure that happens, Sergeant. Joe let's look at the safe."

"While you're looking at the safe, I want to take a few pictures. You were very wise to ask me to come down here, sir."

"Peter. Please. And yeah, I thought it might be a good idea. The safe is under the little rug in front of that chair, Joe."

* * *

Joe the Locksmith goes into locksmith mode. He lifts the rug, then lifts the steel plate. He takes a small high intensity light out of his tool bag, plugs it in and aims it at the dial. Then he plugs a stethoscope into his ears and squats down in front of the safe. He has his back to us and his body blocks our view of what he is doing; I think he planned it that way. After about three minutes, he stands up, removes the stethoscope, stretches, and walks over to me.

"It's like I thought. Figure an hour."

"That long, huh. They always do it very quickly on TV."

"That's on TV. A safe this old will have the door made of two layers of sheet steel with concrete in between to make drilling or cutting harder. You understand that drilling will ruin the safe?"

"I just need to get it open."

"Okay. I just wanted to make sure you understood. I'll go get my tools."

"And I've got to leave," interjects Sergeant Lewis. "Please make sure your son calls." He hands me his business card.

"Will do. And thank you."

"We'll keep an eye on the place."

"Please make a note that Nora, the woman who lives next door, has a key. She used to keep an eye on Uncle John. I will stop over and warn her that the State Police will be keeping an eye on the place. I suspect that word will get around the neighborhood."

"That'll probably be good. And good luck with the safe."

* * *

About forty-five very noisy minutes later, Joe stands up, groans, leans back down into the hole in the floor and comes back up with the door to the safe in his hands. "That's it!"

CHAPTER 5

I write a check to Joe the Locksmith. As I'm walking him up the stairs, I say, "I assume that 'Bonded and Insured' also includes discrete."

"What do you mean?"

"As I told Sergeant Lewis, you are one of five people who know that Uncle John's Arsenal exists. I want to keep it that way."

"Oh. Sure. No problem."

We get to his Astro van. I thank him. We shake hands. He gets into the van, makes a U-turn, and heads down the driveway.

I watch him go. I'm already thinking about digging into the safe.

I go over to my GMC Yukon, get a couple of Banker's Boxes I brought, and head back downstairs.

* * *

I sit down on the floor next to the now lidless safe. The first things I see are a bank night deposit bag and a zippered bank currency bag. I take these out and set them aside. Now I see a half a dozen file folders and several 9 by 12 manila envelopes, all standing on edge. Before I check out the paperwork, I take another look at the bank bags.

The night deposit bag has a lock, but it's not locked. I open it and find several personal checks from people I never heard of made out to John Bradovich, and a small amount of cash. There is a deposit slip with all the checks and cash itemized and totaled. Seven hundred twenty-six dollars and twelve cents total. The deposit slip is dated the day before Uncle John died.

The zipper currency bag turns out to be very much more interesting. It contains crisp new hundred dollar bills – a hundred of them. Ten thousand dollars in cash. I have no idea why Uncle John kept this much cash in his safe. He had a bank account with what Attorney Bianco said were reasonable balances. I think that this stash of Benjamins will not be inventoried – no point in complicating things -- $3300 for George, $3300 for Beth, and $3300 for me will work just fine. I'll put the extra $100 in the next charity collection container I see.

Well, that was a pleasant surprise. Now, on to the paperwork. I take out all of the folders and envelopes. There is nothing else in the safe. I get up, go out into the workshop, clear off a space on the workbench, stack up the envelopes and folders, pull up a steel stool, and dig in.

The manila folders are first. Each folder has a hand lettered label like HOUSE or TRUCK or WARRANTIES or TAXES, and each contains documents pertaining to the label. Nothing exciting; certainly nothing as exciting as the $10,000.

The envelopes are next. Some of them look old; I start with what is the newest looking one. It's well used, and it has TROPHIES printed on the front; I open the flap and look inside – photos. I dump them out on the workbench – there are about two dozen photos of all sorts of American big game animals; some just of dead animals hanging from trees, some with Uncle John; some with other men; all of them with legends on the back stating animal type, date, location, and hunter. I saw some photo albums upstairs. These must have been photos that Uncle John thought were special; I'll never know why.

The next envelope is labeled FAMILY, and it contains very old photos of people dressed in early nineteen-hundreds attire. None are labeled; I recognize a few of the people; most I do not. I wonder who they are; there is nobody left to ask -- pity.

The label on the next envelope is WWII. More photos of people and places that will be lost to obscurity. A few old coins; a few European banknotes. Several embroidered cloth patches; the kind that adorn military uniforms; these are obviously of Nazi origin. I know that during World War II, Uncle John fought in North Africa and Italy. I assume that these are a few souvenirs that he collected.

The next envelope is labeled STAMPS; odd. It contains dozens of very old postage stamps with most still affixed to a piece of an envelope. I wonder why he was saving these. These should be passed on to someone in the family, not auctioned off. A lot of this stuff should be.

The last envelope, and obviously the oldest, has the label RED D; the label means nothing to me; Red D? I open the flap and slide out the contents, a smaller and very old sealed white envelope with a phrase written on it in what appears to be Cyrillic: *червоних діамантів.*

CHAPTER 6

The white envelope is about eight by ten with the flap on the shorter side. I try to carefully peel the flap open. That's not going to work. The glue is old and very tenacious. I get a razor sharp utility knife from one of the work bench shelves, and carefully slit the envelope along the side with the flap. If Uncle John thought that this was important enough to keep in his safe, I need to be careful. I slide out the contents.

It's some sort of packet of documents. There are several sheets of heavy paper a little smaller than our standard eight and a half by eleven sheets. They were once white, but now they're a little yellow. The sheets are folded in half and act as a wrapper for several other pieces of paper that appear to be tri-folded. I remove the tri-folded stuff, set it aside, and look at the outer sheets. They are a hand printed letter – the letter is dated "September 1st, 1924," and the salutation is, "My Dearest Ivan." The printing is very small and badly faded, but it's readable. The third page ends with a phrase in what looks to be Cyrillic – *Будьте здорові* -- and the name "Fedor." I think Fedor was my grandfather's cousin. He lived in Pueblo, Colorado, where my father was born. And I think I remember that the old people called Uncle John, "Ivan." Do I remember that John is English for Ivan? I'll come back to the letter; I want to see what else is here.

I unfold the first tri-fold; three more pieces of paper. It's the same kind of paper as the letter, and like the letter, it is covered with fading, but readable, small printing. It looks like the printing was done by the person who did the first letter. Fedor, I assume. At the top is the title "OLEKSANDR." Oleksandr was my grandfather. This gets curiouser and curiouser.

The next trifold is four sheets of paper. The first two sheets are identical to the others; same size and type; same printing, but page one is titled "MITRI." The next two sheets are completely different. They are very thin, almost tissue paper. It reminds me of what we used to use for air mail letters when I was young. Yes, we wrote and mailed actual letters. This sheet has been folded and unfolded many times; it is covered with printing in a different language; I think it's more Cyrillic. Could the first and second sheets be a translation of the third and fourth sheets?

The last item is thicker than the others. And it is bigger; about twice as big. It's a hand-drawn map. It shows a small village, a river or stream, some mountains, and a line from one of the buildings in the village up into the mountains. The village is labeled *Великий Березний*, and there are several notes on the map in the same language. Somehow, this language doesn't quite look like Cyrillic – but it's close.

I have no idea of what this stuff is all about. Why did Uncle John think it important enough to keep it locked up in his safe? The cover letter is dated 1924. He has kept this package of documents locked away for almost a hundred years. I pause for a minute and try to remember if Uncle John or my father ever mentioned anything that might be related to this stuff...

Nothing. I definitely never heard anything about letters or a map from my ancestors. My father never said anything that might have even suggested something like this. Uncle John was a man of few words, unless it was about guns and hunting or tackle and fishing. He did not like to talk about his early life at all. I think it might have been painful.

A hundred years? This really sounds clichéd, but it feels like something out of my childhood readings. Robert Louis Stevenson. A map to buried treasure. Yeah, right.

It's getting late, and I have a long drive to Youngstown. I'd better get Uncle John's Arsenal secured and get out of here.

I doubt that I've got a treasure map, but the guns are definitely a treasure. They have got to be worth a lot of money. I don't know what to do with them. I don't know what they're worth. I know you can't sell guns on eBay. Sell to a dealer? Can I auction them off with everything else? Do I remember some gun auction sites on the Internet? I definitely need help on this one; I hope Mike has some ideas.

CHAPTER 7

It's late afternoon, Denver time. Mike just might be in the office. I call the Denver Office of the U.S. Marshals Service.

"U.S. Marshal Service, how may I direct your call?"

"Is Marshal Mike Bradovich in? This is his father."

"Yes, sir, he's in the office today. One moment, please."

Five minutes of elevator music...

"Hi, Dad. Sorry to keep you waiting. I was down at the indoor range poking holes in paper bad guys."

"No big deal. I know you're busy. I will get right to the point. I am calling about Uncle John..."

"Dad, I'm sorry I couldn't stay longer when I was there for his funeral. I was actually flying from Berlin to Denver, and managed to do a re-route & long stopover in Pittsburgh."

"It meant a lot that you were able to get there at all. Come back when you can stay a little longer. And bring Lauri. Anyway, I am the executor of Uncle John's will. I think I need your help."

"My help? How?"

"I will keep it brief. Uncle John had a secret gun room in his basement. I am calling it Uncle John's Arsenal. I counted fifteen hand guns, eight shotguns, twenty-seven rifles, five hand grenades of various kinds, a few bayonets and swords, lots of hand loaded ammunition, and various other lethal odds and ends. I showed the room to the Pennsylvania State Police, and they are a little concerned."

"Well, I guess. It always kind of surprised me that there were no guns visible whenever we visited him. Now I know why. Who knew about this room?"

"Just Kate and me. Maybe George, but I don't think so. And now Joe the Locksmith from Sharpsville. I had to bring him in to drill a safe mounted in the floor of the gun room. As executor, I've got to deal with his arsenal now, and I don't even know where to start. When I realized what I had here, I immediately thought of you. You're the gun guy."

"A safe in the floor?"

I make a quick decision *not* to tell him about the contents of the safe. At least not right now. "Yeah. But that is another story. Let's talk about the guns right now."

"So what has to happen with them?"

"His will says that Beth, George, and I can take anything we want to keep as mementos, and then everything else, including the house and land, gets auctioned off. The three of us will split the proceeds of the auction. I don't think Beth and George would object to us keeping a couple of the guns, but I am not sure; I will have to ask them.

"The big question is, 'How do I dispose of the guns we don't want to keep?' I don't think I want to auction the guns off as part of a regular household goods auction, but..."

"You definitely do not want to do that. The long guns could be sold at auction, but you'll do better by selling them to a dealer who knows their worth. The handguns are a whole different can of worms. They can only be sold by going through somebody with an FFL."

"FFL?"

"Federal Firearms License; a dealer. I think the first thing we do is inventory everything. Then we get an appraiser in. Then, depending on what we have, we contact some dealers, and maybe some wholesalers."

"You keep saying 'we.'"

"Well, yeah. You said you needed help. And you told me to come back when I could stay longer. And to bring Lauri. Well, this looks like the perfect time."

"You're sounding like you're planning to come now. Can you do that?"

"I just need to shuffle my schedule a little. I'm sure Lauri can do the same. Give us tomorrow to figure it all out. I'll get back to you tomorrow night."

"That is great. And completely unexpected. Plan on staying with Kate and me. It is a long drive to Clark, Pa, but Kate will demand that you stay at the Lakehouse with us."

"Good enough, Dad. I'll talk to you tomorrow night, your time. I've got to go kill more paper bad guys now."

"'Kill some for me. Bye, son."

"Bye, Dad."

CHAPTER 8

I need coffee before I head for Youngstown. There's a little restaurant about a quarter mile from Uncle John's place. I put everything except the outer pages back into the white envelope, close the door to the gun room, lock the house, and look around -- half expecting bad guys to jump out of the bushes and demand the guns *and* the treasure map.

I definitely need coffee.

In five minutes, I'm sitting in an old and somewhat uncomfortable wooden booth in Rudy's Righteous Restaurant. I am not kidding – that is its name. And I think Rudy himself served me. He certainly looks "Righteous." He's a leftover from the seventies: ponytail, jeans, tee shirt advertising some group I never heard of, and a somewhat unrighteous and sort of white apron.

Okay. Back to the letter – the outer document in the package – the letter written in 1924 to what had to be a very young Ivan (Uncle John?) by a quite old Fedor (my grandfather's cousin?). This is hundred-year-old paper; it won't take much handling. First order of business tomorrow is to make good copies of all these pages and quit handling them. Reading the letter is a challenge. It's badly faded; the printing is somewhat crude; the English in places is poor, but the content is utterly amazing. I think I need to call it unbelievable. There is no reason to believe that the content is fictitious. But it simply can't be true...

The letter tells the story of Fedor's uncle. His name was Metodyj, and he lived in the village of Velykyi Bereznyi on the northern slopes of the Carpathian Mountains. I think the Carpathian Mountains are in southwestern Poland or southeastern Ukraine now. Could that be the village shown on the map -- *Великий Березний*?

Anyway, it seems that, according to Fedor, Uncle Metodyj was a jewelry maker – a renowned jewelry maker – a world renowned jewelry maker -- jewelry maker to Alexandra, the wife of Tsar Nicholas II, the last Tsar of Russia!

And it gets even more amazing. It seems that Alexandra summoned Metodyj to the Hermitage in Petrograd, now Saint Petersburg. She gave him some priceless red diamonds, and instructed him to, "Create for me the most magnificent necklace ever seen." The key diamond was a fifty carat blood-red diamond, the likes of which had never been seen before. Designing and fabricating the necklace could take a year or more.

Metodyj spent several months at the Hermitage, but when war between the armies of the Tsar and the Austro-Hungarian Empire threatened his village, he was allowed to return home – accompanied by a detachment of the Tsar's palace guard.

The story goes on. While Uncle Metodyj was creating Alexandra's necklace, the Russian Revolution happened! The Tsar and his entire family were murdered by the Bolsheviks, and Metodyj was left holding the bag – the bag of diamonds!

Fedor describes the bag of diamonds as it was described to him by Metodyj's son. There was over 250 zolotnik of pure gold. I kind of want to question that amount; I looked up zolotnik on Safari and 250 zolotnik translates to something like 35 ounces – over two pounds of gold. But I guess that's no more unlikely than Metodyj's estimate of the main red diamond; fifty carats would make it ten times larger than the Moussaieff, the largest red diamond now in existence. There were six smaller red diamonds, about ten carats each, but they seemed almost trivial compared to the red diamond.

I've read the letter about four times, and every time it sounds more unbelievable.

Fedor's letter goes on. With the death of the Tsar, the detachment guarding Metodyj and the diamonds disappeared. Their boss was dead and unless they disappeared quickly, they would soon be dead as well. Metodyj spent the rest of his life waiting for the Bolsheviks to show up at his door and demand the return of Alexandra's diamonds. But they never did, and as time passed, he devised a plan to keep the diamonds out of the hands of the Bolsheviks. He hid the diamonds in the hills outside the village. He swore that he would die before he disclosed their location to the Bolsheviks.

Metodyj knew that his two sons, Oleksandr and Mitri, could never escape from the new Russia with the diamonds; but they might escape with the location of their hiding place. After the war, and hopefully after the end of the Bolsheviks, they could return and reclaim the red diamonds. The gold he had been given to fabricate the necklace would make his family fabulously wealthy! The diamonds themselves were beyond price.

To prevent one son alone from being arrested and tortured to reveal the hiding place, Metodyj made each son memorize half of the directions to the hiding place. He sold a small portion of Alexandra's gold, went to the nearby town of Przemysl, and bought his sons steamship tickets. He sent them on their way to America by different routes. Oleksandr was to go north through Saint Petersburg, to Finland, to England, and from there on to America. Mitri was to go south to Italy, across Europe, and to America.

They were to meet at the home of their father's nephew, Fedor, in Pueblo, Colorado, and wait for peace to return to Velykyi Bereznyi. Then they could formulate a plan to bring the treasure -- and perhaps their parents -- to America. Metodyj's plan had many uncertainties. He gave Oleksandr and Mitri instructions on what to do if they could not complete their journey. They were to write down their half of the directions, hide the directions wherever they were, and send the location of the directions to cousin Fedor in Colorado.

Here comes the finale: Mitri never made it to the United States. He died in Venice, but he drew a map, hid it in a Venetian cemetery, and mailed the location to cousin Fedor.

And Oleksandr? Oleksandr made it to Colorado. He got a job at the Colorado Fuel and Iron Company, Pueblo's biggest industry. He met a young woman named Julia who had emigrated from the city of Przemysl, very near to his home village. They were married in the Archangel Michael Orthodox Church, and bought a modest home near the mill. Oleksandr became very active in the governance of the church. For a while he even considered becoming a priest. He never went back to the old country, but he and Julia prospered in their new country. They had two sons, Ivan and Fedor. Then tragedy struck: Julia died of influenza during the great epidemic of 1921. Oleksandr was crushed. His life spiraled downward into alcoholic despair, and he took his boys to live with a cousin in Sharon, Pennsylvania. When he died, cousin Frank and his wife Anna raised the boys. The boys were named Ivan and Fedor, but as they grew up, they took American names – John and Frank – they were my uncle and my father.

The letter ends with a list of the contents of the white envelope that Uncle Ivan/John guarded all his life. There is a letter from Fedor that tells the story of Oleksandr, and of his trip to the United States. And there is the map that Oleksandr drew from memory; it is the first half of the directions to the hiding place of the red diamonds. Lastly, there is the letter from Mitri with an English translation by Fedor; it tells of Mitri's travels, of his illness, and of where in Venice he hid his half of the map.

CHAPTER 9

After reading Fedor's letter about Metodyj, I decide to go back to the house and get the rest of the contents of the white envelope. I can't wait 'til tomorrow. I pay Rudy for the coffee, and go back to the house. I unlock the house, go downstairs, unlock the door to the workshop, move the drill press and bench grinder, open the door to Uncle John's Arsenal, go in, find the manila envelope labeled RED D, turn to leave the workshop -- and stop.

I go back in and grab the bank zipper currency bag and its $10,000. No point in taking any chances.

I turn to leave again – and stop again. I'm looking at the wall full of handguns. I take down a Kimber Model 1911 forty-five. I get a box of shells from one of the drawers. I tuck the Kimber under my belt in the small of my back and leave. I don't know why I'm taking the gun. It's very unlike me.

I reverse my steps back to Rudy's. When Rudy looks up from sorting silverware, and sees me come back in with a manila envelope, he says, "More paperwork, huh? More coffee?"

I shake my head yes and go right back where I was sitting before. Rudy hasn't gotten rid of my cup from before, so I move things out of my way, and take the white envelope out of the manila envelope. I leave the bank zipper currency bag and its contents in the manila envelope and set it on the seat beside me.

Rudy brings me a fresh cup of not too fresh coffee. I find the trifold with the heading Oleksandr, and put everything else back in the manila envelope.

* * *

Oleksandr – my grandfather. This letter is his story: as told to and transcribed by Fedor. I suspect this story was the result of many hours of comparing immigration stories over many glasses of Vodka.

Oleksandr's father, Metodyj, had bought him a steamship ticket from Turku in Finland to Hull in England, and another from Liverpool in England to New York City. When he went to Przemysl to buy the steamship tickets, he also visited a money changer. He gave Oleksandr small amounts of markkas and pounds, and a larger amount of dollars for his land journeys in Finland, England, and America. His mother sewed these into secret pockets in the lining of his coat. He could remove each as he needed it, and he prayed he could keep the others safe until he needed them. Metodyj went over and over the details of the land voyages that Oleksandr would have to make until he believed that he had a good chance to succeed in making the very long trip to Pueblo, Colorado, America.

Finally, Oleksandr said goodbye to his mother and his brother Mitri, and went with his father to the train station. They bought him a second class ticket to Saint Petersburg. He hugged his father one last time, kissed him on both cheeks, and got on the train. He knew he would never see his homeland again. He prayed he would see his brother Mitri again – in Pueblo.

The train ride to Saint Petersburg was long, but uneventful. Oleksandr made his way from the train station, across the Neva River, and to the port on the Gulf of Finland. He bought a ticket on the overnight ferry to Helsinki, and spent the day wandering the streets of Saint Petersburg.

In the evening, after a very suspicious customs agent examined his papers and his belongings, Oleksandr boarded the ferry. He found his way to his berth and slept until the noise and jolts of landing in Helsinki woke him. He got off the ferry into a cold and gray new country. The Finnish customs officer didn't even look at his papers. He just waved him through the gate and onto the street.

Oleksandr had removed his Finnish markka from their hiding place in his coat lining before he left the ferry. He found a little food and some hot tea at a sidewalk vendor, and asked directions to the train station. He and the vendor had no common language, but after many hand gestures and choo-choo sounds, he was pointed in the right direction. He bought a train ticket to Turku, the port where he would board the steamship for England. It was only a hundred miles to Turku, but it took most of the day on the local train that stopped at every farm village on the way.

The train pulled in to Turku at dusk. He had two nights before his ship departed, and he had no idea of how or where to spend them. He wandered the streets for a while, and then he heard Russian voices coming from a pub. He went in. It was noisy and crowded, but it was warm. He went up to a customer about his age who had been speaking Russian. He introduced himself and explained his problem. His new friend said that the pub had rooms upstairs. They were small and noisy, but cheap. Oleksandr decided to make the pub his home for the next two nights.

The next day, his plans changed. He learned that he would be able to board his ship the evening before he was to depart, so he gathered up his belongings and walked to the port. There were several steamships berthed at various piers. He showed his ticket to an important looking uniformed man, and was directed via sign language to the right pier. Again, the Finnish customs agent didn't even bother to look at his papers. Hundreds of people from all over northern Europe were emigrating every day; he didn't care where they were from or where they were going; he only cared that they boarded the right steamship and left.

The S/S Astraea was not a huge ship, but at 230 feet, it was the largest thing Oleksandr had ever seen. He boarded, found his berth in steerage, and settled in for the two-day trip to Copenhagen and Hull.

At Hull, Oleksandr repeated what he had done in Finland: find the train station in Hull; buy a ticket to Liverpool; wait until nearly departure time; find the train; find his seat in third class. It was a five-hour trip, and he got in to Liverpool in the late afternoon. He found his way to the docks in Liverpool, and found his ship. The S/S Teutonic, the ship that was to take him to America, made the Astraea look like a skiff. It was almost 600 feet long, had two huge smokestacks, and carried almost 1500 passengers.

The Teutonic was leaving on the morning tide, so he could board this evening. "Leaving on the morning tide," was a tradition carried over from the days of sailing ships. In these days of coal-fired steamships, it was no longer necessary, but it was a tradition. And nobody saw a reason to change it. The journey would take about a week

The journey was uneventful. Steerage was divided into separate very large cabins. Cabins for men on the port side and for women on the starboard side. Each side had berths for 600 passengers. The seas were not rough, but enough of the passengers got seasick that there was a terrible stench in steerage. Oleksandr spent most of his time on deck watching the waves and the frigate birds. He met several other Russians, both men and women. Talking with them about their troubled pasts and their dreamed of futures passed some of the time.

One afternoon, Oleksandr started to see sea gulls instead of frigate birds. He wasn't the only one who had noticed. Soon, there were hundreds of people on deck looking for their first glimpse of the landmark they had dreamed of for so long – the Statue of Liberty. A great shout went out as they saw it – Lady Liberty – and America!

The Teutonic docked at the East River Pier. First and second class passengers underwent a cursory examination and questioning aboard ship, and were free to disembark in New York City and go on their way. Oleksandr and 1199 other steerage passengers were taken to Ellis Island by barge. They stood in line for hours, underwent the famous six second physical examinations, and were quizzed on their answers to the twenty-nine questions.

Eventually Oleksandr got his papers stamped, and he was ferried back to the city. His father had given him the address of a family from his village that lived in the city. There he could rest up after his voyage, perhaps learn a little English, and make plans for his train trip to Pueblo, Colorado.

All went well. Two weeks later, he stepped off the train at the platform in Pueblo.

CHAPTER 10

Oleksandr's map is on a piece of paper roughly twelve inches by fifteen inches, folded to fit in the white envelope. The paper is a little heavier than the paper Fedor used for his letters. It feels brittle; I gently unfold it. This definitely needs to be copied and preserved.

Everything has the slightly fuzzy look that you got a long time ago when you used a fountain pen on paper that was just a little too porous. Near the top of the paper are the words *Великий Березний.* In the upper left hand corner is a simple compass rose with the primary direction labelled П and pointing up on the page.

The map itself runs generally from the lower left hand part of the page to the upper right hand part. At the lower left is a village. There are several streets shown on the map. A couple are labelled; most are not. The village has maybe 30 buildings: some small, some large; some rectangular, some irregular; some with labels near them; some without. One of the largest buildings has a cross; an orthodox cross with the extra crossbeam at an angle.

The river is labelled Уж Річка. There is no indication of which way it flows, but it seems to get smaller as it goes northeast. There are several branches going off to the north and east. No obvious bridges cross the river, but a couple of the streets go right up to the river's edge and continue on the other side. Ferries? Fords? Bridges?

A dotted line starts at the church, goes east to the river, and then goes northeast along the river bank. There is no scale, so I have no idea how far the line goes. But if I assume that a city block is fifty yards, the town is less than a quarter mile across. At least it was a hundred years ago! If the dotted line is drawn to the same scale, it is a little over two miles long.

The dotted line ends at an ornate drawing of three peculiar looking trees on the east bank of the river. There is no writing near the trees. This map is a hundred years old. Chances of those trees still standing are slim to none. The good news is that the map shows what looks like a small pile of rocks several feet upstream of the trees, another pile downstream of the trees, and yet another pile several feet inland from the trees. If I can figure out where this village is, I can go on Google maps satellite view and see what the area looks like today. If the area is not built up, the landmarks may still be there.

There is little else on the map except for a few short notes along the river, and a short paragraph in Cyrillic across the river from the trees. Actually, I'm not sure that the writing is in Cyrillic. Somehow it doesn't look quite right. When I get home, I'll try using Babelfish or Google Translate on it.

I get another cup of coffee, ask Rudy for a menu, and move on to the next trifold.

CHAPTER 11

Fedor's translation of Mitri's letter is shorter than Oleksandr's story. But then, so was his trip.

In some ways, his trip was more arduous. He first journeyed south across the Carpathian Mountains and into Slovakia. He got rides from locals when he could and walked when he had to. He ate when and where he could, and slept in the woods. As he got farther from his home, his accent became stranger to the local people, and in this time of war, he found himself under more and more suspicion. He was very happy when he got to the city of Kosice and could board a train for Vienna.

He found a cheap hotel with a Russian-speaking proprietor, and spent a couple of nights resting and exploring. Vienna was the largest city he had ever visited, and he found it amazing. He bought new clothes for the next phase of his journey: he would take the train to Salzburg. And then take another south, across the Alps and into Italy.

The trip across the Carpathian Mountains had taken a toll; it left him very tired and felling generally unwell. The hotel proprietor sent him to a Russian-speaking doctor. The doctor pronounced him travel worn and with a mild case of the flu that seemed to be going around, but well enough, and encouraged him to get on with his journey.

And so he did. The 150-mile journey from Vienna through the farmlands of Austria to Salzburg was uneventful and somewhat boring. But the next 150 miles south across the Alps was unlike anything he had ever imagined. He had been born and raised in the mountains, but the Alps were different. There were times when the tracks going up to the passes were so steep that he could have walked faster than the train moved. And there were times going down that they coupled engines to the back of the train to keep it from running away. And the passes themselves: awesome. So high that they were above the tree line. And so high that the snow never melted. By the time he got to Trieste, he was exhausted from the experience.

His plan was to go to Venice to rest up before continuing his journey. His family had some distant relatives who lived in the Cannaregio Sestiere -- the Venetian Ghetto. From there he would travel across northern Italy and across France to Calais. Mitri would cross the English Channel and take the train to Liverpool where he would buy his ticket to America.

But as the days went by, he grew more tired, not less. The flu that he picked up during his travels was getting worse. He came to realize that he was a victim of the great flu epidemic sweeping Europe. In time, he knew that he would never leave Venice.

Mitri drew a map of his half – the second half -- of the directions to the red diamonds. He sealed the map in a cloth pouch impregnated with bees wax to protect it. He put the pouch in a small leather folio. And he took the folio to the Venetian cemetery island at San Michele. He hid the folio behind a loose brick at the base of the wall of the Orthodox section.

He wrote and mailed two identical letters to cousin Fedor; two just in case one got lost. He told the story of his journey and of his illness. He explained that just in case he could not continue his journey, he had drawn and secreted the map. He gave very detailed instructions about how to find the loose brick. It was behind the gravestone of one "Princesse Troubetzkoy." He promised to write again when he was well enough to continue his journey. And he was never heard from again.

* * *

Fedor goes on to say that only one letter from Mitri arrived. The other must have been lost.

He wrote to the "distant relatives" in Venice, but never got an answer. These were difficult times in Europe. The Great War was followed by a great flu epidemic. Then came two decades of giddy peace followed by another World War. During that war, Stalin starved millions of ethnic Ukrainians. After the war, letters to Velykyi Bereznyi went unanswered. Fedor assumed that they had no living relatives left in the old country. The Bradovich family had always been small; now it numbered less than a dozen. It could die out completely.

Fedor carefully translated the stories of Oleksandr and Mitri. His English was not great; but it was passable. He didn't dare ask for help. The story of the red diamonds must remain in the family, and only in the family.

His letter ends with statements that make it sound like Fedor wasn't sure that the red diamonds even existed. He questioned whether Metodyj's story was fact or fiction. But he did write that Oleksandr remembered his father's trip to Petrograd; and he remembered the Tsar's soldiers guarding his father 's workshop when he returned.

* * *

When Ivan – now John -- came back from serving in the Army during World War II, he visited the old people in Pueblo. He spent several months there before he returned to western Pennsylvania to be near his younger brother. Fedor sat him down and told him the story of the red diamonds. John would soon be patriarch – Fedor would pass the responsibility on to him. Before John left Colorado, Fedor gave everything to him for safe keeping.

Eventually, the Pueblo branch of the Bradoviches died out. My dad and Uncle John are both gone. I guess I'm the patriarch now. That left my brother and me to carry on the family name. George never had children. I had Mike and Gabe. Gabe had two daughters, but no sons. Mike had only Eric. The line would continue through Eric or not at all. The secret of the red diamonds could die with him.

CHAPTER 12

I talked to Mike on Tuesday. It's early Friday evening. And Mike and Lauri are sitting on our deck overlooking Lake Erie. I still can't get over how quickly they got here.

Kate read the letters Wednesday night. She's more than a little skeptical. So am I. The likelihood of the whole story of the red diamonds being true is close to zero. Then again, why would my ancestors make it all up – and then keep it a secret for a hundred years?

We decided that we had to let Mike and Lauri in on the story of the red diamonds. And we're sitting here watching the boats go by while they read. Mike has read Fedor's letter to John and passed it on to Lauri. He's reading Oleksandr's story now. The look on his face is textbook bemusement. Lauri is frowning deeply.

"Dad, how long have you known about this?"

"Since Tuesday, Mike, when I opened the safe."

"But this is crazy. How could…"

"You need to read all three documents and look at the map before we talk."

"Got anything to drink?"

"I will look. Read."

And from Lauri, "Me, too."

Mike picks up the map and studies it. I go inside to see what I can find them to drink.

I come back with a couple of Great Lakes Brewing Company lagers for Mike and Lauri. While they read, I play around some more with some on-line translator programs. I found out yesterday that what I thought was Cyrillic – Russian – is not. Babelfish couldn't translate it. Google Translate has an auto-language-detect feature. Auto-detect thinks it's Ukrainian, but the translations are weird. Apparently, Ukrainian has changed a lot in a hundred years.

* * *

By the time Mike and Lauri finish, I've given up on translator programs. I think I'll have to come up with another way of translating hundred-year-old Ukrainian.

Mike just looks at me – still bemused. Lauri breaks the silence. "Is this for real?"

"I don't know. I found this stuff in Uncle John's safe on Tuesday. I knew nothing about it before then. I just don't know. And I don't know how to find out."

She continues. "Well, we can fact-check the general history. Maybe we can find out if there were any missing Red Diamonds. We can try to figure out if the story fits the history of that place at that time. But I want to say, 'So what?'"

Lauri says Red Diamonds like it's a proper noun; like it should be capitalized. Fifty carats plus six times ten carats – maybe it should be…

Kate joins the conversation. "I've had twenty-four hours to think about this. The whole story sounds unbelievable. But it's too unbelievable to be made up -- if that makes any sense. Why do that? Why make this whole thing up? And then keep it a secret for a hundred years. I have this crazy feeling that it's true. But I don't know what to do about it. Like Lauri just said, 'So what?'"

I offer my opinion. "Everything we know is based on the story told to Fedor by Oleksandr. There is collaboration in the supposed letter from Mitri. It *is* possible that the whole thing is a fantasy invented by Oleksandr. But somehow, I don't think so. I just don't know what to do about it. Short of going to Venice and finding part two of the map, and then going to Velykyi Bereznyi and looking for the diamonds."

I continue. "That is not happening right now. Let's all see if we can come up with other ideas. In the meantime, I have an estate to dispose of. Mike, let's go check out Uncle John's Arsenal tomorrow. Ladies, you want to come along?"

Kate answers for them. "We're going to the Grove City Outlets. It'll be a lot more interesting than a bunch of guns. You guys want to meet somewhere for dinner?"

"How about the Springfield Grill south of Mercer?"

"Great idea."

Mike says, "Sounds like a good plan to me. I'll start digging into the saga of the Red Diamonds."

I'm trying to think of something dramatic like "This meeting of the Red Diamond Search Team is adjourned" when Mike interrupts my thought. "Dad, have you tried to translate the notes on the map?"

"According to Google Translate, the notes are in Ukrainian but some of the translations are sketchy. I think Ukrainian has changed a lot in the hundred years since they were written. I need to find someone who speaks – actually reads – old Ukrainian."

"How about the church on Clark Street? In Sharon. By the old Westinghouse plant."

"Excellent idea. We will stop there on our way to Sharpsville."

CHAPTER 13

I was raised in Sharon, Pennsylvania. We went to Sacred Heart Church. It's a fair sized Roman Catholic Church in downtown Sharon.

My mother told me that when she was young, they went to Saint John's Carpatho-Rusyn Orthodox Church. But her father switched himself and his family to Sacred Heart when he realized that most of the supervisors at the mill were Irish Catholic. And Roman Catholic, not Orthodox Catholic...

Her father had ambition. He wanted to be a supervisor someday. He knew that he would be more accepted as a Roman Catholic than as an Orthodox Catholic. He didn't want to be just another "Mill Hunky." It must have worked. He wound up as Superintendent of the Pipefitter's Shop in one of Sharon's steel mills.

Saint John's is a small church. It sits on a hillside overlooking the remains of the now defunct Westinghouse Transformer Plant. The outside is white lap strake. It has a small steeple with a single bell in it. The doors are red; somebody once told me that meant the mortgage was paid off. From the outside, its stained glass windows look black in the morning sun; from the inside, they would be on fire. My guess is that the church is early nineteen-hundreds.

Mike and I knock on the door of the rectory. A priest answers. He's in his late thirties and looks just like he should. He's about five foot eight, a little chubby, and has a grizzled beard. He's wearing a floor length black cassock; he greets us with a big smile. If his costume was red instead of black and his beard whiter, he'd make a great Santa Claus.

"Welcome to Saint John's. Please come in."

We enter a small foyer. I introduce myself and Mike, and explain that many years ago my father attended Saint John's.

"I am Father Basil. Basil Pataki. I've only been here for five years, but we have many old records, and many old photographs. Do you live here in Sharon?"

"No, we are just visiting, but we need some help."

I explain the history of the Bradoviches and their attendance at – and departure from – Saint John's. Father Pataki is not surprised. "That happened a lot in the old days. Are your parents still with us"?

I tell him that they are all gone now, and that we just buried my uncle. "That makes me the Bradovich patriarch, I guess."

"I see. So what can I do for you?"

This will be a little difficult. "I live in Lorain, Ohio, and Mike lives in Denver. We're here cleaning out Uncle John's house in preparation to selling it. I found this old map. I know that the notes are in Ukrainian, but I have not had a lot of success in translating them."

"What do you know about the map? It looks very old."

"Virtually nothing. It was with some old letters that were dated about a hundred years ago. Do you read Ukrainian?"

"I do, but these notes are in a very old dialect. We would do better to have one of our older parishioners look at it. This may sound silly, but my first impression was that it looks like a treasure map. Stevenson's *Treasure Island* came to mind…"

"Funny. I had exactly the same thought."

"Maybe it is!" Father breaks into a Santa Claus laugh.

"Maybe. Until I find out exactly what it is, I am not sure I want to circulate it very much."

"So what do you have in mind?"

"Perhaps I can make a copy of the map, cut out the notes, and give them to your translators. See what they come up with."

"We're a very modern church. We have a copier. We even have Wi Fi!" The Santa Claus laugh again. It's infectious. I like Father Basil.

The map is too big to fit on the platen of the copier. We copy it in pieces, and cut out the notes. I give them to Father Basil and gather up the remainder of the copies.

The good father notices. "Don't you trust me with your treasure map?"

"More than most people, actually. If it is a treasure map, you will get my tithe."

"We could certainly use it. But I won't start planning where to spend it just yet. Give me until next week at this time to circulate the notes among some of our parishioners."

CHAPTER 14

I've spent the last week trying to keep up with work and trying to get Uncle John's place ready to sell. Mike was here for a couple of days and that was a big help. He has taken over the burden of disposing of Uncle John's Arsenal. Actually he's doing the paperwork and I'm doing the grunt work. But it's getting done.

I think that John kept everything he ever acquired. Some of his trophies are older than I am – and like me, showing their age. I remember the mounted albino weasel from when I was a kid. And how much is a thirty-year-old moose head worth? The auction should be interesting.

I've got another month before the Riemold Brothers auction. I'll get everything done, but it will be a challenge.

It's been a week, so I go back to see Father Basil. He's done a great job. Each Ukrainian label is pasted to a separate sheet of paper. And there are one or more English translations pasted below each Ukrainian label.

"Some of the notes were simple. 'One versta from the last branch. Follow the main river at this branch.' That kind of thing."

"One versta?"

"I asked the same question. A hundred years ago, the Ukrainians used three units of measure for length: the arshin, about twenty-eight inches; the sazhen, about seven feet; and the versta, 1.0668 kilometer, about 3500 feet. Literally, a versta is 'a turn of the plow.'"

"I see."

"Some were harder. The old people are still arguing over them. And they want to know what this is all about."

"Can you tell them that the notes are on an old map of Velykyi Bereznyi, the village of my grandfather? That is the truth. Do you know if any of your parishioners are from the village?"

"No, but they already figured that much out. One of the notes – the title of the map -- was *Великий Березний.* It translates to 'Velykyi Bereznyi.' Some of them are from nearby villages. And they told me something interesting."

"What is that?"

"They said that during the troubles as they call them, a small detachment of the Preobrazhensky Regiment took up residence in Velykyi Bereznyi. Why they were there was a secret."

"Who took up residence? When were 'the troubles'?"

"The Preobrazhensky Regiment was the elite palace guard of Tsar Nicholas, the last Tsar of Russia. And 'the troubles' was the period from World War I to the Russian Revolution. It was then that Nicholas and his family were assassinated by the Bolsheviks. About a hundred years ago. I find it very odd that the Preobrazhensky Regiment was in Velykyi Bereznyi at that time. It's a long way from Saint Petersburg."

"Saint Petersburg?"

"The home of Tsar Nicholas and his wife Alexandra. A thousand miles away."

"I'm afraid you are losing me on the history. All I know is that I have an interesting old map that I am trying to figure out. "

"Speaking of interesting, the most interesting note is the one across the river from the end of the dotted line."

"Oh?"

"It says, 'Cross the river to the spot due east of the stone in the tree. Mitri's map to the Red Diamonds begins here.'"

"Red Diamonds?"

"Yes. Interesting." Father Basil watches me intently.

"Yeah... I guess... Interesting... Well, I have a long drive ahead of me. I will redraw the map and add the English notes. If I figure anything out, I will certainly let you know. Thank you. And thank all of you parishioners. Goodbye, Father."

"I'll do that. Godspeed."

* * *

Father Basil knows more than I would like. But he is probably more trustworthy than a lot of people. I hope.

We have a large platen copier at work. I made several copies of the map. On one, I whited out the Ukrainian printing and copied it again. So now I can add the English text, and see what we've got.

* * *

Well. It's a treasure map. Complete with the proverbial dotted line. Or more correctly, it's half of a treasure map.

The dotted line starts at the church in Velykyi Bereznyi and follows the west bank of the river Uzh upstream for about four miles. There are several notes about which way to go at branches in the river. The dotted line ends with an X at a very distinctive bend in the river. A note there says, "Look for the three hornbeams. There are stones upstream, downstream, and to the west. You will find a white stone embedded in the middle tree where the eastern branch leaves the trunk."

And just as Father Basil said, there is a note across the river on the east bank. It says, 'Cross the river to the spot due east of the stone in the tree. Mitri's map to the Red Diamonds begins here." Nearby are several small crude circles. There is another note that says simply, "White Stones."

And thus it ends. Now what?

CHAPTER 15

I can't believe that I'm even considering this. It's crazy. A quest for a lost treasure. Seriously?

First we'll have to go to Venice and find Mitri's map. And the chances of it still being behind a loose brick in the cemetery wall are? Zero. Or very near zero…

And let's assume it is still there; and still readable after a hundred years in the dampness and decay that is Venice. Then what?

So then we go to Ukraine; or to Poland; or to Belarus; or to wherever Velykyi Bereznyi is these days. The town hasn't moved, but the borders have. I'm pretty sure that Velykyi Bereznyi is in Ukraine again. But that's subject to change; not while we're there, I hope.

So let's assume that we find the secret location of the red diamonds; that they haven't already been found; that the diamonds aren't under a factory or a mall or something now. It's been a hundred years; Ukraine has changed.

So we find the diamonds. If they're still where Metodyj hid them. And how likely is that? Another zero…

But if they are there – we're rich. And stuck in Ukraine. I remember the "Customs Officials" when we were in Russia. They all carried Kalashnikovs. We're just going to stroll out of Ukraine with a zillion dollars' worth of diamonds. Yeah right.

So we smuggle them out of Ukraine; and into Italy. Then what? We smuggle them out of Italy and into the United States; yeah, that'll be easy. But if we do; how do we dispose of them? Sell them on eBay? Have a garage sale?

This whole enterprise is one near zero probability after another; one impossibility after another. And yet I think we just might try to do it. If nothing else, it'll be a great vacation…

CHAPTER 16

"Kate, we have to talk."

"Yes?"

"We need to make a decision about the Red Diamonds."

"And what decision is that?"

"Do we go after the Red Diamonds or not."

"And?"

"We need to decide before we talk to Mike and Lauri."

"And?"

"Oh, stop it. You're not helping."

"I am helping. And I think you've already made your decision."

"But it is a fool's errand. There is a near zero chance of success. It'll be expensive; and probably illegal. And maybe dangerous."

"And you know we have to try."

I sigh. "Yeah."

"Or we'll spend the rest of our lives wondering."

Another sigh. "Yeah."

"So let's do it. Talk to Mike. See if they're in."

"What do you mean, 'See if they're in?'"

"My suggestion is that all four of us go to Venice. If nothing else, it'll be a great vacation! I want to stay at the Londra Palace again. A canal-view suite again, please."

"You knew we were going, didn't you? And after Venice, then what, my little Project Manager?"

"Of course I knew. We have to go. Then, if we find the map, you and Mike go to the Ukraine. What's the name of the town again?"

"Velykyi Bereznyi. You're not coming with us? And what do you and Lauri do while we're in Ukraine, may I ask?"

"While you boys are discovering your roots, we'll go to Florence or maybe Paris. Lauri and I will let you know."

"Have you set the date yet?"

"No, that's your job, my little tour guide. But I am thinking early spring. I love Italy then."

CHAPTER 17

"Hi, Mike. Is this a good time to talk?

"Actually, no. How about I call you back this evening?

"That works. It is about maybe doing that trip to 'discover our roots.'"

"I figured. I'll call you this evening, Dad."

* * *

"Hello?"

"Hi, Dad. 'Discover our roots'"?

"That is the euphemism Kate came up with. I like it."

"So it's a go, then? What are you thinking?"

"Well. Kate's suggestion is that the four of us spend a few days in Venice. Then they go to Florence and we go to Russia."

"Florence? Russia?"

"I think that Kate and Lauri might have been talking about this. She said that they have no desire to go to Russia. They are planning a week or so in Florence – or maybe Paris – while we're 'discovering our roots' in Russia."

"You've said 'Russia' a couple of times. I thought our roots were in Ukraine."

"You are right. Our home village, Velykyi Bereznyi, is now in Ukraine. But old habits die hard. I grew up saying we were from Russia; from the USSR. I am not used to being from Ukraine yet."

"I still tell people I'm Russian, too. It's easier."

"If you really want to confuse them, you can tell them we are Rusyn, aka Lemko, from the north slopes of the Carpathian Mountains."

"Dad, it may not matter what we call it. I'm not sure I can go."

"Huh?"

"I *am* a U.S. Marshal. I'm not sure how my superiors will react to my going there. I mentioned it to my boss, and he got a weird look on his face. I need to get definite, official permission."

"I never thought about that. When will you know? I am thinking late spring; perhaps May. I will want to start planning."

"Give me this week to get an okay. Regardless of how our 'roots' turn out, it sounds like a great trip. I really want to go, and I know Lauri will feel the same way. She's never been to Europe. It's on our list."

"I can't think of a better introduction to Europe than Venice and then Florence or Paris."

CHAPTER 18

The Ukraine will be new to me, but going to Venice will be like going home. Why do I say "the Ukraine"? I don't say "the Italy" or "the France." I think that started before Ukraine was a country; when it was part of the USSR. It's something to Google.

Italy. When I was in the Air Force, I spent fifteen months on a small site in the Colli Euganei; about 30 miles west of Venice. I went to Venice every chance I got. Then, as a civilian contractor, I spent some time in Trieste; about 50 miles northeast of Venice. People find it odd that I speak Italian, but not Russian.

More recently, Kate and I spent three weeks in Italy with our friends Susan and Ted. I played tour guide for three weeks in Rome and Florence and Venice. We enjoyed it so much that Kate and I went back last year; a week in Florence and a week in Venice. Going again will be easy. And it won't raise any questions.

Venice will be easy. If Mitri's map is still there, finding it will not be a problem. I know San Michele; it's a small island just north of Venice; it's Venice's cemetery. I've been there.

CHAPTER 19

Venice will be easy. But the Ukraine will be new and exciting. And challenging. Kate and I were in Russia about ten years ago. We spent most of our time in Saint Petersburg, but we took the train to Moscow for a few days.

During the train ride, as we travelled through the small towns, I remember wishing that we had time to visit them as well as the big cities. Well, it looks like I'm going to get my chance. From what I've seen, western Ukraine doesn't look too different from the farmlands southwest of Moscow. Hillier, perhaps, but the same small town look.

Before we went to Russia, I bought some cheap CDs and learned a little of the language. It was a disaster. I *look* Russian. When I spoke a little Russian, the locals assumed I *was* Russian and spoke to me as they would to any other native. And then they got mad when I didn't understand. I quit trying after a while.

In Ukraine, the most common languages are Russian and Ukrainian. I know Rosetta Stone does Russian; I wonder about Ukrainian. I've had good luck with Rosetta Stone Italian. Maybe this time, I'll learn more Russian or Ukrainian before we go.

Whether or not I do, the trip will be a challenge. We'll have to act like tourists exploring our roots. But we'll have to follow Mitri's map to the Red Diamonds. And then get them out of the country.

And into Italy. And out of Italy. And into the United States. It *will* be a challenge.

CHAPTER 20

It's good to have Mike and Lauri back in town, if only for a few days. They're going to help get Uncle John's place ready for the auction. And we're going to make a decision on what to do about the Red Diamonds. They are the only people we've told. Nobody else knows about the safe – or what I found in it.

Mike has been in touch with an arms dealer in the Pittsburgh area. They will sell all of Uncle John's guns on consignment. But we have to do a detailed inventory: make, model, caliber, serial number, and a photo of every firearm. And we have to deliver the guns to West Mifflin.

We spend two days going through every cabinet and drawer gathering up personal and family stuff that we do not want auctioned off. We pack up all of his business records and personal files. Most we'll destroy, but I have to go through them first. And I'll need to talk to Bianco to see if there is anything "legal" that I need to do.

Mike and I each pick out a gun to keep as a memento. I'll keep the Kimber I grabbed the first day I was here. Mike selects a beautiful Steyr Mannlicher match rifle. I'll ask Beth and George if they want to select a gun – or anything else -- before the auction. I'll also ask them if Gabe can pick out a gun. He always loved Uncle John. I'm sure he'd like a gun as a memento.

* * *

Dinner at the Hickory Grille. It's owned by the same guys who own the Springfield Grille, but it's not quite as nice. It's still what I call a "White Tablecloth Restaurant." That Bradovich Scale ranking has nothing to do with whether or not it actually has white tablecloths; it has to do with service and the menu choices and the wine list – and with ambiance. There are few restaurants in the Shenango Valley that I rate as "White Tablecloth Restaurants."

It's a bit noisy. Bad acoustics kind of noisy, not big crowd kind of noisy. But the noise covers the very serious discussion the four of us are having. About the red diamonds. Fact or fiction? Truth or fabrication? History or myth? Real or fake? Still there or gone? Go or no go?

And we decide to go. Just the four of us. Like the song. Sort of.

We'll go on "vacation" to Venice. It's my favorite city in the world, anyway. Kate loves it, too. Mike and Lauri have never been there. We'll go in late May. The crowds are still down and the weather is balmy.

Then Mike and I will go "discover our roots" in western Ukraine. And Kate and Lauri will go shopping in Paris.

Of course whether or not we go to Ukraine depends on whether or not we find the map in Venice. Chances of it still being behind a loose brick in a wall on San Michele after a hundred years are slim to none. Even if it is still there, the chances of it still being readable after a hundred years in Venice's dampness are slim to none. What's slim to none times slim to none? Slim to none squared? Slim to none factorial? My brain says it's dumb to go; my heart says we have to try.

And after discussing about a million reasons not to, we all agree – we have to try – we have to find out.

CHAPTER 21

I've done this all before. Kate says I'm a great travel planner. I'm not; it's just that I've lived in Europe. I know where I want to stay; I know how to get from place to place. I know what to preplan and what to do on the spot.

We'll fly Cleveland to Venice on a European flag carrier; I like them better the American carriers, especially for the trans-Atlantic hop. Probably two stops: Detroit and Paris seem to pop up a lot.

We'll leave on Saturday in the middle of May. A late afternoon departure works well. It makes the long trans-Atlantic flight a night flight, and that gets us into Venice late Sunday morning.

I'll need to book a water taxi from Marco Polo Airport to the hotel. Kate has already decided that we're staying at the Londra Palace. And that's fine with me. It's a five-star hotel on the water overlooking San Giorgio Maggiore. And it's a five-minute walk west to Piazza San Marco, the center of the tourist world in Venice.

I figure five nights in Venice: a day to get over jet lag; a day to play tourist; a day to find the map; a day to prepare for the next legs of our quest.

Where the next legs take us depends on whether or not we find Mitri's map.

If the map is gone or if it's unreadable, we all go to Paris… We'll be bummed out; we might as well make a vacation of it and let the City of Light cheer us up. After Paris we can either pay the fees and change our flights back to Cleveland, or go back to Venice for more vacation.

But if Mitri's map is there… The girls go to Paris and Mike and I go to Ukraine. The adventure continues…

CHAPTER 22

Depending on whether or not we have a map, either just the girls or all four of us will be going to Paris. The night train is great, if you have a private compartment. It's city center to city center (almost), and you pull into Paris in the morning, well rested and even having been fed breakfast.

The First Class compartments sleep two. I'll book two compartments. If Mike and I are going to Ukraine, we'll cancel one.

This leg is easy. The concierge at the Londra Palace can arrange a water taxi to the Santa Lucia train station. And we (just the girls, or all four of us) can take a regular taxi to the Hotel in Paris.

And speaking of the hotel in Paris, I know a great one near the greatest landmark in Europe, the Pullman Paris Tour Eiffel. It's near the tower and the Seine. It's an easy walk to the Metro station, and to great shopping and touristing.

We (two or four) can be very happy there for a few days.

And where next? TBA. I used to work for a large company that was always in such a state of management flux – read management chaos – that the Organizational Chart was always full of positions held by TBA: To Be Announced.

I'll book two first class compartments on the night train back to Venice just in case.

CHAPTER 23

This leg will be the hard one. I've only been to Eastern Europe once. And that was to Saint Petersburg and Moscow after the fall of the Soviet Union – when Putin was very firmly in charge. The political climate is different now. It's more like it was before the World Wars. In many countries, various factions are vying for control; sometimes with words; sometimes with demonstrations; sometimes with guns. The Ukraine is pretty stable right now. But Russia is eyeing Crimea; it was vacation central for Russian apparatchiks during the Soviet era. And like many of the *nomenklatura*, Putin had a dacha there. I'm sure he'd like it back.

And you can't get there from here… To get to Velykyi Bereznyi, we'll have to fly to Kiev (no easy task, itself), then take the train to L'viv (two hundred fifty miles of notoriously unreliable state run railroad), and then drive the last hundred miles to Velykyi Bereznyi.

Plane tickets to Kiev (via Frankfurt) won't be a problem. Travelocity and Amex work fine in this part of the world.

I can book train tickets in advance, but once we get to Kiev, determining whether the train will actually make the trip to L'viv will be another TBA. When we make it to L'viv, we'll spend the night at the Eurohotel, and hopefully get an early start to Velykyi Bereznyi.

The more I think about the last leg of the trip – a hundred miles of mountain roads – the more I think I'd like to get a car *and* driver – and "leave the driving" to a native. I'll email the Eurohotel and see if they can arrange it. And see if we can afford it. And we'll need to make the return drive six days later.

I'm figuring one day to settle in; one day to explore the town and get known; one day to make friends and ask about relatives; one day to find the diamonds; one day to hide the diamonds; and then one day to drive back to L'viv.

From there, it's the train to Kiev, and the flight to Venice. And a glorious reunion with the girls.

But between us and the girls will be Ukrainian and Italian Customs. I'm hoping that the Ukrainian Customs officials will be like the Russian Customs officials I faced ten years ago. Customs officials carrying Kalashnikovs looked scary, but I found out later that they were more interested in bribes than contraband.

Italian Customs are – well – Italian. Fancy uniforms, lots of bluster and lots of red tape. But their basic attitude is either, "Welcome to Italy; we hope you brought lots of money." or, "Come back soon; bring lots of money." They will not be a problem.

The biggest challenge will be U.S. Customs. We'll have to figure out a way to smuggle the Red Diamonds past the Customs Inspectors. And I don't have a clue. I'm hoping one of us has a flash of inspiration…

Of course this all assumes that the map is still in place in San Michele. And that it's still readable. And that the diamonds are still where Metodyj buried them. And that we get them out of Ukraine and into Italy. And a thousand other ifs.

This whole expedition sounds more and more like a fantasy adventure. It sounds more and more like a wild goose chase. But we've got to try.

CHAPTER 24

If all has gone well, if we have the diamonds, we need to get them back into the United States.

And Lauri has had the flash of inspiration I was hoping for! She will wear the diamonds!

Lauri has a friend who makes custom, mainly costume jewelry. She does it for Hollywood, and for a few friends. Breeze Johanson's shop is in Boulder, Colorado. Breeze -- where else but Boulder? The aging hippie, liberal wacko, drug fogged capital of the US. And that was before they legalized pot.

Lauri will have her make a gaudy fake gold pendant and bracelet. The pendant will have a single red glass stone the size of the real Red Diamond. The bracelet will have six red glass stones the size of the smaller Red Diamonds. When we're back in Venice with the Red Diamonds, we'll remove the glass stones and replace them with diamonds. Lauri will *wear* them on the trip home!

I don't know, though. I don't have a lot of confidence. I don't know if Laurie can walk through customs wearing several million dollars' worth of diamonds without looking at least a little nervous. But it's the best we have come up with.

I'll plan on another three nights at Hotel Londra Palace: a day to hide the diamonds in plain sight; a day to prepare to come home.

Getting out of Italy will be no big deal; getting through U.S. Customs will be the challenge. Is it easy to tell real diamonds from fake diamonds? Do the various TSA scanners and detectors detect diamonds? My research says no.

But there *are* a couple of hand held diamond detectors that work pretty well. Two I have learned about are the Thermal Probe and the Reflectometer. They're not even very expensive –a couple hundred dollars will buy a good one. But in all my years of going back and forth through customs, I've never seen anything that looked like it might be a detector. I'll have to ask Mike.

CHAPTER 25

I've done all the planning I can. It's time to start making reservations. Good reservations in Italy require a long lead time. Cheap tickets to Italy require a long lead time. The time is now.

I remember a few years ago when I started making reservations for the trip Kate and Sue and Ted and me went on to Rome and Florence and Venice almost a year in advance, they questioned the necessity of that much lead time. I told them, "Try to get a nice room at the River Palace or the Berchielli or the Danielli or the Londra Palace three months from now, or even six months from now." I don't know if they actually tried, but they got the point. And we got great accommodations.

Before I start spending money, before I start making non-refundable commitments, I need to get everybody's buy in – one more time.

I text Mike and Lauri and Kate; I tell them we need to have a phone conference. We agree on next Sunday afternoon. Afternoon for them and evening for us.

* * *

I go over the schedule with everyone. We will leave the third Saturday in May and be gone two weeks.

Everyone will tell friends and coworkers this is a vacation – with the boys making a side trip to research the Bradovich family origins.

Five nights in Venice. If we find the map, and it's readable, the girls go to Paris for a week and Mike and I go to Ukraine. Then we all meet back at the Londra Palace for another three nights. Then home – with or without the Red Diamonds.

* * *

Everyone agrees: let's do it. I'll start making reservations next week.

CHAPTER 26

Kate talks to Sue almost every day. They have been best friends for years and years –longer than we have been married – and that's a long time.

When Kate mentioned that we were going back to Italy in May, Sue got all excited. She started talking about her and Ted going along.

Kate had to kind of let her down gently. She explained that we were going with Mike and Lauri; that it was a "family" thing; that Mike and I were going to Ukraine to "discover" our roots. Sue pouted a little, but she got it. If there is one thing Sue understands, it's family. She even wound up telling Kate that she'd get the word out to our friends

Funny thing is, I've enjoyed our trips with Sue and Ted. Both to Russia and to Italy. I'd love to do another trip with them. Especially if we come back with a boatload of diamonds – Red Diamonds.

CHAPTER 27

Kate has done some serious research into the sizes of the Red Diamonds. She figures that if they were Alexandra's they were cut in the nineteenth, or eighteenth, or even seventeenth centuries. They would not be modern round "brilliant" cut diamonds. They would be Mazarin or Peruzzi cut. The Mazarin is square or rectangular; the Peruzzi is kind of square or rectangular, but with rounded corners – sort of like the modern "cushion" cut diamond.

It's kind of interesting that Peruzzi was a late seventeenth century Venetian who invented a more brilliant way of cutting diamonds. Venice was the center of the world's diamond cutting industry then. And the story continues…

Kate figures that a fifty carat Peruzzi will be about 50 mm across and the ten carat stones will be about 15 mm across. She'll ask Breeze to make the stones in the costume jewelry those sizes. And hope that she doesn't ask too many questions about why. Beyond, "They're to go with a great new dress I bought to wear to some really fancy places in Venice!"

Next comes our first test. Lauri will wear her new jewelry on a test run through U.S. Customs.

CHAPTER 28

Mike and Lauri always have lots of frequent flyer miles. The plan is for them to visit us in Key Largo, and then test the fake jewels by heading for a long weekend in Jamaica.

* * *

They leave Denver. Lauri is wearing her new fake jewelry as she goes through security. She's a TSA Pre✓™ traveler so she doesn't have to take her shoes off and go through the scanner. She gets to go through the Express Lane. But there's still a Metal Detector. And she trips the Metal Detector. Lauri acts surprised, pauses, and points to her pendant. The young female TSA Attendant smiles, and says, "Go back, take that – and the bracelet – off, put them in a tray, and try again."

She complies, and on the second try, goes through with no trouble. As she's retrieving her jewelry, the Attendant says, "Unless those are worth a lot of money, next time you probably should put them in your checked baggage." Laurie smiles and mumbles something about them being cheap bling, and that being a good idea for next time.

TSA test passed. But the real test will be customs – on the way back *in* to the US.

* * *

Mike and Lauri spend the night with us. We do dinner at Mrs. Mac's; cheap and easy. Tomorrow, they're off to Jamaica. They'll do two nights in Jamaica, and then fly back to Miami Airport. I've never paid much attention, but Miami has got to be one of the better equipped airports. Better equipped for interdicting drugs and all kinds of illegal things. Like contraband jewels. And Mike agrees with my assessment!

As a U.S. Marshal, he goes around security, but he is intimately familiar with what they do and what equipment they have. It's his job. Lauri, on the other hand, is just another civilian. She'll have to go through Immigration and Customs. As will her baggage. And her jewelry.

* * *

Mike and Lauri have had their two days in Jamaica. They deplane at Miami and head for U.S. Customs and Border Protection. Now it's time for the *real* test.

They show their passports to a bored Customs Officer. Mike's maroon Official U.S. Passport causes the agent to look up only briefly. He stamps their passports and hands them back.

Mike could go through the special Customs line for aircrew and other "special" people. He chooses to stay with Lauri. They stand in line for ten minutes, looking bored, tired, and just a little irritated. Just like everybody else. When it's their turn, they follow the procedure others have been following. They put their suitcases up on the table, open them and turn them around. But then Mike lays his U.S. Marshal's Badge on top of his open suitcase. The Customs Agent's head snaps up. Mike says, "I decided to keep my wife company."

Lauri is first. The agent makes a show of searching the Marshal's wife's bag. He finds nothing. He closes her bag, puts a little sticker on it and looks up at Lauri -- approvingly. She's been working out a lot and looks pretty buff. He looks at her pendant and asks, "Nice pendant. Did you get it in Jamaica?" He's not fishing. He's just making conversation with an attractive woman.

Then he remembers the Marshal. He looks at Mike a little sheepishly, closes his bag, puts the sticker on and says, "You're free to go, sir. And you, too ma'am."

Customs test passed. Mike realizes that that's exactly how he wants to do it coming back from Italy.

* * *

Mike told me to try to schedule our return through JFK. It's International Arrivals Building is old, crowded, staffed by too few surly baggage handlers and disgruntled INS and Customs Agents, and should be one of the easier airports for us to get through. He's the expert. He knows.

PART TWO:

ITALY

CHAPTER 29

It's time to go. Kate and I take a taxi to Cleveland Hopkins Airport. It's about a forty-five-minute ride, and we're nervous. And quiet. We are each lost in our thoughts about this trip; this quest; this wild goose chase. I'm not sure why. The outbound trip will be easy. Maybe we're already anticipating the inbound trip…

We arrive at the airport and check our bags at the curbside US Airways facility. We each have one rather large suitcase to check; mine green, Kate's pink.

Kate has her iPad in her carryon along with her usual traveling stuff. She flies often for her employer and is a seasoned traveler. She's good at taking what's necessary – and no more. She has a spreadsheet of what to take, whether it's a day trip, an overnighter, a few days, or an extended stay. Today she's got her Vera Bradley print wheeled carryon computer tote packed for two weeks in Europe playing tourist.

I'm not quite as organized. But I have what I need in my small Chaps duffel with wheels and a handle. My laptop and a manila envelope stuffed with notes, maps and miscellaneous paperwork are critical. I also have my hand held Garmin GPS. I've downloaded a general map of Europe and city maps of Venice and Paris. The coverage in Ukraine is not great, but it's better than nothing.

We watch our luggage carefully as we're waiting our turn. We're more than a little paranoid since we had Kate's computer tote stolen here at the curbside check-in a couple of years ago. It only took a few minutes of inattention. She lost her work laptop, her Apple Air, and her iPad! But today everything goes smoothly and we're inside and on our way to TSA security. It's Saturday morning and the crowds are lite. But we planned it that way.

Going through security is a non-event. Even though we're both TSA Pre✓™ travelers, we have to go through the regular screening process because we're continuing on to Venice. But we have no issues at all. We gather up our stuff, put our shoes back on and head for our gate.

We're flying US Airways from Cleveland to Detroit; we'll meet Mike and Lauri there. They'll be coming in on a United flight from Denver. If our flights are on time, the four of us will have several hours to have dinner in Detroit before we board the KLM night flight to Paris.

We spend fifty minutes waiting to board our fifty-minute flight to Detroit. As with most flights these days, the flight is overbooked. US Airways fixes the problem by giving free travel vouchers to a couple of travelers who don't mind waiting for a later flight, and we finally get aboard and seated. It's a typical domestic flight – a minimum of room, a minimum of service, a maximum of passenger grumbling. By the time everyone finally settles in, we're on our descent to Detroit. We deplane in Detroit and check the arrivals TV monitor for the United flight from Denver.

We're at the United gate when Mike and Lauri deplane. We all greet each other and sit for a minute. Mike knows the airport well – he flies here often "on business." I asked him once, "Why Detroit?" His answer was, "Because Detroit has the largest Muslim population in the United States." And he would say no more.

Mike says that Champps is about as good as any place here, so we head for Champps. I agree with his choice; it'll be my last hamburger for a couple of weeks.

After dinner, we head for the KLM gates. We get to the gate just as the flight starts boarding. I chose an aircraft that has a few two-five-two rows. Kate & Lauri have the A seats in rows twenty-five and twenty-six and Mike and I have the B seats -- we each have a window or an aisle. The KLM Airbuses are fairly roomy, even in economy, so we should have a reasonably comfortable flight to Paris. The cabin crewmembers are pleasant and helpful – and young -- unlike most American flag carrier aircrews these days.

They feed us an actually edible dinner, and tuck us in for the night. The girls sleep. Mike and I read, and watch TV, and read, and watch TV, and snooze. Eventually we sleep, too.

We all wake up when they turn the cabin lights on and prepare to feed us breakfast. By the time we each go to the head and eat breakfast, the Airbus has started its descent into Paris and the Charles De Gaulle Airport.

We have about ninety minutes to get to the Alitalia gates and find our flight to Venice. It's ample time, but we can't goof off too much.

I can't help but remember the last time Kate and I were in Paris. Ten years ago, the two of us, along with four friends, were coming back from two weeks in Russia. When I first planned the trip, we had a four-hour layover in Paris. Zoe asked me if four hours was long enough to go outside, jump in a cab, go to the Eiffel Tower, take a selfie, and get back to the airport. I told her that she wouldn't be allowed to clear customs in mid-journey. The women had several long discussions and the result was that I extended the layover from four hours to four days! It was a great trip.

This time, our layover is just enough time to get to the gate and board our Airbus to Venice. It's a ninety-minute flight over the Alps, and almost before we know it, we're descending for our landing at Marco Polo Airport.

CHAPTER 30

Clearing customs is a non-event. We claim our checked suitcases and head for the Customs Hall. At the first kiosk, a uniformed customs agent compares the photos in our passports to us, stamps our passports, says, "*Benvenuti in Italia,*" and waves us on. Mike's Official Passport seems to cause no reaction from the agent.

We move on to the long low table where travelers are having their suitcases searched. We place our suitcases on the table and start to open them. An agent spots us, rushes over, looks at the covers of our passports, says, "*Va via,*" and waives us on. Either they trust Americans or they are just eager to get our dollars.

It's about a two hundred yard walk from customs to the water taxi docks. Several locals, some in uniform some not, descend on us as we leave the building. They offer taxis, buses, lunch, souvenirs, hotels, tours; about anything we could want. I see one with a four wheeled cart, call him over, and greet him in Italian. He seems a little surprised that I speak Italian, but he recovers quickly and asks how he may be of service.

I explain that I have ordered a water taxi to take us to our hotel. He says he can take us and our luggage to the dock for only ten Euros. I tell him it's only two hundred meters, and offer him five. He shrugs and says, "*Si. Si. Va bene.*"

We've been sitting most of the night and morning. It's almost noon, Italian time, and we're stiff, tired, and a little grumpy, but we're excited to be here. We welcome the opportunity to walk. The weather is perfect and by the time we get to the docks, we're all feeling awake and ready to go. I tell our porter that our water taxi is waiting to take the Foxes to the Londra Palace. The porter looks suitably impressed. Mike says, "Still using that alias, Dad?" I just smile and nod as the porter finds our water taxi. He puts our luggage on board, helps the women get in, smiles broadly, and waits for his money. I give him the ten Euros he originally asked for. He smiles even more broadly, thanks me profusely, tells the taxi driver to take care of us, his good friends, and helps shove us off from the dock.

Our water taxi driver is about twenty-five, and his boat is immaculate. These guys own their own boats, and they are very proud of them. As we move away from the docks at idle, he introduces himself as Luciano and asks if it is our first visit to Italy. I tell him in Italian that we have been here before and that Venice is my favorite city in all of Italy. He agrees that Venice is the best city in the world! He tells me that we have chosen a great hotel, asks us all to sit and hold on. He brings the boat up on a plane, and we're off to Venice.

We head east at about twenty knots toward the island of Murano. Then Luciano turns a little south and takes us between Murano and San Michele. We pass by the Arsenale and make a broad turn south and then west around the eastern end of Castello. Luciano throttles back and brings his boat down off of plane as we pass the Giardini and approach the mouth of the Canale Grande. We see the Campanile that marks the Piazza San Marco just ahead as Luciano brings us in to the dock at San Zaccaria. He helps us ashore, loads our luggage onto a cart, and leads us on the thirty yard walk through the light crowd of tourists to the Londra Palace.

CHAPTER 31

Luciano holds the door open and we troop in to the relatively small but elegant lobby of the Londra Palace. I've already collected everybody's Passports. As Luciano busies himself with our luggage, I lay the Passports on the counter at the front desk. The desk clerk sees that they are American and says, in excellent English, "Good morning, sir. I am Paolo; how may I be of service?"

I tell him in Italian that though I speak Italian, his English is much better than my Italian. He tells me that my Italian is excellent – that my accent is even that of Veneto – "True Italian." I tell him that I learned Italian when I lived near Padova many years ago. I thank him for the compliment and switch to English. "We have two fourth-floor Junior Suites reserved, Paolo."

He is looking at my Passport. "Very good Mr. Peter." He enters information from our Passports into his computer, hands me one key, and hands another to Mike. "You have two of our best rooms. The view of Bacino San Marco and San Georgio Maggiore from your terraces is marvelous. Is there anything else you need at this time?"

"No, thank you. We would like to go up to our rooms and freshen up."

He calls over two bellmen. Each is pushing a brass hotel cart. "Please identify your luggage for Aldo and Franco."

We do as he asked. "Aldo and Franco will escort you to your rooms. Then they will bring your luggage."

Aldo leads Kate and me to the elevator. The elevator is not big enough for six, so Franco waits to bring Mike and Laura up. As we make the quick ride up, Kate asks, "Did Paolo say terrace? I thought we had a junior suite with a balcony like last time."

"Last time, we were on the third floor. This time, we are 'movin' on up' -- to the fourth floor. Wait 'til we get there; then decide which you like better."

Aldo unlocks the door, pushes it open, and stands aside so we can go in. The suite is stunning. It looks exactly like a five-star hotel suite in Venice should look. The furnishings all say old Italian class. Kate just stands there for a minute taking it in. Aldo comes in, pulls the curtains aside and opens the French doors leading to the terrace. Kate walks out onto the terrace; I follow. Our third floor suite last time had a small balcony – just big enough for us to stand on and take in the view. This suit has a terrace with several potted plants and a table set for two. I can see the tears in the corners of Kate's eyes. She hugs me and says, "Peter, you done good."

"Mike and I decided to do it right. If we find the Red Diamonds, we will be traveling like this all the time. If we don't find them, this is our last luxury vacation for a while. So let's enjoy."

Aldo says, "I go bring luggage, Signore."

We sit at our little table holding hands. We hear the doors to the adjoining terrace slide open. We can't see the terrace because of the intervening privacy wall, but we recognize Lauri's voice. "Oh shite." After a minute, "Are you guys over there?" We hear Mike's laugh.

Kate walks over to the railing. "I don't know who you're expecting, but your neighbors are the King and Queen of Ohio."

Lauri counters with "It's only fitting that the Prince and Princess of Colorado should have you as neighbors."

I walk over and lean over the railing a little so I can see Mike and Lauri. "What do you think?"

Mike smiles. "It'll do."

* * *

We shower and change clothes. We're refreshed – and hungry.

I call Mike's room. "Are you guys up to a ten-minute walk through Piazza San Marco? I know a good restaurant."

"Sounds like a plan. Give us five minutes."

"We will meet you downstairs."

CHAPTER 32

We walk west along the Riva degli Schiavoni, probably the most famous walk in Venice. We have the Grand Canal on our left and some of the most photographed sights in Venice on our right. We pass the Bridge of Sighs and turn right past the ornate pink Palazzo Ducale. We have to keep stopping as Lauri or Mike or both play tourist and gawk at something or snap a picture. It *is* their first time in Venice. It *is* worth gawking at.

We walk through the Piazza San Marco, past the Basilica di San Marco, and through the passage under the Torre dell'Orologio – the Clock Tower. We turn right onto Calle Larga San Marco and push our way through the tourists. It's May, not yet high season, but there are always crowds of tourists in Venice. At least until about ten pm. Then most of the tourists go back to their mainland hotels or back to their cruise ships. That's when Venice, the tourist mecca becomes Venezia, the home of the Veneziani, the city I love.

We come to the Ristorante All'Angelo. It has changed over the almost forty years that I've been coming here, but it will always be a place I remember fondly. I was a twenty-two-year-old kid, in the Air Force, away from my wife of one year for the first time, stationed on a small radio site in the hills west of here. We worked four days on and four days off. I had no friends there and Venice was an hour's train ride away. I came here whenever I could afford it. The Hotel All'Angelo was at best, a one-star hotel back then, but it was reasonably clean and the staff was friendly. They were pleased that I was learning to speak their language and I quickly became a regular, both at the hotel and the ristorante.

Like most restaurants in Venice, they have a multi-lingual menu posted outside, and a multi-lingual waiter standing next to it inviting us in. "This is it," I say to the group. I steer us toward the front door; the waiter smiles broadly. "Welcome. You are four?"

We have a light lunch. Cantaloupe is in season and the *Prosciutto e Melone* is marvelous. We follow it with pasta dishes. Everybody tries something different -- I have my usual Pasta Carbonara. After a couple of glasses of house wine each, everybody is thinking nap.

I lead our little group through some of the back streets east of Saint Mark's, and we emerge back on Riva degli Schiavoni right next to the Londra Palace.

Lauri is a little surprised. "I was sure we were lost. How long has it been since you were here?"

"About four years. Kate and I spent a week in Florence and a week here."

"You remember it amazingly well."

"Not really. If you pay attention, it is hard to get lost. On our way to lunch, we crossed two canals going west and then turned north. To get back here, I took us east across two canals and then turned south. We had to come out close."

The wine brought out the jet lag. We agreed to meet about seven, and headed up to our rooms.

CHAPTER 33

I'm not really sleeping, just sort of drifting in and out – on the edge of sleep. Too many thoughts are fighting for my attention. My iPhone dings: incoming text message. I bought European SIM cards for all four of our phones. Mike and I put them in on the plane. But I've been wondering if I should have bought burner phones, instead. It's unlikely that anyone is tracking us or listening in. Then again, I said the same thing before the NSA wiretapping scandal broke at home…

I look at my phone: "Are you up, Dad?"

I text back, "Meet me downstairs. Bar. 5 min."

I get up quietly, splash some water in my face, write a quick note to Kate, and go out into the hall. Mike is just leaving their room.

"Couldn't sleep?"

"No sir. Too much to think about. You?"

I hit the elevator down button. "Same thing. I'm surprised that the jet lag isn't bothering me more."

"I think people make a bigger deal of it than is justified. I travel back and forth from the US to Europe almost constantly. My body seems to adjust quickly."

We get into the empty elevator and I hit 1. "With all your travel, I'm surprised that you've never been to Venice."

"Venice may be high on the tourist list, but it's low on the government business list."

"I understand. During my first stay in Europe, I was very fortunate to get stationed on a six-man radio site about thirty-five miles west of here; I came here frequently. I could have wound up like many of my friends – one of hundreds or even thousands of GIs on some big NATO base. To live in a small Italian village, and to be within commuting distance of Venice was amazing. 'Oh, the stories I could tell…'"

"I suspect that we'll have a new bunch of stories to tell when this quest is over."

"I expect that you are right!"

The elevator door opens on the ground floor. We walk twenty feet to the small bar. Like most bars in Italy, in addition to alcoholic beverages, it serves coffee, and light snacks. Mike and I each order an expresso and a brioche and move to a small table tucked into the corner near the end of the bar.

"So refresh my memory. What's the plan?"

"Tomorrow we play tourist. The main part of Venice is divided up into six sistieri or neighborhoods. The Canale Grande does a big "S" shape through the middle. Here. I've got a map."

"So where are we?"

I point. "We are in San Marco – one of the six sistieri. Here is where we walked this morning."

"We're going to see the other five sistieri tomorrow?"

"No. That would take a week; or a month; or a lifetime. I thought that in the morning, we could walk up here to the Rialto – probably the most photographed bridge in Venice. Well, maybe second. The first is probably the Bridge of Sighs."

"That *was* cool."

The waiter brings our coffee and sweet rolls to our table. I fold the map some to make room. "We will have lunch around the Rialto, and then hop on a vaporetto – water bus – for a trip out to Murano and Burano. And if you're up to it, to Torcello."

"You lost me."

I point out the three islands on the map. "From the Rialto, the vaporetto will go this way, around Sant'Elena to Murano. We came that way this morning. We can stop at Murano if you want to check out some of its glass factories. Burano, up here, is known for hand made lace; and houses painted in all different pastel colors. Torcello is the oldest settlement around. The church was built in something like 650. Not 1650 – 650. It's an amazing place. Torcello was founded somewhere around 450 by mainlanders trying to escape from attacks by Attila the Hun. It grew to 10,000 people and then started sinking into the mud. It is mostly swamp now and the population is about ten. But the church is awesome."

"Sounds like a very full day."

"We can do as much or as little as you guys want. But right here is something that is the key to everything."

I point to San Michele. As I've been talking, I've called up a photo on my iPhone. I lay my phone on the map next to San Michele. "This is the grave of Princesse Troubetzkoy. The map is hidden in the wall behind it. We hope…"

"So when do we go get it?"

"Day after tomorrow."

CHAPTER 34

Time to eat again.

We stroll back to the Piazza san Marco. "Do you guys want fine dining, atmosphere, or good Venetian cooking?"

Lauri says, "I'm still full from lunch. How about one of these sidewalk cafes?"

"That's the 'atmosphere' choice." I lead us through the piazza to dinner and music at the Gran Café Chioggia. We choose an outside table near the Grand Canal. A waiter comes rushing over. "*Buona sera, signori.*"

He hands out the usual multilingual menus. I smile at him and try out my still slightly rusty Italian. "Drinks, for now. A light dinner later."

The waiter looks reasonably pleased; we'll be here a while. In the United States, the waiters depend on tips for most of their income, and they maximize income by turning tables quickly. In Europe, waiters make a reasonable hourly pay, and tips aren't their driving factor. They assume that when you sit down, you'll be there for a long time; the longer you stay, the fewer new diners they'll have to deal with. The whole dynamic is different.

We order a carafe of house red wine, and a bottle of San Pellegrino. The band –orchestra? – quartet? –starts playing.

This earns another "Oh shite" from Lauri. "You read about this. You see it in movies. It really *does* exist!"

We enjoy the music and the atmosphere. Eventually we all have a pasta dish. Mine is the Pasta Carbonara – again. Pasta here is usually considered a first course or a side dish. But again, we make it our main course.

By the time we're fed and paid up, it's dark. The crowds have thinned out. Venice is turning into Venezia. Kate says, "I hope you guys have saved a little room for dessert. Follow me."

We walk across the piazza to the Torre dell'Orologio. I should have known. Kate's favorite gelateria is right beneath the clock. I laugh. "I should have known. Kate always has room for gelato."

We're stuffed and tired as we slowly walk hand in hand back to the hotel. It's still fairly early, but we're tired. And we'll have a long day tomorrow.

CHAPTER 35

We meet for a light breakfast at Do Leoni, the Londra Palace's restaurant. The veranda overlooks the Riva degli Schiavoni; it's a great place for people watching.

The Rialto Bridge is less than half a mile from the hotel as the crow flies, but this is Venice. The trip takes us through Piazza san Marco again, along many narrow streets and alleys, across numerous bridges, (and into a couple of accidental dead ends), but we get there. We've probably walked a mile; it's taken us over an hour; this is Venice.

The bridge is another photo opportunity. We take pictures with each other's cameras and phones. We ask a stranger to take a photo of the four of us. She is French, I think. But with a short pantomime, she understands what we're asking. She takes several pictures, and then asks us to take a picture of her with her camera. We oblige her. Then Kate and Lauri join her to make a threesome and Mike and I take several pictures of the three of them with her camera and ours. I wonder how many times this little brief passing connection is repeated in Venice. The city brings that out in people.

We decide that it's way too early for lunch, so we walk to the Fondamento Nove vaporetto dock. It's another less than half a mile as-the-crow-flies jaunt that is really more like a mile and takes another hour. But we're in no hurry – this is play tourist day.

We buy our tickets and board the number 12 boat. Nobody really wants to see the glass factories or buy glass, so we bypass Murano and head for Burano. It'll be a great place for lunch.

The first stop the number 12 makes happens quickly. A few passengers, some carrying flowers, leave the vaporetto here. I play tour guide. "This is San Michele – the cemetery island of Venice.

"San Michele is about a quarter mile square, and sits just north of the main islands of Venice. For at least 200 years, it has served as Venice's cemetery. There is a section reserved for Orthodox Catholics – the "Greci" section. In that section is the grave of the Princesse Troubetzkoy. And buried in the wall behind her grave is Mitri's map. Well, maybe. It was put there a hundred years ago. Is it still there? Is it still readable? Tomorrow, we find out."

We stay on the boat for the trip to Murano -- another quarter mile. About three quarters of our fellow passengers disembark at Murano. They are mainly tourists with money to spend at the glass factories. Murano has been inhabited since Roman times, but in 1291, the Venetian government, afraid of fires, forced all glassmakers to move to Murano. It has been the center of the world of ornamental glassmaking ever since.

We stay aboard with the now mainly Italian passengers for the two-mile trip to Burano. We disembark and walk the hundred yards to the center of Burano. Burano, like Murano and Venice itself, is really a small group of islands, complete with canals and bridges. I'm not sure why, but the buildings in Burano are all painted with a rainbow of pastel colors. That, and its lace works are its claim to fame.

We find a restaurant with outdoor tables overlooking the small central square and settle in for lunch.

* **

Full and refreshed, we stop in a couple of lace shops, buy nothing, and head back for the vaporetto dock. Torcello is the next island, less than a hundred yards from Burano, but you can't get there without a boat.

So we wait for the next vaporetto, make the short hop across the canal and walk to the little palazzo and its group of ancient churches.

These are some of the oldest in northern Italy. If there is a word that describes Torcello, it is quiet. The whole island sort of demands quiet. And the churches demand reverence. It's hard to describe -- I felt it once before, at Notre Dame in Paris. We're walking with the ghosts of Torcello's past.

We visit the little round Church of Santa Fosca; there are a dozen tourists, and it's dead quiet. The tenth century mosaics are awesome. We move on to the Cathedral of Santa Maria Assunta; more tourists, more quiet. We sit for a while in one of the pews. No one says anything. We can feel God's presence. We think or meditate or pray. After a while, without discussion, we get up and walk out into the sun. Kate smiles. Lauri says, "Awesome."

We take a few pictures and head back along the little canal to the Vaporetto dock. We pass an odd little stone bridge over the canal. It has no railings; just a humped walkway. More pictures. I suspect that this bridge has a story; it might be worth Googling.

More importantly, we pass a little trattoria. Well, we almost pass it. Time for a coffee break. Actually, the girls share a small carafe of the local red wine and Mike and I each have an espresso. Then it's back to the dock to wait for the next vaporetto home – to the Londra Palace.

And dinner.

CHAPTER 36

I had planned on dinner at the Alle Carone. It's a truly outstanding restaurant in a city of great restaurants. But it's another walk back to the Rialto bridge area. We're tired, and excited about tomorrow. We decide to eat at a small trattoria we saw on the little street behind the hotel.

It turns out to be a great choice. It's quiet, the food is simple but good, and we feel comfortable talking about tomorrow. After dinner and coffee, I ask our waiter, Vincenzo, if we may stay a while and talk. He smiles and says, "*Naturalmente. signore.*" It's late enough that the tourists have gone back to wherever they are staying, and there are just a few small groups, mostly Italians, doing what we're doing. Talking.

Vincenzo cleans off the table, and I lay my map of the Venetian lagoons out on the table. "The first stop on the vaporetto today was San Michele. As I said then, the entire island is one big cemetery. Several hundred years ago the Venetian government decided that the practice of burying their dead under the pavements was not a good idea and they decreed that all burials would be on San Michele."

That gets Kate's attention. "You mean under the streets?"

"Yes. As the city started to sink and the high tides started to flood the some of the streets, they realized that the needed a better solution. Hence San Michele."

Mike adds, "After 'several hundred years,' isn't it getting kind of full?"

"As a matter of fact it *is* full. Only Venetians can be buried there, and only the very wealthy can afford a *permanent* grave or crypt. Most Venetians sort of rent a space. After ten years, they move your bones elsewhere, and rent your spot to a new corpse. I've not bothered to research just *where* they move your bones."

I replace the bigger map of the lagoons with the eight and a half by eleven PDF that I printed. "Anyway, here's a map of San Michele that I found on the internet.

"You can see that the cemetery is broken up into sections. I have no idea what most of these section titles designate, but I do know that this is the one we're interested in. The 'Greco' section is for Orthodox Catholics – as opposed to Roman Catholics – and that's where the Princesse Troubetzkoy is buried. Mitri hid his map behind a loose brick in the wall behind her grave.

"Tomorrow we look for the brick – and the map."

Mike looks dubious. "After a hundred years, I doubt that the loose brick is still loose. It's more likely that it fell out or that it got cemented back in."

I agree with him. "You are absolutely right. We were here the last time we were in Venice. I remember that the cemetery walls were in good condition. I don't know what we're going to find. I do know that tomorrow will determine whether we continue our quest or not."

CHAPTER 37

It's eight o'clock. We're at Do Leoni having an "American" breakfast. The Italian idea of breakfast is coffee, either cappuccino or café al latte, and rolls or bread with butter and jam. We're almost certain to have a long day and there is no food on San Michele, so we're fueling up with ham and eggs and potatoes and toast.

It's quiet at the table. We all know that the results of this trip will affect the rest of our lives. Without Mitri's map, the quest ends here; with it, we continue in Ukraine.

* * *

The number 12 vaporetto is crowded, so we've opted to stand amidships. The boat makes a couple of stops as it takes us around the eastern end of Castello and back west to San Michele. We disembark with a small group of mostly Italians. San Michele is not high on the Trip Advisor to-do list. Most of the women who get off are dressed in black, and most of the men wear black arm bands. We've tried to dress conservatively, but we still stand out. Many of the Italians carry flowers; Mike carries a backpack.

The vaporetto dock leads directly to the cemetery. I take a quick look at the map to orient myself. "This way."

We stroll past sections reserved for priests and nuns and military. The hole-in-the-wall entrance to the Greco section is clearly marked. We walk through the entrance and stop. The Greco section is about forty yards square. It's completely surrounded by a brick wall about eight feet tall. And it's deserted; we are the only visitors this morning.

The Greco section is filled with burial plots, some with little walls around them; some with gravel; some with grass. A few have flowers; all have markers of various sizes.

We make our way along the path that follows the row of graves along the wall. We know exactly what we're looking for. I actually found a photo of the gravestone of the Princesse Troubetzkoy on the internet. Her grave is surrounded by a low wall with granite corner posts and a heavy chain defining the perimeter. The gravestone itself is a rectangular block of granite about two feet square and three feet high. It's surmounted with a six-foot-high granite cross.

Lauri has been leading the way. She spots it first. "I see it!" And she takes off at a slow trot.

We catch up in a couple of minutes. She's right. This is the grave of the Princesse Troubetzkoy.

CHAPTER 38

The wall behind the Princesse's grave is in a good state of repair. The bricks have been pointed and nothing appears to be loose. It looks like there is a break in the age of the brickwork. The first five courses above the gravel look older. The bricks are crude and vary in size. Many are stained with splotches of gray and black. Above that the bricks are more consistent in size and color. It's pretty obvious that the upper wall was rebuilt fairly recently. This could be bad.

Mitri's directions were very specific. "Stand at the feet of Princesse Troubetzkoy. Look past her left shoulder. The brick you see is protecting the map."

Assuming that I am about Mitri's height and assuming that "her right shoulder" is the top of the granite block, I locate the brick. It's in the older part of the wall; and it's right at ground level. It is not loose. As Lauri would say, "Shite."

The backpack Mike is carrying has a few tools. I bought a small gardener's hand shovel and a three-tonged hand rake during our wanders the first day we were here. I added a couple of screwdrivers yesterday. But we'll need more than that to break through the pointing and remove the brick.

Kate has a suggestion. "I saw what looked like a tool shed. At least there were some tools and tool carriers outside."

I hadn't noticed it. "Where at?"

"Just past the entrance to this section. Not more than fifty feet further."

CHAPTER 39

We leave the Greco section and walk down the path to the shed that Kate saw. It does look like a maintenance worker's shed. There are garden tools of various sorts and a wheelbarrow near the entrance.

The door is padlocked. I rattle it in frustration. Mike says, "Let me look, Dad."

He takes a very close look at the lock. "Never thought I'd need my set of lock picks."

"Why am I not surprised that you own a set of lock picks?"

"That's a story for another day."

Mike goes into military mode. "What we need here is a little brute force. Let's break out the walkie talkies. You guys establish a perimeter. Double click the talk button if somebody is approaching. I'll get us in. I'll do four clicks when you can come back."

Kate, Lauri and I head down the main paths that lead to the shed. I just get back to the entrance to the Greco section when I hear four clicks. I turn around and head back. The door to the shed is open. By the time I get back to the shed, Mike is standing outside holding some hand tools.

"These should do the job." He holds up two cold chisels and a small hand sledge hammer

"Yeah. That's great."

"There's a small crowbar just inside and to the right, Dad. Grab that too."

"Will do. Let's head back."

Mike closes the door and replaces the now broken hasp. It won't pass a close inspection. But from the path, it looks fine.

We walk back to the grave. "I am really glad you saw that place, Kate. You saved the day."

CHAPTER 40

We get back to the Princesse's grave. I stand at her feet again and look over her shoulder. "Go point to a brick, Mike."

He uses the point of his toe. "This one?"

"Two to the right and one down."

He moves his toe. "You got it."

Mike stoops down to look more closely. "Okay. I'll remove the brick. We'll have to post lookouts. Same signals as before."

There is still nobody in the Greco section. The walls hide us from people outside of the section. All we need is a lookout at the entrance. I volunteer. Kate says she'll come with me.

There is a stone bench just outside the entrance. We sit and try to look like we're resting. We can just hear the clink of metal on metal coming from the Greco section.

An old woman dressed in black and carrying flowers comes down the path. She stops at the entrance and looks at the brass plaque mounted on the wall next to it. I double click the walkie talkie. She turns and continues down the path. "False alarm. And we don't have an all-clear signal."

Kate says, "I'll go talk to them."

In what seems like forever but is really less than five minutes, Kate comes back. "I told them what happened. Two clicks for intruder warning. Three for all clear. Four from Mike still means return."

We wait. We're too nervous to even chat. I look at my watch. We wait.

We wait. It's been almost a half hour. If we listen carefully, we can hear the clinking. Another fifteen minutes. The clinking stops. Another five minutes. Suddenly the walkie talkie clicks four times. We almost run. This is it.

CHAPTER 41

Mike and Lauri look disappointed.

"Well?"

"Nothing."

Kate looks ready to cry. "Nothing? Now what? Is it over?"

Mike looks at his hole in the wall. "We may have the wrong brick. Let me look. You figure I should stand here and look over the right corner of the block. I thought Mitri said look over her left shoulder."

"She is buried face up. Her left shoulder is on your right."

"Got it. I'm tall enough that I'm looking at the brick below the one I dug out. Let's remove that one. Back to your lookout post!"

We just get settled on the bench when a uniformed guard walks purposefully down the path and turns in to the Greco section. I click twice. Did someone hear the noise? I click twice again. I wait thirty seconds. I click twice again. We wait.

In a few minutes, the guard comes back out, looks at us somewhat suspiciously, and returns the way he came.

We go back to the grave. Mike looks a little shaken. "What happened?"

"The guard walked up to me and said, 'Signore, we have reports of noise from this section. What are you doing?'

"I stammered a little and told him that my great-grandmother's grave stone was leaning a little. I said, 'I fix.' Thank God I put my backpack in front of the hole in the wall when Lauri saw him coming."

"Then what?"

"He said very pointedly, 'You are not permitted to do that. Report the problem to the office. Our workers will fix it.'

"I told him I would put things back the way they were and he said, 'You must do nothing more. Our workers will do it.'

"I said, 'Okay, got it,' and made like I was paying my respects. He left."

Lauri had been silent until now. "I don't think he really believed us. His look said 'I know you're up to no good.'"

Kate broke in. "He'll probably come back to check up on you. What do we do now?"

I have an idea. "Let's put everything back and wander around the cemetery for a while and make sure we're seen elsewhere. Then we can come back. Mike, did you get the second brick out?"

"I just got it out when Lauri alerted me."

"No map?"

"No map, but it looks like there's a hole behind the next brick to the left. I want to take it out."

"Okay. Let's play tourist for a while."

CHAPTER 42

We wander the cemetery for a while, making sure that we are seen in various places. We see the guard who confronted Mike at least twice. He still looks suspicious of us.

After a while, I ask another uniformed guard for the location of the oldest graves. I ask him in English. He doesn't understand, and I pretend to not understand his response in Italian. I try the classic tourist gambit of speaking slowly and loudly. "Old … grave … sites…" It doesn't work, of course.

His eyes say "Stupid American tourists," but his mouth says, "*Asspeta un po'*. You wait." He says a few words into the portable radio mike clipped to his epaulet. The only word I catch is *Americani.* The response comes quickly. "*Dove sei, Paolo*?" Paolo answers, "*Il secondo.*"

"*Dammi cinque minute, Paolo.*"

"*Grazie, Aldo.*" And to us, he says, "You wait."

We wait. Aldo turns out to be the guard who confronted Mike. He looks even more suspicious when he sees us. He walks up to Mike and says, "How can I help you? More gravestones to fix, perhaps?"

I quickly step between Aldo and Mike. "Excuse me, sir. I am his father. Mike is retired military; he can be '*come se dice*?' rash. I'm sorry that we caused a problem at my grandmother's grave. We were only trying to help."

"Military? I was military. I understand. It is nothing."

"I am writing a book about the Princesse and we wanted to see her grave. Your cemetery is amazing. I would like to get a better understanding of this remarkable place by visiting its oldest sections. If you can point them out on our map, I would appreciate it."

"Certainly, signore. I would take you, but I have other duties just now." He points to several sections on the south-western part of the island. "You must see this, and this, and this. And perhaps here, as well."

I thank him profusely and comment on his excellent command of the English language. He beams. "Thank you. It is important that I speak English well. I hope to study in America soon. Forensic Science at the State University of Ohio. I have family in Columbus, Ohio."

I tell him that we are from Ohio. I introduce myself and Kate. I tell him that my son and his wife are from Colorado, and introduce them as well.

The suspicious look is gone. We are friends now. Aldo takes a minute to explain all of this to Paolo, then turns back to me. "I'm sorry to say that I must leave to attend a meeting in Venice. Paolo will escort you to the old sections."

I thank Aldo again, and tell him that we do not wish to take up any more of Paolo's valuable time; that we can find our own way. But he insists. We say our good byes; handshakes for the men; hugs for the women. After all, we're almost neighbors. Kate has even gotten his Facebook address so she can keep in touch.

Now all we have to do is ditch Paolo and we can get back to the Princesse's grave.

* * *

We've seen enough old grave sites to last a lifetime. When Paolo is finally satisfied that he has done his job, he smiles broadly and points down a gravel path. He says, "*Uscita*. Exit."

We thank him with words and smiles. After handshakes and hugs all around, we start slowly down the path to the exit as Paolo heads down another path.

* * *

Soon we are back at the Greco section. Kate and I take up residence on our bench and Lauri and Mike head for the Princesse's grave.

This time there is no discernable noise. We wait. And wonder. And wait.

It's only been ten minutes when we hear the four clicks that mean come here.

We almost run.

Mike is grinning. Lauri is so excited she's bouncing up and down.

As we get close, Mike holds up a moldy looking leather pouch about the size of a brick and an inch thick. "It was behind the next brick. Apparently, they never removed the brick. They just secured it by filling the spaces around it with a layer of mortar. One good tug with the crow bar and it popped right out."

"Let's put the bricks back in case somebody comes in."

"I've already done that. And I've filled in the spaces between the bricks with a paste I made of dirt and water. It will deteriorate fairly quickly, but we'll be gone by the time Aldo notices it and figures out that we really were up to something."

Lauri says, "Let's open it. It's killing me not to look."

I say, "Let's get out of here and find some place private."

"This is Venice. There *is* no place private!"

"Then we will go back to the hotel if we have to. Nobody else can see this."

"Shite."

Kate looks almost mad. "I agree. Shite. Let's move."

And we do.

CHAPTER 43

It's only a hundred fifty yards to the vaporetto dock. I look over my shoulder every ten yards. No pursuit. We get down the ramp to the floating dock without incident. I don't know how often the boats run. Once again, we wait. I keep expecting a bunch of guards to come running down the gangplank and arrest us.

I'm jittery. I buy us four tickets and pass them out. The tickets are 7 € each and are good for travel anywhere the vaporetti run for up to one hour from the time of purchase. We've spent quite a bit of money on the vaporetti in the last couple of days. But it's either that or swim, and the water doesn't look particularly inviting.

The next boat comes alongside the dock before my imagined hoard of guards. We quickly board and find seats in the stern. As soon as we sit down, Lauri wants to open the leather pouch. "Let's take a quick look. Nobody will know what it is."

I caution against it. "We are talking about a hundred-year-old piece of paper. It has to be delicate. I don't want to take a chance with the wind. We will be back at the Londra palace soon."

"Shite."

Mike has been looking over the stern. "I need to get rid of these tools. Toss them overboard, you think?"

I take a quick look around. The boat is fairly crowded. "Somebody might see or hear. We will take a walk tonight and dump them in a canal somewhere."

* * *

The vaporetto ties up at the San Zaccaria dock. We're first off of the boat, and Mike and Lauri take off for the Londra Palace. They're almost running. A couple of obvious locals scowl and grumble about rude tourists. I say, "*Gabinetto,*" and shrug my shoulders. It doesn't help.

Kate and I head for the hotel at a quick walk. We catch up with Mike and Lauri at the elevator. "Your room or ours?"

Kate says, "Our desk is clear. Let's use that."

As soon as we get into our room, Mike takes the leather pouch from his backpack and tosses the backpack on our bed. He sits down at our desk and lays the pouch on the blotter. It's time.

CHAPTER 44

We all drag chairs up to the desk. Mike pulls what looks like a dark grey credit card from his wallet. He unfolds it into a very sharp looking knife with about a two-and-a-half-inch blade. "Handy thing to have."

The leather pouch is shaped roughly like a #10 business envelope. The leather is dry but it has an almost soggy look. I think it was originally brown, but now it's covered with green and black splotches. The flap of the envelope looks like it's pretty well fused to the envelope itself.

Mike tries to insert the knife blade under the tip of the flap. No luck. He tries along the side of the flap. Again, no luck,

He stands the pouch on edge, long side on the table, and says, "Hold it in this position, Dad."

I do, and he carefully cuts the leather between the flap and the envelope proper. It only takes a minute, but it is a very long minute.

Mike puts his two thumbs into the cut and gently opens the envelope. I look inside, reach in with two fingers and two thumbs, and gently extract a yellowish brown cloth pad. I know the feel – it's beeswax. Natural waterproofing! Mitri had planned this well.

I lay the pad on the blotter and hold it while Mike peels it open to expose a yellowing folded up piece of paper. We carefully separate the cloth from the paper. The paper is yellowed but not brittle or even very faded. The leather and beeswax have preserved it well for a hundred years. We have a map!

I carefully unfold the paper. Like Oleksandr's map, this one is about twelve inches by fifteen inches, but this paper is quite thin. Almost like today's onion skin. It's not brittle, but I know it won't take much handling. We have to get copies made as soon as we can. The important thing is that the map is perfectly readable. Well -- it would be perfectly readable if you read old Ukrainian.

The map has a compass rose drawn on the top right hand corner. Like Oleksandr's map, it has no scale. On the left hand side of the map there is a drawing of three trees near the west bank of a river. There are three small groups of small circles north, west and south of the trees. The middle tree has what looks like a stone where a large branch leaning toward the river joins the trunk. The drawing is almost identical to Oleksandr's. This map starts where Oleksandr's ends!

A dashed line starts at a small group of circles on the east bank of the river opposite the trees. It continues east two thirds of the way across the paper, then turns northeast for about two inches, and then goes east again for another inch. There are no landmarks, but there are six notes along the dashed line. We need these translated. And soon. The dashed line ends at an X, just like on Oleksandr's map.

This X is surrounded by a small rectangle. From the centers of the two short sides of the rectangle are perpendicular lines with arrows on the ends pointing away from the rectangle. One line is about twice the length of the long side of the rectangle. The other is about twice as long as the first. At the end of each line, the arrow points to another small circle. Each circle has a short note near it.

My guess is that the six notes refer to landmarks along the way. The X and the rectangle are the red diamonds, probably buried in a box. The circles are more stones marking the burial spot. But without translating the notes, we'll never find the diamonds.

We need translations – and quickly.

I don't know why we didn't expect this. There is nobody here in Venice like Father Pataki.

But I have an idea.

CHAPTER 45

"I have an idea. Let's scan the map to a BMP file, and use MS Paint to crop each of the notes to a PFD file. I can email them to Father Pataki."

Lauri always sees the problems. "And how are we going to scan them?"

"I am going to go buy a small scanner. Paolo will know where there is a computer store."

"Does email even work here?"

"Yes. The hotel has free Wi-Fi. I have already checked my email."

"You should make copies of the map while you're at it. I don't think it will take much handling."

"Good idea, Lauri. Want to come along?"

"No. I think I hear a glass of wine calling me. And something to eat."

"Kate?"

"I think Lauri has a great idea. It's been a very long morning. We could all use something to eat and a glass of wine. Or two."

"You are right. Where? Downstairs?"

"Let's go to the trattoria where we ate last night, Dad. Then I'll go with you to the computer store and the girls can go wherever."

* * *

Ten minutes later, we're in the elevator heading down to the lobby and the short walk to the trattoria.

Paolo is working the front desk. "Wait a minute. I want to ask Paolo about computer stores."

At the mention of his name, Paolo looks up from what he is doing. "*Buona giornata, Signore.* What is it that you need?" My three companions continue past the front desk to wait outside.

I explain to Paolo that I am doing a little work while we are on vacation. Paolo says that that is a pity, but if it is necessary…

"Yes, unfortunately, it is necessary. I need to make copies of some documents. I need what we call in America a Copy Center. Then I need to scan some other documents so that I can email them. I have my laptop computer but no scanner. I think that I will have to buy a small scanner. Can you direct me to businesses that will help?"

Paolo smiles broadly. "I can do more than direct you. We have a fully equipped Business Center on the second floor. You can copy, print, scan, fax, use our computers; do whatever you need. There is, of course, no charge for our guests."

I thank Paolo in Italian and English and tell him I will use their facility either this evening or tomorrow morning. I head outside to pass on the good news.

CHAPTER 46

Fifteen minutes later we're back at the Trattoria da Nino. Vincenzo remembers us from last night. "*Buon pomeriggio. Come va oggi?*"

"*Va bene. E lei?*"

"*Bene. Bene,*" He seats us at the same table we had last night. I order a carafe of house red wine and a bottle of sparkling water. I tell Vincenzo that we'll be having a late lunch in a bit. He goes off to fetch our drinks.

Kate vocalizes the question we're all thinking. "So what's next?"

They all look at me. "As soon as we get back to the Hotel, I'll send Father Pataki an email. I'll tell him I have more notes that I need translated, but that I won't be able to get them scanned until later tonight or tomorrow. I'll also tell him that I need a quick turnaround because I'm going out of town on business. I will *not* tell him that I'm in Italy."

Kate frowns. "I don't like it."

"Why?"

"We're giving Father Pataki too much information. He'll want to know where the new notes come from. He'll suspect that we found another map. He knows where we're headed."

"What do you mean?"

"The last note on the map he saw said, 'Mitri's map to the Red Diamonds begins here.' And now you're going to give him more notes to translate?"

Vincenzo returns with our drinks. I tell him that we'd like to relax some before we eat. He says he understands, and moves on to another table of somewhat loud tourists. "So what else can we do?"

"Let's go back to the hotel after we eat. You make copies of the map and also scan it. As you said, you can crop each of the notes into PDFs. I'll get on the Internet and see what I can find in the way of translation services that can handle old Ukrainian."

Lauri says, "I'll help you."

Mike says, "I'll work with you, Dad."

And I say, "Let's eat."

The group at the next table is getting noisy. Vincenzo takes the bill to their table. He stands there waiting while they talk amongst themselves and figure out who owes how much. Vincenzo looks pained. His expression says, "Please pay and go away. Please."

Finally, they get it figured out, pile their money on top of the bill and start to get up. Vincenzo scoops up the money, says a quick "*Grazie*," and heads for the register. As he walks past our table, he looks me in the eye. "*I giapponesi sono i peggiori.*"

Mike overhears him. "What did he say?"

The noisy ones are going out the door as I smile and translate. "The Japanese are the worst..."

* * *

By the time we get back to the Londra Palace, we are all in agreement that we've had enough for one day. We have all day tomorrow. It's our last day in Italy and we have almost nothing planned. We'll get a fresh start at dealing with the map in the morning.

We decide to take a walk to the Piazza San Marco and have gelato. Venice has what Kate thinks is the greatest gelato in Italy.

The gelateria beneath the Torre dell'Orologio has at least 20 flavors – and she is determined to try them all!

CHAPTER 47

After breakfast, Mike and I go downstairs to the front desk. There is a new clerk at the desk. I tell him that I talked to Paolo yesterday about using the Business Center. I ask him its location on the second floor, and how I gain access.

He stumbles a little with his English, and I tell him in Italian that I speak a little Italian. He grins, and apologizes for his poor English. I tell him that his English is better than my Italian. He disagrees, but continues in Italian. He introduces himself as Lorenzo and tells me that the Business Center is at the end of the hall to the left from the elevator, and he gives me a metal plate the size of a credit card with a hole in one corner. A ring goes through the hole and has a key on it. He hands me two flash memory sticks with the hotel logo on them and says that if I need more, to just ask. I thank him and we head back upstairs to our rooms.

We both go to Kate's and my room. I knock lightly and open the door part way. "If you are not decent, go hide. Mike is with me."

"I'm decent; I'm decent. What's the plan?"

I tell her that we're heading for the Business Center. She picks up her laptop and announces that she is going to work in Lauri's room. "I want to check their room out, anyway."

I get the folder of papers from our in-room safe, gather up my laptop, give Kate a quick kiss, and Mike and I head out the door.

* * *

The business center has everything we need. The copier even does A3 copies. A3 is a European paper size close to eleven by seventeen and perfect for our map. We make several copies of the map.

Mike snips the Ukrainian language notes from a copy of the map while I play with the DPI setting of the scanner to find the best compromise between resolution and file size. We have made everything we need within an hour.

* * *

Upstairs, we find the girls hard at work. Mike asks what I was about to ask. "Any luck?"

Lauri answers. "We found a couple of sites. Including the Ukrainian Embassy in Rome. There's also an Honorary Consulate in Padova, about twenty miles west of here."

It's my turn to be wary. "I am not sure that I want to ask the Ukrainians to translate for us. I don't want to warn them that we're up to something besides playing tourist and 'discovering our roots.'"

"Good point. Can we have more time to look?"

"Sure. Mike and I need to go try to buy some burner phones that will work in Ukraine and Paris."

"What's wrong with using our phones? You put European SIM cards in them."

"I don't know that there is anything wrong with using our phones. Maybe I am being paranoid. I would rather be able to communicate between Ukraine and France anonymously. That's all"

"I guess that makes sense."

CHAPTER 48

When Mike and I get down to the lobby, Paolo is back. "*Ciao, Paolo*... Is it appropriate to say 'Ciao'?"

"*Si. Si.* Formality is not necessary. We are becoming friends. Can I help you with anything?"

"Yes in a couple of days, my son and I are making a trip to Ukraine and our wives are going to Paris. We will meet back here at the Londra Palace in a week or so."

"And I can help, how?"

"I need to buy some inexpensive cell phones so we can keep in touch. I'm told that our American phones won't work in Ukraine."

"You want to buy what?"

I remember reading that "cell phone" is an American colloquialism. The European equivalent is "mobile telephone" with mobile pronounced in the British way – with a long "i." I try again. "I need to buy some mobile telephones that will work between Paris and the Ukraine."

"I do not know about Ukraine, but I do know someone who can help you."

Paolo unfolds a tourist map of Venice and marks a location no too far from the other side of the Piazza San Marco. "My friend Mario owns an electronics store; he sells many mobile telephones. I will call him now and tell him that you are coming to his shop. He will treat you well."

"Thank you, Paolo. Is there a house telephone that I can use to call my room and ask if our wives want to come with us?"

He points to a phone at the end of the counter. "Use this one. Dial your room number."

I do. Kate answers. "*Pronto.*"

"Wow. You sound like an Italian."

"No. I've just seen a lot of movies. What's up?"

"Paolo has a friend who owns a cell phone store. Of course. It is less than a half hour from here and we will go past the Venice Yacht Club. Want to go for a walk?"

"No. Lauri and I are still surfing the web. Have fun."

"Okay. See you in an hour or two. Love you."

"Love you, too."

* * *

Another walk along the Riva degli Schiavoni. This time we follow the Grand Canal past the Piazza San Marco. In less than a hundred yards we reach the *Compagnia della Vela di Venezia* – the Venice Yacht Club. In all the times I have been to Venice, I have never stopped here. I would love to have a burgee from the club.

The building that houses the club is exactly what you would expect. It's an ancient four story stone edifice directly across the Riva degli Schiavoni from the mouth of the Grand Canal.

We go up the eight stone stairs to the very old and ornate doors. They are closed and locked. There is no sign, but there is a burgee painted on each of the double doors, and there is a bell next to the right hand door. I push the button. In a few minutes, we hear the door unlock. The ancient door swings open to reveal an ancient gentleman in livery that would look fitting in late nineteenth century England.

He looks us up and down, and says, "*Mi dispiace, ma il club è aperto ai soli membri.*"

Mike looks at me. "Members only?"

I open my wallet, get out my Vermilion Yacht Club membership card, and hand it to the door keeper. I explain in Italian that I'm a member and past Commodore of an American Yacht Club, and that I would like to buy one of their burgees. I struggle with the Italian for burgee. I settle for Italian for flag and point to the painted burgee on the door.

He looks at the card for several minutes. He's considering his response. "*Si signore. Capisco. È possibile acquistare un Burgee durante la sera quando negozio della nave è aperto.*

Mike looks at me for a translation.

"He says I can buy a Burgee in the evening when the ship's store is open." I thank the doorman, and turn and head back down the stairs. "Let's head for Mario's cell phone store."

* * *

Buying four disposable phones turns out to be very easy.

Mario has done a little research and is prepared for our visit. When I identify myself and tell him that Paolo from the Londra Palace sent us, he smiles broadly, nods his head, and reaches under the counter. His English is almost as good as Paolo's. "These will work anywhere in the Unione Europea, as well as in Ucraina and most of eastern Europe."

I compliment him on his excellent English. He smiles even more broadly. I continue. "And the cost?"

"Only 25 € each, complete with chargers and 60 minutes of call time. You can easily buy more time with a credit card by calling the telephone number in the instructions."

I look at Mike. He smiles. I turn back to Mario. "Excellent, but I need four of them."

More smiles. "Bene. Bene. I have more in the back room."

* * *

In less time than it takes to tell it, the deal is done and we're heading back to the hotel.

CHAPTER 49

As we're walking back to the hotel, we pass a luggage shop. "Mike, do you have any experience with flights within Europe?"

"Some. Why?"

"Some years ago, when we flew from Saint Petersburg to Venice, we ran into problems with weight restrictions. The intra-European weight limit was less than the trans-Atlantic weight limit and we had to jettison stuff at the airport to meet the lower weight limit."

"That sounds ugly."

"It was. I'll have to tell you the story someday."

"Let's check with Paolo when we get back. I'd like to leave some stuff here anyway. Maybe we can pick up a couple of smaller suitcases and stash our big ones here until we return."

"Good idea. The girls may want to do that, too.

* * *

According to Paolo, airline checked bags can be the size and weight of ours, but carry-on luggage size and weight is very limited. He goes on to tell us that on the trains, there are no limits, but there are usually no porters, so the girls will have to carry everything themselves.

Paolo also tells us that we may leave suitcases at the Londra Palace until we return. Lauri and Kate like the idea of leaving some stuff here, too.

So -- we walk back to the luggage shop we passed and buy four European sized suitcases, and two carry on valises. The girls will be able to take the carry-ons they have on the train, but Mike's and mine are too large to take aboard our flight to Kiev.

So we spend the afternoon packing and repacking and organizing. We leave tomorrow.

* * *

Kate and Lauri have had some success with translation sites. They found two with what look like American home pages that say they can translate old Ukrainian. And there is still the Ukrainian Embassy and the Consulate.

I've got another idea. Though he's not been a big part of this enterprise, I've kept my younger son Gabe in the loop. He's the financial person in the family, and I've already asked him to discretely look into ways to auction off the Red Diamonds, should we find them. Instead of going through the Ukrainian government facilities in Italy, I'll email the PDFs to Gabe and ask him to contact the Embassy in the US. It'll keep more distance between us and the Ukrainian government. But we have to move quickly – we'll be in Velykyi Bereznyi in a couple of days.

The girls email the PDFs to their translation services. All we can do is wait for responses.

* * *

Tomorrow morning, we head for Ukraine and the girls head for Paris. Our reservations are made and our tickets paid for and printed. All we need to do is get girls to the train station and us to the airport. And go.

We decide to have our last dinner at the Ristorante Quadri on the Piazza San Marco. And we decide to dress up a little: jackets for Mike and me, dresses for Lauri and Kate. Where to sit is a toss up. Their inside dining room overlooking the Piazza is one of the most elegant in Venice. But the outside tables are *on* the Piazza, as is the quartet. We opt for outside.

We choose a table on the edge of the dining area and near the quartet. The night is warm and there are tons of tourists milling around. But few dine here. Some check out the multi-lingual menus that are posted in frames around the perimeter of the dining area. Most decide that the Quadri is too pricey and move on. A few groups of tourists check us out, too.

A waiter comes over, welcomes us in Italian, and introduces himself as Giorgio. When I return his greeting in Italian, he looks a little surprised, but recovers quickly. He asks if we live in the Veneto. I explain that we're Americans here on vacation, but that I used to live here a long time ago.

I tell him that we'll be having dinner in a little while, but that for now, we'd like a carafe of house red, a carafe of dry house white, and a bottle of *acqua minerale*. He nods, says "*Subito signore*," and heads inside to get our drinks.

* * *

Two hours later, we are finishing our cappuccinos and expressos. It's been a truly epic dinner; we're full and ready for the short walk back along the Riva degli Schiavoni before bed.

Kate announces that she has saved room for one last gelato, so we take a slight detour to the gelateria under the Torre dell'Orologio.

CHAPTER 50

The girl's train leaves at eleven. We have plenty of time to get them to Santa Lucia Station.

There are night trains that do the Venice to Paris run in just at ten hours, but Kate and Lauri have opted to travel during the day and see the countryside. They'll take the *Frecciabianca* to Milan today, stay overnight, and then take the TGV over the Alps and on to Paris tomorrow. It's almost 700 miles from Venice to Paris, but the high speed trains make it smooth and relatively fast trip.

Paolo has ordered a water taxi for ten. We're down in the lobby when the driver comes in. He introduces himself as Mario. He's brought a two-wheeled cart. Paolo tells him our destination, and that I am fluent in Italian. The way he says it implies that we are more than common tourists. Mario loads the girls' luggage onto his cart, and off we go.

Twenty minutes later we're at the wharf in front of Santa Lucia. As I pay Mario, he asks if he should wait. I tell him that Mike and I will stay with the girls to help them onto the train, and that we'll take the vaporetto back. He thanks us, wishes the girls safe travels, and heads back to his boat. Mike and I take the suitcases; Kate and Lauri take their carry-ons, and walk the fifty yards to the entrance. We go inside, consult the large LED sign, and head for platform seven. We only have a ten-minute wait until the conductors allow us to board.

The girls are traveling first class. European high speed trains have assigned seats just like airliners. We find the girl's first class coach, and their seats, and get them settled in. In a few minutes, we hear the announcement telling all non-passengers to leave the train. We trade hugs and kisses all around. Almost as soon as Mike and I return to the platform, the doors close, the whistle blows, and the train starts to move.

Mike and I stop at the station bar for expressos before we head for the vaporetto dock and the Londra Palace. We're next out of town.

CHAPTER 51

Our first order of business is to deliver the four suitcases that we are leaving here to the hotel staff. We drag Lauri's and Mike's into our room and call the desk. In a few minutes, Franco arrives with his cart. He loads the suitcases and heads for the elevator. We follow him down to make sure that everybody understands that these are to be stored for a week.

Now that that's done, our next order of business is to get us and our luggage to Marco Polo Airport. Paolo has ordered our water taxi, and the driver arrives as we are checking out. We say our goodbyes to Paolo get ourselves and our luggage aboard the water taxi for the half-hour ride to the airport. As is often the case, our drive Matteo is anxious to show off his boat. As we round the east end of Saint Elena and pass the island of Certosa, Matteo grins and asks, "You like to go fast?" I tell him to show us what his boat can do. He slams the throttle forward, and we're off. The bay is flat and my guess is that we hit fifty knots as we pass Murano.

In a very short time, Matteo throttles back and we're all laughing as we pull into the dock at Marco Polo Airport. I pay Matteo, thank him for the ride, and we head up the slope to the terminal building.

There are no direct flights to Kiev. Our choices were Aeroflot through Moscow, KLM through Amsterdam, or Lufthansa through Munich. We definitely don't want to go through Moscow; especially on the return trip. I chose Lufthansa; the hops were shorter.

We enter the terminal building and find the Lufthansa counter. I present our tickets to Kiev to the agent. When she finds us in her computer, I explain that we're actually going to Lviv and show her our tickets from Kiev to Lviv.

Lviv is the largest city in western Ukraine; it's about a hundred miles northeast of Velykyi Bereznyi. It has a population of about 700,000 people so it has pretty much everything we will need. There is actually a Ramada Inn near the airport, but I booked us at the Hotel Leopolis near the center of old Lviv just because it looks – well, Ukrainian.

Originally, I thought we were going to have to take the train from Kiev to Lviv. But it turns out that Ukrainian International Airlines has a one-hour flight from Kiev to Lviv. Apparently, Ukrainian International is pretty independent – I couldn't get tickets from Venice to Lviv. I got tickets from Venice to Kiev, and then two additional tickets from Kiev to Lviv. The trip should be interesting.

The Lufthansa agent speaks excellent English. She explains that the Kiev to Lviv tickets are meaningless to her. As far as Lufthansa is concerned, our final destination is Kiev. We'll have to work out our transfer with Ukrainian International in Kiev. As I said, the trip will be interesting.

We check our bags and head for the gate.

PART THREE:

UKRAINE

CHAPTER 52

Since we're flying to Munich, clearing Italian customs is a non-event. The flight is within the EU – it's like flying from New York to Chicago – one big happy family.

The one-hour flight to Franz Josef Strauss Airport in Munich is equally uneventful. The aircraft is a Brazilian Embraer 195, and the flight is typically German – spotless aircraft, and young, attentive, but businesslike and somewhat cold air crew.

Clearing German customs for our flight to Kiev is also a non-event. I get the distinct impression that they are much more concerned about who is entering Germany than who is leaving.

The flight from Munich to Kiev is *also* a non-event. Another Embraer; another German crew.

Then we land in Kiev. It's a whole different world. Like many European airports, Boryspil Airport does not have jet ways. The aircraft park on the tarmac. Airport workers roll stairs up to the door and the passengers walk down the stairs, across the tarmac and into the terminal building.

Waiting at the bottom of the stairs are two uniformed guards with Kalashnikovs. I'm not sure if they are Police, Customs or Military. And I don't ask. There are two more uniformed guards with Kalashnikovs at the entrance to the terminal. As we walk from the plane to the terminal, I turned to Mike. "Welcome to the Ukraine."

"I'm beginning to see why our ancestors left."

We enter the terminal and follow the crowd and the signs to the baggage claim area. More guards with Kalashnikovs. I approach the nearest guard. "Do you speak English?"

I get a blank look. Then he says, "*Nee*," and points to another guard.

The guard he points out does not have a Kalashnikov; he has a pistol. From his fancier uniform, my guess is that he is an officer. I walk up to him and smile. "The guard over there said that you speak English."

"*Trishky*. A little. What do you need?"

"We just arrived on the flight from Munich. We have another ticket to fly from here to Lviv. How do we get ourselves and our luggage onto that flight?" I hand him my ticket.

He studies the ticket and me. "*Pishly zi mnoyu*. Come with me." He heads for the luggage carousel. I wave Mike over.

When we get to the carousel, he points and says, "Pick suitcases. Bring with me." We grab our suitcases, put our valises on top and follow the officer to a long table where other passenger's bags are being examined. He points to an empty spot and says, "*Tut*. Here." He calls a luggage examiner over. They have a short discussion. He turns to us. "After Sasha examine luggage, he will lead you and luggage to Departures. You will be okay."

I thank him in English and Russian, and he walks briskly away. He looks pleased that he has handled us foreigners efficiently.

Sasha goes through our luggage very thoroughly. He examines our laptops, our cellphones and our cameras carefully. He ruffles through my folder of maps, notes and letters. He slips my Garmin out of its case and looks at me questioningly.

"GPS."

He nods and puts it back in its case. Sasha closes our suitcases and affixes a small sticker with some Cyrillic writing on each suitcase and each valise. He says, "*Vy pryyshly*. You come," and starts to walk along the long table.

We grab our luggage and follow on our side of the table, then through an unmarked door, up a flight of stairs, through another door and into what appears to be the public part of the terminal. Sasha checks a large monitor on the wall and repeats, "You come."

He takes us to the Ukrainian International Airlines ticket counter and has a brief discussion with the agent. He looks at us, says, "You are okay now," and walks back the way he came.

The agent points to her scale, says "Checked bag here, please."

When I comply, she says, "Your ticket?"

I give her my ticket. She types something into her terminal; a printer dispenses a baggage tag and a boarding pass. Mike goes through the same process. When the agent is finished with Mike, she points to a seating area not far away. "You wait twenty minutes, yes?"

Mike smiles at her. "Yes. Thank you. *Spasibo*." Then he smiles at me. "You're not the only one who knows a little Russian."

"Good for you." And we sit. And wait.

CHAPTER 53

The gate attendant announces our boarding in several different languages. About seventy-five people get up and start shuffling toward the door. Mike and I join the crowd.

Eventually, we go through the door, down a ramp, through a long drab hallway, and out a door onto the tarmac. Another agent checks our boarding passes and waves us on. Past two guards with Kalashnikovs. We walk fifty yards to the boarding stairs pushed up against the Boeing 737. And two more guards with Kalashnikovs.

We clamber up the stairs and are greeted by a very attractive young stewardess. In English. How she knew to greet us in English, I don't know. I'm of Ukrainian descent. Mike and I *look* Ukrainian. Maybe it's our clothes. If I get a chance, I'll ask her. Her name tag identifies her as "Аліна -- Alina."

Alina is what they called in Saint Petersburg, a "light eyes." It's not an ethnic group; they're randomly mixed in with the population. Perhaps it's a recessive gene. Most Russians (and Ukrainians) have brown eyes, brown or black hair, and a swarthy complexion. We just look eastern European. Think Josef Stalin. But there are a small number of Russians who have light complexions, blond hair, and startling light blue eyes. The women are stunningly beautiful. The regular Russians call them "light eyes." My son Gabe has two daughters; one is a "light eyes."

We find our seats and settle in. The aircraft is only about one third full; something we never see on American carriers anymore. When all of the passengers are seated, another stewardess asks us if we need anything; if we'd like a complimentary drink. I ask for sparkling water; Mike asks for vodka.

In a few minutes, she's back with our drinks and a small tray with breads, cookies and crackers; and a small jar of caviar. And this is tourist class.

The 737 is a little tired, but the air crew makes up for it with their enthusiasm and attentiveness. And their freebies.

In a few minutes, the door is closed, and we hear the usual safety information in several languages as we taxi toward the runway.

* * *

It's only a one-hour flight. The pilot gets us to altitude quickly and heads west. We relax a little.

"Hey Dad, back there in the customs hall where Sasha examined our luggage."

"Yeah?"

"Did you watch what the other agents were doing?"

"Not really. I was busy watching what Sasha was doing."

"They were being extremely thorough. Emptying suitcases completely. Checking linings. Opening everything. Even unwrapping gift-wrapped packages, I have a real concern about leaving with the diamonds. If we find the diamonds."

"Me too. Did I ever tell you about the last time I left Russia? The fish knife incident? The time Kate and I went to Saint Petersburg?"

"I think you mentioned it. Remind me."

"I'll tell you the details some other time. Condensed version: they hassled me about leaving Russia with three filet knives for you, Gabe and Devin."

"Oh yeah. You worked your way up the chain of command until you got the okay to export them. And your friend from the embassy told you later that the examiner could have cared less about the knives. He just wanted a bribe."

"I'm going to buy three more knives and repeat that incident when we leave. I hope that the knives will act as a decoy to divert attention from the matryoshka dolls I intend to use to hide the diamonds. I don't know how else to do it."

* * *

As we start our decent into Lviv, I turn to Mike. "This may be our last comfortable night for a while."

"What do you mean?"

"Tomorrow, we go where no tourist has gone before…"

We land at Lviv's Danylo Halytskyi International Airport without incident. And we deplane as we did in Kiev. Down the stairs, past two guards with Kalashnikovs, across the tarmac, past two more guards with Kalashnikovs, and into the terminal.

The airport is quite new and very western. There are restaurants, bars, duty free shops, money changers. I stop at a money changer and check the exchange rates. The basic unit of currency in Ukraine is the hryvnia, with about 35 hryvni to the US dollar. We need to exchange a bunch of euros for hryvni, but we'll get a much better rate at a bank than here at the airport.

We follow the signs to the baggage claim area. No customs this time, but there are guards. With Kalashnikovs. I'm not sure if they're for show or for real. I think I'll not ask.

We collect our luggage and make our way outside to the taxi stand. There is a small kiosk with a dispatcher. Mike walks up and asks him if he speaks English.

He nods vigorously. "A little."

"Do the drivers accept euros?"

"*Da. Da.* Yes. Yes."

Mike turns to me. "What's the name of the hotel?"

"Leopolis."

He turns back to the kiosk. "How much to the Hotel Leopolis?"

"Only five euros per person. Bags free."

He calls a driver over and talks to him for a minute. "Dima will take you and your luggage to Hotel Leopolis. Very nice hotel."

CHAPTER 54

The airport is less than four miles from the hotel, so it's an easy taxi ride. In less than four miles, we go from the modern airport surrounded by new looking light industrial buildings to drab apartment blocks to semi-slums to the historical center of Lviv. To the old city. The Hotel Leopolis sits near the center of the old city.

The hotel is elegant. And old. It's listed as a UNESCO World Heritage Site. I'm not sure exactly what that means; I wish we had more time in Kiev. This is a "business" trip, and as soon as we get settled into our rooms, I'll get down to "business."

Dima double parks on the street, hops out, opens the sidewalk-side taxi door for us. A uniformed hotel employee comes over with a brass cart and Dima piles our stuff on it. He smiles and waits for his money. I give him a ten euro note and two one euro coins; he looks a little puzzled. "It is a tip. You keep it."

His smile widens. "*Dyakuyu. Dyakuyu.* Thank you." He bows slightly, then nods twice and gets back in his taxi.

I keep forgetting that European service workers are not used to getting much in tips.

The porter starts in with his cart. We follow.

At the front desk, the clerk greets us in passable English. How do they know? Her nametag says Оксана -- Oksana.

I tell her that we have two rooms reserved and that I asked for rooms near each other. We give her our passports. She says that she will return them when we come back down. My guess is that she will copy them for the SBU before we come back down.

Oksana gives two room key to the porter, and says, "Stas will take you up."

We ride the elevator up with Stas. It stops at the third floor. Mike takes the first room. "I'll give you ten minutes, Dad. Then I'll be over." He waits at his open door until he sees where my room is.

My room is right next door. Mike goes into his room. Stas opens my door and waits for me to enter. My room is like the lobby. It's old, but elegant. As soon as I tip him, Stas leaves and I flop on the bed. It's been a long day.

* * *

In what is probably exactly ten minutes, I hear three nocks -- twice. I get up and open the door. As I expected, it's Mike. "Now what?"

"We go downstairs and enlist Oksana's help. I emailed the hotel and asked them to get us a car and driver to take us to Velykyi Bereznyi. It's just at a hundred miles. I didn't even check to see if there's a train; I figured that we'd see more from a car, but I really didn't want to rent one. We can rent scooters or bikes in Velykyi Bereznyi."

"That's it?"

"Not quite. I've reserved us rooms at a hotel called the Hotel Perlyna Kraslia, but it's some sort of resort and it's outside of town. I'd rather be right in town; that's where Oleksandr's map starts. I'm hoping that Oksana can help. There have to be hotels in town."

"How big is Velykyi Bereznyi?"

"Around 7,500, but I don't know if that is just the town or if that includes the surrounding area."

"That's fair sized."

"Yeah. Google maps makes it look like a reasonable town. The photo mode shows what looks like some light industry."

"We'll find out tomorrow. Let's go down."

* * *

Oksana is still at the desk. She smiles as we walk up and waits for one of us to talk. I start. "Oksana, I reserved a car and driver to take us to Velykyi Bereznyi tomorrow. My grandfather was born there and left in 1918. We want to explore his town."

Oksana types something into her terminal. "Your car will be here at eight o'clock in the morning. Is that good?"

"Can you change it to noon? We would like to visit in Lviv for a while first."

"Noon?"

"Twelve o'clock. Mid-day?"

"Twelve o'clock. I understand. I change."

"Perfect. One more thing. I have reserved rooms at the Hotel Perlyna Kraslia, but we would rather be in Velykyi Bereznyi center. Can you find us two rooms for six nights in the center of Velykyi Bereznyi?"

"I will try. You come back. One hour?"

"Yes. We will come back. *Dyakuyu, Oksana.*"

I look at Mike. "Let's go explore."

* * *

By the time we get back, it's supper time and we're hungry. As we enter the lobby, Oksana waves us over. "I change car time to 'noon' and I move you to the Hotel Gold. It is in town center and very nice. You will like it much."

"Perfect. We would like to eat now."

Oksana points the way and we head for the dining room. The host is a fifty-year-old gentleman in a cheap black suit. I hold up two fingers. "Two, please."

He nods. We follow him to a table by a window overlooking the main street. White tablecloth. White cloth napkins. Heavy silver plate utensils. Nice. The host hands us each a menu and leaves.

A bus boy – actually another fifty-year-old -- comes over and fills our water glasses. I'm still not used to the fact that in Europe, restaurant workers are not kids. These are jobs for adults; jobs that are considered quite desirable.

The menu is multilingual. Thankfully. Mike orders *Holubtsi* – what my mother used to call "pigs in a blanket." I order *Guliash* – goulash. Our meals are excellent – just like mom used to make.

By the time we're finished with desert and coffee, we're both ready for bed. We agree to meet at eight for breakfast, and head back to our rooms.

CHAPTER 55

Western Europeans tend to eat a light breakfast. Not so with the Ukrainians; they believe in a hearty breakfast. Since we aren't sure of when or where or even if we'll have lunch, we do breakfast Ukrainian style: orange juice, sausage, eggs, potato pancakes, coffee. The only thing that disappoints is the orange juice; but then, we're a long way from Florida.

We leave the hotel for a walk and look at Lviv. From the taxi, the city center looks like a very typical old European city.

* * *

Our driver, Vova, shows up promptly at noon in a Škoda Superb. Vova speaks a little English; the car is the eastern European idea of a "family car." The back seat is good for kids, dogs and groceries. Not so much for adults. Mike and I will take turns in the back. Vova crams our suitcases and valises into the small trunk. I ride shotgun as we pull out onto one of the main street of Lviv.

We're soon out of Lviv and its suburbs, and into farm land. I've done some research on our route. The first half of our trip will be through the Roztochia Uplands; the photos I found on line reminded me of western Pennsylvania and eastern Ohio. The second half of our trip will be into the eastern Carpathian Mountains; think central Pennsylvania. Oksana, who seemed to be at the front desk all the time, told us to expect a two to three-hour trip, so we settle in and watch the land of our ancestors go by.

The first part of our trip follows the M06 motorway. It's a major four-lane, limited access highway. If you've ever driven in the northeastern United States, you know about potholes. M06 has grown a fine crop of potholes over the winter. Cars and trucks of all sizes are moving at speeds pushing a hundred miles an hour and swerving all over the place to avoid the potholes. I'm glad we opted not to rent a car. I hope Vova gets us there in one piece.

After about forty-five minutes of craziness, Vova turns off of M06 and onto a two lane road. As we approach a small town, Vova turns to me. "We stop for snack?"

"Great idea, Vova."

He pulls into the parking lot of what looks like a bar and restaurant. We get seated on the patio behind the building. Our table overlooks the break between farms to the east and mountains to the west. There is a small menu, but it's in Ukrainian. Vova looks at it, and then at us. "You want coffee or wine or beer or maybe vodka?" Mike and I both opt for coffee. Vova orders for us.

Mike has brought his laptop from the car. I watch as he powers it up and opens a map of eastern Ukraine. He zooms in on the area southeast of Lviv. He looks at Vova and points to the map. "Where are we right now?"

Vova touches a spot on the screen. "You zoom a little."

Mike does. Vova points again. "Here. Pidpolpzzya."

"Where do we go now?"

"You zoom out a little?" Mike does.

Vova traces a line with his finger. "First northwest toward Pol'shcha, and then southwest toward Slovachchyna."

He touches another spot. "Zoom again."

And Velykyi Bereznyi pops up! Mike says, "How long?"

"One hour. Maybe two hours." He holds his hand palm down in front of himself. He waves it left and right and up and down like a car moving. "Mountain roads. We must go slow sometimes."

"No problem. I was just curious. Slow is good." I know what Mike is thinking. After the craziness of the M06 motorway, slow will be a welcome change.

The waiter brings our coffee and a basket of what looks like donut holes. I look questioningly at Vova and point to them.

"Pampushky. You like."

Mike and each take one and taste it. Poppy seed and walnut. We like. We nod. "We like."

After our coffee break, we hit the road again. I offer to sit in the back, but Mike says he's fine. We're on a broad flat plain and Vova makes good time. After a half hour, the road starts to go up and down and left and right like Vova's hand did earlier; we've hits the foothills of the Carpathian Mountains. These are old mountains like the Alleghenies, not new ones like the Rockies. I feel at home here. I'm beginning to understand why so many of "my people" settled in western Pennsylvania. It felt like home.

After a while we drop down into a narrow river valley and follow it for what seems like forever. The road signs say H13.

After about an hour, we stop at a small bar and restaurant for a stretch and a potty break. Then it's back into the car. We continue to follow the river downstream.

All of a sudden, the mountains end and we see flat land ahead. Vova pulls over. He points to the town ahead. "Velykyi Bereznyi!"

I just look for several minutes. "My grandfather lived here."

"And my great-grandfather."

"And now you return!"

"And now we return."

CHAPTER 56

Vova pulls up in front of what must be the Hotel Gold. At least I think it's the Hotel Gold. It's an old building near what appears to be the center of town. There is a sign, but it's in Ukrainian.

We've been on highway H13 since before our last break, and the highway has become the main street of Velykyi Bereznyi. This is it; home for the next few nights; our base of operations.

Vova unloads the trunk. A fiftyish porter comes out of the hotel with a two-wheeled hand cart. He loads our luggage on and heads inside.

I dig into my pocket to get money to pay Vova. We could have rented a car in Lviv for a week for about 250 €. Vova's company charges 150 € for their car and his services for the day. Having Vova do the driving was well worth the cost. I ask him if he will be here next week to take us back. He shrugs. "I think so." I'm not sure if he expects a tip; I give him 175 €; his smile says that he is very pleased. We shake hands.

While I've been dealing with Vova, Mike has gone into the hotel. I follow him in. The lobby is small, but functional. Mike is standing at the small counter talking to the porter. He hears me close the door and turns to face me. "This is Sasha, porter, desk clerk, and owner of the Hotel Gold. He speaks excellent English."

I walk to the counter and extend a hand. "Hello, Sasha. I am Peter."

"Welcome to the Hotel Gold." Sasha speaks English with a New York City accent.

"We're glad to be here. Your English is excellent. You accent is..."

Sasha interrupts me with a laugh. "I was born here in Velykyi Bereznyi. When I was five, my family moved to Long Island. Ten years ago, I returned here and bought the Hotel Gold."

"Wow! That's great news for us. I am very glad to meet you. I am of Ukrainian descent, but I speak no Ukrainian and only a little bit of Russian. I have been concerned that communication was going to be a problem. You are a godsend."

"I am honored to have you here. We rarely get Americans."

"The girl at the Leopolis in Lviv did the booking. You should thank her; her name is Oksana."

"I will do that. Mike tells me that your grandfather came from Velykyi Bereznyi?"

"Yes. He left here in 1918 with his parents and older brother. They settled in Colorado."

"Do you have any relatives still living here?"

"I don't know. I am the oldest living Bradovich in the United States. That's one of the reasons we're here."

"Perhaps I can help you answer that. I will make enquiries."

"Excellent."

"Let me take you to your rooms."

CHAPTER 57

My guess is that the hotel has a dozen or so rooms; ours are on the second floor; there is no elevator.

Our rooms are across the hall from each other; they're small but comfortable, and have all the necessities. My window looks out at the foothills of the Carpathian Mountains. I'm again reminded of Pennsylvania. This could be somewhere around Somerset.

I unpack a few things and fire up my Toshiba Ultrabook. It boots in less than ten seconds, and I can see several Wireless Networks. All are secure. I'll have to ask Sasha for the hotel's SSID and password.

I walk across the hall and knock on Mike's door. He opens the door with his burner phone next to his ear. "Hang on Lauri."

"They made it okay?"

"Yes."

"I'll go call Kate. Come over when you're ready for dinner."

"Roger."

* * *

I go back to my room, slouch into a fairly comfortable recliner and call Kate. Arrived okay – miss you already – looking forward to our time in Paris/Velykyi Bereznyi – be careful – keep in touch – let me know as soon as you hear/know anything – take care – be safe – love you – bye. The usual stuff.

There's a knock on my door; I recognize it as Mike's; he always knocks three times twice. I open the door. "Ready to eat?"

"Yeah. Let's go see what Sasha recommends."

We go to the staircase and Mike looks up before we head down. "One floor above us. Eight rooms on this floor. Probably the same above us. Another set of stairs at the end of the hallway."

"Do you always reconnoiter?"

"Yeah. Old habits. And don't ask me to sit anywhere other than with my back to the wall."

"I remember seeing that when you visited us in Key Largo."

* * *

Sasha is at the front desk. We ask him to recommend a place for dinner. "You should eat here tonight. We have a small dining room with a very complete menu and daily specials."

"Sounds good. When does dinner start?"

"Whenever you wish."

"Mike, let's take a walk first. I'd like to walk off the stiffness from the ride. After that we need to go back upstairs for a few minutes. I want to check email. Then dinner."

When I say email, Sasha looks up from his computer terminal. "Let me give you the password for our free Wi-Fi service."

He hands me a small piece of paper with the hotel SSID and password on it. "I change the password every Monday because we have many poachers."

"Thank you, Sasha. We won't be long."

We walk out the door and arbitrarily make a left. At the end of the block we make another left. At the end of this block is the river Uzh. At this point, it's about thirty feet wide and moving swiftly left to right. Its muddiness says recent rain.

I point upstream. "The maps say go that way. Getting across could be a challenge."

"We passed a couple of bridges. How about we go up this side and find our landmarks. Then we can cross on one of the bridges and go up the other side and continue?"

"That makes sense. I plan to rent scooters or motorbikes or if necessary, regular bikes. We need local transportation."

"I agree. Sasha should be able to help."

"I'm hungry. Let's go eat."

* * *

Sasha is still at the front desk when we get back to the hotel. "Ready for dinner?"

"Yes. And we're hungry."

"Let me seat you. This way please."

We follow him into the dining room. "Are you our waiter, too?"

He laughs. "No. My nephew will be your waiter. The chef is a cousin. Nepotism is rampant in Ukraine!"

As he seats us, a young man comes to our table. Sasha introduces him. "This is Artem; he works most evenings. His English is pretty good. Artem, these are our American guests, Peter and his son Michael.

"It is good to meet you. Welcome to Velykyi Bereznyi and to the Hotel Gold."

Mike answers for us. "It's good to meet you as well. What do you recommend for dinner?"

"Here are our menus, but tonight's special is Kotleta po-kyivsky. It is very good."

Sasha jumps in to translate. "Americans know it is Chicken Kiev. However, it's not really a dish from Kiev. Tradition says a chef in Saint Petersburg invented it in the early nineteen-hundreds, and gave it that name to make it sound exotic. Wherever it was invented, it is very good. I recommend it."

Artem's turn. "You should have the Kapusniak first. Excellent soup."

My turn. "Sounds perfect. We will take your advice."

"Dinner is very cheap. I will add the cost to your room account if you like."

"That will be fine, but I would also like to see the bill."

"As you wish." Sasha bows slightly and leaves us in Artem's hands.

* * *

An hour later, we're finishing our dessert and coffee. We're comfortably full. Sasha was right about "very cheap." Our bill for soup, Chicken Kiev with potatoes and some unidentifiable vegetable, desert, and wine and coffee was 300 Hryvnia for each of us. A little under ten dollars per person.

CHAPTER 58

This morning, we have a light breakfast; continental style rather than Ukrainian style. Artem is our waiter again.

After breakfast, I ask Sasha about renting motor scooters or small motorcycles. He says he can get us two good scooters for about eight euros a day. I tell him that today we will walk, but that we'd like the scooters for about five days starting tomorrow morning. He says he will have them for us after Mass.

The main unit of money in Ukraine is the hryvnia, but prices seem to be often quoted in euros. I ask Sasha about it. His answer seems to make sense. "People believe that the euro is more stable, more safe than our hryvnia because the worth of the hryvnia was very uncertain after the fall of the Soviet Union. I don't think that's really true anymore, but it *is* the perception. I should warn you -- don't try to pay for anything in Russian rubles. The Ukrainian people hate them."

I can't resist. "Rubles or Russians?"

"Both, I think. At least here in the west. In the east, perhaps not the people so much."

Before we left the States, Mike printed maps of "downtown" Velykyi Bereznyi. But we ask Sasha if there are any tourist maps or guides, and he loads us up with stuff. I thank him.

I tell Sasha that I want to buy three really good quality, engraved knives for my three sons. "I'm thinking hunting knives."

"That's easy. This is farm country. Everybody uses knives." He circles a spot on the city map. "Go here. Another cousin! I will call him and tell him to treat you like family!"

So we're off to explore the town. And to find the church where the map starts.

We do tourist things. We walk; we look; we smile at people; we take pictures; we shop. I get the impression that the whole town knows that we are Americans who have come to discover their roots.

Speaking of discovery, we discover that in western Ukraine, the general dislike of Russia and things Russian makes it difficult to find matryoshka dolls. We finally find what we need -- three sets: one large and two smaller.

We take our loot back to the hotel at about noon, and decide to stop for lunch. Artem is our waiter again.

* * *

Before lunch, we went north from the hotel. After lunch, we decide to head south. Almost all of the town is west of the river; certainly all of the older parts. The church on the map has got to be here somewhere. Unless it was destroyed during one of the world wars.

As we wander south, we come across a church. It's a lovely brick and masonry building, but it looks too new to be our church; my guess is early nineteen-hundreds, maybe even post World War Two. We're standing in front of the church, when a priest comes out. He smiles at us. "You must be Sasha's Americans. Would you like to come in?" His accent is heavy but he is understandable.

"Does everyone in town know about us?"

"Yes, I think so. We do not get many Americans, especially Americans who trace their ancestry back to our town."

We follow the priest up the stairs to the church entrance. He stops at the doors, introduces himself as Father Lazarenko, and the church as Saint Michael's. "I am Peter Bradovich and this is my son Michael. I don't know the proper protocol for entering an Orthodox church."

"Don't worry. God will understand. Come in."

We enter the narthex. It is cool, dark, and quiet. I look around and then at Father Lazarenko. "My ancestors left Velykyi Bereznyi in 1918. This church doesn't look old enough to have been the church they attended."

"Unless they were Jews, this definitely would have been their church. It was built in the mid-eighteen-hundreds, heavily damaged during World War I, and repaired after the war. It was almost completely destroyed during World War II, and again completely rebuilt."

Father Lazarenko continues. "There are several newer churches in our town, and even some Protestant ones, but this is the one that dates back to 1918. There is also an old wooden church by the river a few blocks from here, but there have not been Masses there since Saint Michael's was built. Come in to the nave." The priest goes first, dips his fingers into the Holy Water Fount, bows and crosses himself. Mike does the same; he's a practicing Russian Orthodox Catholic. I am not; I just go in. The nave is quiet and smells faintly of incense. There are no pews; just the hard stone floor. I stand and look around; the nave is impressive, but the Iconostasis is absolutely incredible.

I whisper to Father Lazarenko, "How old is the Iconostasis? It looks much older than the church."

"It is. It is perhaps four hundred years old. It was brought from a monastery in the Carpathians. Their church was destroyed during the wars, but the brothers dismantled the Iconostasis and hid it in a cave beforehand. We are blessed to have it."

"It is beautiful."

"Come to Mass tomorrow. We would be honored."

"We may do that. What time does Mass start?"

"We have two, a shorter and more modern Mass at ten o'clock, and the traditional High Mass at twelve o'clock."

"We will try to attend the earlier Mass. Can you show me on our map exactly where this church is located?"

He points out the location. I put a cross on the map. "And the old wooden church?"

He points again. I add a cross with a circle around it. "Thank you. We do not have dress clothes with us. Are casual clothes okay for Mass tomorrow?"

"No shorts. No bare shoulders. Those are the main restrictions. Sasha can advise you."

"We will be here tomorrow."

We take our leave and go back out into the afternoon sunshine.

CHAPTER 59

Mike looks at me with a slightly puzzled smile. "Why did you commit us to Mass tomorrow?"

"I'm not too sure. It seemed like a good idea. It will get us known to a lot of people."

"You know we have to stand?"

"Yeah, and that may be a problem for me. I should have asked Father Lazarenko."

"Sasha can probably help us out. In the United States, they set up a few chairs around the perimeter of the nave for new mothers and for the old and infirm." He grins.

"I don't know about infirm, but old, definitely." We both laugh.

"Let's check out the wooden church. Even though it wasn't used in Oleksandr's time, it was probably a landmark."

* * *

We walk the three blocks to the wooden church. It is a remarkable structure. Constructed of unpainted wood, its footprint is perhaps twenty-five feet by fifty feet. Our first impression is that it is all roof. The walls are only about eight feet high, but the roof is three times that. The roof has three peaks, each with a traditional onion surmounted by an orthodox cross. The door is closed and locked; there is no sign or anything like one. I look through the brochures that Sasha gave us. There is nothing about a wooden church. Another question for Sasha. I take a couple of pictures with my Digital Nikon.

Mike is looking through his collection of maps. He compares a copy of Oleksandr's map to the tourist map that Sasha gave us. I see his face brighten. "This is Oleksandr's church. This is where we start."

"Show me." And he does. There is no doubt. This *is* Oleksandr's church.

* * *

As soon as we get back to the Hotel Gold, we go to our respective rooms to call our respective wives. Cell phone service was sketchy in the mountains, but it seems fine here.

"Hi cutie. How is Paris?"

"As beautiful as I remembered. The weather is warm and the flowers are just coming out. How is … Wherever you are?"

"Velykyi Bereznyi, hometown of 'my people.' It is interesting, to say the least. It is definitely not Paris, but if we find the diamonds, we can visit Paris again. Any time we want. For as long as we want."

"That sounds good to me."

"We found the church today. The starting point of Oleksandr's map!"

"Hurrah! When do you go after the diamonds?"

"Not until Tuesday. We want to make it look like we are here to explore the town. Sasha, the owner of our hotel grew up on Long Island. I think the entire town knows us as Sasha's Americans who trace their ancestry back to Velykyi Bereznyi. We are very visible and need to not do anything out of character."

"But Tuesday?"

"I know. It will be hard to wait. We got invited to go to church tomorrow. By the parish priest, no less. It was hard to say no."

"What about Monday?"

"We are supposed to look for relatives. Sasha has volunteered to help us. I haven't run this by Mike yet, but I am thinking that we are going to start our trek on Monday. Maybe do Oleksandr's map on Monday and Mitri's on Tuesday."

Our conversation turns to Paris. Things to do. Things to show Lauri. It's her first time in Paris; maybe in Europe. Kate will make a great tour guide.

We say our goodbyes and I head downstairs to talk to Sasha about dinner tonight.

* * *

"Sasha, can you suggest a place for dinner tonight? Please do not misunderstand. Dinner here last night was wonderful, and the price was lower than I expected. We just want to try different places."

"I do understand. You must go to Hinkalnya na Fedorova. It is the best dining experience in Velykyi Bereznyi. It's a restaurant that would be considered five star if it were anywhere in Western Europe. It is only two blocks from here."

"What about dress? We didn't bring suites, sport coats, dress shirts, or neckties. Are casual clothes okay?"

"Casual is fine. Just not sloppy."

"Do we need a reservation?"

"This is our slow season. But I will call anyway. Is seven o'clock good?"

"Perfect. And what about clothes for Mass tomorrow? We met Father Lazarenko today and he invited us. We're planning on going to the ten o'clock Mass."

"Similar to dinner tonight. Casual is fine. No shorts. No sleeveless tops. Again, not sloppy."

"Again, perfect. I'm going to go up and rest for a while before dinner. We walked a lot today."

Mike agrees with me. "Me too. Rest, I mean."

"Tomorrow you will have scooters."

"Yes we will."

CHAPTER 60

Dinner at the Hinkalnya na Fedorova last night was amazing.

The owner personally escorted us to a table with a view, and introduced himself as Denys Motruk. His English was not great, but we communicated okay. He asked our permission to have the chef prepare a special meal for us. We agreed; he brought out a bottle of very strong red wine; we sipped until the first of many courses arrived.

We started with purple cold soup with gobs of sour cream floating in it. That was followed by some rolled up meat and pastry things. And those were followed by many other courses. Most of the dishes were very good, and most had names I could not pronounce, let alone remember.

Two hours later we were nibbling on some very rich honey cakes (Baklava?) and drinking very strong and very good coffee. We were stuffed – nearly to the point of immobility.

I asked Denys for our bill. He went into the kitchen and came out with the chef. "Vadim speaks no English, but I would like you to meet him. He says it was an honor to cook for you, the American Rusyn. He hopes you have enjoyed."

We shook hands all around, and thanked Denys and Vadim as best we could. There was much smiling and bowing. Denys asked if he could have his daughter take our picture. We said of course and he semi-yelled something to the kitchen. A lovely teenager came out with her digital Cannon. Denys introduced her as Nastya. The four of us posed for several pictures. I asked Denys if I could have digital copies. "Of course. I will bring a memory to the Hotel Gold."

Vadim bowed one more time and smiled all the way back to the kitchen. I looked at Denys. "And the bill?"

"This meal is no charge. It is something for you to remember fondly and think of us. It is an honor to have you as my guest."

I was flabbergasted. I could think of nothing to say except, "*Dyakuyu*. Thank you."

We waddled our way back to the Hotel Gold. It was a meal and a night to remember.

* * *

I'm still full this morning. The walk to church is welcomed and pleasant. The ninety-minute Mass is interesting but not so pleasant. After about a half hour, I sit down on one of the chairs along the wall. I stand when the little old ladies occupying other chairs stand. I do the sign of the cross when they do the sign of the cross. Backwards from the Roman Catholic way that I was raised with. I sit when they sit. I mumble when they mumble. And I have no idea what is going on. But I know that many people were watching me. So I try to kook pious and prayerful.

After Mass is over, we shake hands with Father Lazarenko and two junior priests. We head for the hotel.

Mike says that the Mass was very like a Mass in the United States. He says that he was able at least, to follow the order of the service.

"Maybe you can explain a little of it to me over dinner tonight. You can start with the backwards sign of the cross."

He just smiles. "Be happy to, Dad."

And we walk on, each lost in our own thoughts.

* * *

Waiting at the curb when we get to the hotel are two bright red scooters. They look like Vespas, but are eastern European knock offs. We go into the lobby. "Are those our scooters, Sasha?"

"Yes! They are brand new!"

"They look like they will do just fine."

"I have some papers for you to sign. Then I will show you the fine points of how they operate."

"Great."

We take care of the paperwork and go back outside. The scooters are very straightforward. A child could drive one, but we decide to humor Sasha.

"Have you ever driven a scooter?"

Mike sits astride one. "No, but I have two Harley Davidsons at home."

I sit astride the other scooter. "I used to have a Norton a long time ago. I could use a refresher course on the controls."

"May I?" Sasha and I trade places. He shows us the ignition, the front and rear brakes, and the throttle. He shows us how to open the under seat compartment, how to control the lights, and a few other things.

He gets off and waves for me to get back on. I do. I look at Mike. "What do you think?"

"You know what they say. It's like riding a bike. You don't forget. Let's go around the block. We'll go slowly 'til we get the feel of the balance, throttle and brakes. Follow me."

He takes off – slowly – and I follow. The first couple of minutes are a little shaky. Then I'm okay. I pass Mike. "I'm good."

We go back to the hotel and tell Sasha that we are very happy with the new scooters

We follow route H13 south for a couple of miles to the next town. Malyi Bereznyi is smaller than Velykyi Bereznyi. Mike stops to look at the map on his tablet. "Let's turn right here and do a little reconnaissance."

"Reconnaissance?"

"My map says the border with Slovakia is less than two miles up the road. I'm curious about the frontier. So let's go look."

"You're not suggesting that we cross over into Slovakia?"

"No. Definitely not. I had to specify to my chain of command what countries I was going to travel in and Slovakia was not one of them. I just want to check it out."

We drive our scooters north west on route P53; we're moving away from the river Uzh and following one of its tributaries. In a couple of minutes, we see what has to be the frontier. There is a small parking lot, then some small buildings, then two sets of red and white striped barriers straight out of a Cold War era movie. On the other side of the barriers are another small building and another parking lot. Both barriers are manned by troops in different uniforms carrying similar weapons -- probably more Kalashnikovs.

We stop fifty yards from the frontier. The guards are watching us. One on each side of the barrier goes into their building.

"Close enough?"

"Close enough. Let's head back."

CHAPTER 61

The guards watch us as we turn our scooters around and head back toward Malyi Bereznyi. When the frontier and the guards are out of sight, I breathe a sigh of relief. I pass Mike and signal for him to pull over. "I don't know why, Mike, but that place left me feeling very unsettled."

"It reminded me of what all of the European borders must have looked like during the Cold War. The national borders are pretty much gone in Western Europe, but not here. They have very strong sense of nationalism now that the Soviet Union has collapsed."

"I suspect that many Western European nations wish they had their secure borders back."

"I suspect you're right." He pulls out onto the road again.

* * *

At Malyi Bereznyi we have to make a decision. Left or right; upstream or downstream; return or explore farther. We decide to decide over a cup of coffee. We stop at what looks like a bar with a couple of outside tables. I'm not sure how this is going to work. Neither Mike nor I have picked up much Ukrainian yet, and we're far off of the American tourist track. An English speaking waiter is unlikely.

A very attractive young light eyes comes out of the bar and says – in English, "Good afternoon. What can I bring you?" How do they know?

And I ask her, "How did you know that we are American?"

"Everybody knows about Sasha's Americans and their new red scooters!"

We all laugh. She continues. "We do not get many Americans here. Our big tourist season is winter, for skiing. You are, how do you say, 'Novel.'"

"'Novel' is good. And your English is excellent. We would like two coffees, please."

"Thank you. English is the preferred second language for many young Ukrainians. It is, how do you say, 'Universal.'"

I smile and she leaves to get our coffee.

Mike smiles. "Cute."

"I won't tell Lauri."

In a few minutes, our waitress is back with our coffee and a platter of pastries. I ask about them. "First, what is your name? And second, what are the pastries?"

"My name is Yana, and I am happy to meet you. These are pampushky; you will like them."

"I am Peter and this is my son Michael. We are happy to meet you, too."

"I will return in a while. Enjoy." And we do.

Yana comes back just as we are finishing our coffee and pampushky. I ask her how much we owe her. "Seventy-five hryvnia, please. Or do you have euros?"

I do a quick conversion. Seventy-five hryvnia is about two dollars. "I have hryvnia, but that can't be enough."

"The pampushky were, how do you say – on the home."

"On the house. But free is not fair."

"We are happy to meet Sasha's Americans. Perhaps we can have a photo?"

"Of course. And we would like one of you as well."

Yana turns and yells something into the door. About eight Ukrainians of various ages come trooping out. "These are my coworkers and my family."

Yana introduces us all around. Most of the names are unintelligible to American ears. We smile, nod, shake hands, and hug. And then out come four or five cameras and smart phones. We have our pictures taken with various relatives. Mike takes some pictures of the whole group, and then asks Yana to have someone take a picture of the three of us. A teen aged boy volunteers when he sees Mike's camera.

When that's done, we say good bye and head further south along route H13 and the Uzh River. There's a town called Perechyn about eight miles down the road. It's roughly the size of Velykyi Bereznyi, and we're curious if we'll still be known as Sasha's Americans.

* * *

It takes us just a few minutes to come to the realization that we are not celebrities in Perechyn. We get a few quick looks, but most of the people studiously ignore us. Their behavior reminds me of the behavior I remember in Saint Petersburg and Moscow; don't make eye contact with strangers; definitely don't smile at strangers. It is behavior left over from the communist era; from the cold war days.

We go into what appears to be sort of a general store. It's crammed full of food, tools, hardware, snacks, souvenirs, gifts, videos, magazines, and about anything else you can think of. The two clerks and apparent owner speak virtually no English and are unimpressed with the fact that we are Americans. We look around for a while, smile and thank them – and leave.

We "scooter" to Perechyn's small central square. We dig through Mike's collection of tourist maps and guides. We're about ten or fifteen miles from Uzhhorod, a city of over a hundred thousand, but neither of us feel like tackling a big city.

We decide to head home to Velykyi Bereznyi.

CHAPTER 62

Over breakfast, I tell Mike what I've been thinking. "Mike, our original plan was to spend today still acting like tourists. But I am getting bored -- and anxious to get on with it."

"Me, too Dad. I don't do inactivity well. Especially with something like this 'quest' on the horizon."

"It must be in your genes; I am the same way. Anyway, what do you think of heading north today? Maybe see if we can follow Oleksandr's map."

"I am *so* ready."

"Great. As soon as we are done with breakfast, let's gather up our maps and do it."

As we walk from the dining door to the staircase, Sasha calls us over to the desk. "I have some great news for you. I have found some of your relatives!"

"Really?"

"Not blood relatives. They're related through marriage. I haven't figured out the exact connection yet."

"That *is* good news. Did they know my grandparents?"

"Bohuslav, their patriarch is very old and a little senile, but he remembers your family. Your grandparent's house and barn are long gone, but he can show you their land, and maybe the family burial plot."

"When can we meet them?"

"They live on a working farm just west of our town. They would like you to come to dinner at their home tonight."

"That works out perfectly. We are going to explore to the north today. At what time should we return? How will we find their farm?"

"If you accept their invitation, Bohuslav's great-grandson Andriy will come to pick you up when he finishes his work. He can be here about five."

"Of course we accept. Should we take some sort of gift? Perhaps a bottle of wine?"

"No. A gift is not appropriate; it implies that you do not expect your hosts to provide for your needs completely. A thank you gift tomorrow is appropriate. I will select something and have it delivered with your thanks."

"Great. Thank you. We're going exploring."

Mike has been silent until now. "My great grandfather kept journals. In one of them he mentioned a place called Uzhansky. Do you know it?"

"I do. It is a now a National Park perhaps twenty kilometers north of here."

"What's there?"

"To be honest, not too much. It is noted for its beautiful mountain views and its birds."

"We might go check it out. We'll be back in time to meet up with Andriy."

* * *

It turns out that Oleksandr's map is very easy to follow. His map follows the Uzh River north from Velykyi Bereznyi. Highway H13, the road we followed into town, runs parallel to the river. The river is to the east of the road, and there are railroad tracks between the road and the river. The road, the tracks and the river follow the valley up into the hills. The three are never further apart than a hundred yards or so.

To make it even easier, there is a foot path along the river. The path is wide enough and smooth enough for our scooters. We check off the land marks on the map as we go north.

In a couple of hours, we're about four miles upriver and at the distinct bend in the river where the map has the drawing of the three trees. My guess of two miles from town to the trees was way off, but this is the place. We're sure of it.

There are no trees.

But there are stumps. Three of them. The hornbeams were full grown trees a hundred years ago. These have to be their stumps.

The map shows piles of stones north, south, and west of the middle tree. The ground is covered in thick grass about a foot deep. It will be difficult to find the stones. If they're here.

We scuff our feet through the grass hoping to kick stones. Fifteen minutes goes by. Nothing. I'm about ready to call for a break. "Dad!"

He's five feet west of the middle tree. "What?"

He's down on his knees. "Stone pile. Or what's left of it."

I hurry over. The white softball sized stones are scattered through an area about two feet square. But it must have been a pile a hundred years ago. "Í knew it. This is the spot. Let's take a break and then see if we can find the other stone piles. Just to verify our find."

"Sounds like a plan. Dad, do you realize what this means? We're half way to the Red Diamonds."

"I know... I know... I had hoped… But I never really expected… Wow."

* * *

We spend another half hour looking for the other two stone piles, but find nothing more than a couple of isolated stones. The foot path passes between the river bank and the trees. It probably went right past the stone piles. Walkers on the path have had a hundred years to scatter the stones.

But we're still very certain that this is the spot where Oleksandr's map ends and Mitri's begins. It simply has to be. Everything fits.

The other side of the river looks wild. No roads, no paths, just dense woods. It looks like the second half of our quest will be much harder than the first half.

But we have an amazing bit of help. Less than two hundred yards south of here, the railroad tracks cross the river. We can cross the river on the railroad bridge. We'll have to leave the scooters on this side, but we'll be able to get to the starting point on Mitri's map.

Tomorrow.

CHAPTER 63

We get back to the hotel with just enough time to call the girls with a progress report, and to clean up for dinner with the "cousins."

"Hi cutie, I was hoping to catch you before dinner."

"What's up Peter? Is everything okay?"

"More than okay. Mike and I couldn't stand the inaction any more, so we followed Oleksandr's map north."

"And?"

"We found the three hornbeams, or rather their stumps. And we found the stone pile. We now know the point where Oleksandr's map ends and Mitri's map begins."

"That's great. Now what?"

"Tomorrow we cross the river and follow Mitri's map! Or try to. How are you going on the translations of the notes on his map?"

"Stupendous! We now have English translations of *all* of the notes on Mitri's map. Some are pretty clear; some are kind of vague; some are confusing. Lauri has a bit map of Mitri's map on her laptop. We'll replace the Ukrainian notes with English ones and email it to you."

"That's good news, but don't do it that way. Let's assume that we are numbering the notes on the map with '1' nearest the origin and 'n' nearest the destination. Email us the notes in order from '1' to 'n'."

"Why do it that way? And what do you mean by note 'n'?"

"Maybe I'm being paranoid, but I don't want to make it easy for anyone to figure out the map and what we're doing with it. And 'n' is the last note – nearest the destination. Like 1, 2, 3, 4, … n."

"Okay. We'll do it your way. You'll have the translations of the notes tonight."

"That is great, Kate. You guys have done well."

"Thanks. But I miss you."

"Me, too. I have one more bit of news. Sasha, the hotel porter / desk clerk / owner has found some distant relatives living here. We're having dinner at their house tonight."

"Cool. But what are 'distant relatives'?"

"He's not too sure; we are related through marriage. Sasha said that they know where my family farm used to be, and that they may know where the family burial plot is located."

"Again, cool."

"To tell the truth, I would rather be following the map than meeting with distant relatives. But that is why we are supposed to be here, to discover our roots. We will do what we have to."

"It could be fun: meeting relatives, finding your homestead, finding your family plot."

"We'll see. I have to get cleaned up and changed. Do you want me to call you when we get back from dinner?"

"Not if it's late. We had a long day, too. Playing tourist. And shopping! We're going to crash early. But respond to my email so we know you got the translations."

"Will do, cutie. Love you."

* * *

Mike and I meet in the lobby at almost exactly five. Mike is always exactly on time – the result of years in the military. I'm always a little early – the result of a childhood with a father who was always late. Andriy is not here yet. We quiz Sasha on what to expect. He says, "Lots of food! Lots of vodka!"

I ask him if any of the people we are visiting speak English. He says that virtually all of the younger generation speak some English, and he understands that Julia Oparowski is pretty fluent.

I'm startled by the name. "I think that was my grandmother's name!"

"Julia Oparowski?"

"Yes."

"This Julia is in her late teens or early twenties."

"But that was my grandmother's maiden name. I know it."

"Then that's the connection. I believe that Julia was named after her great-grandmother."

And just then, Andriy walks in to the hotel. He is in his late twenties and could have been one of my nephews. The family resemblance is remarkable.

Sasha does the introductions all around. Andriy speaks a little English. "My sister Julia speaks very good English. She will be our translator. We go now?"

It's a twenty-minute drive to their farm and I'm reminded again of how much it looks like western Pennsylvania.

As we pull into the hundred-yard-long drive, Andriy honks the horn several times and about ten people of various ages come out of the house

We stop on the gravel parking area in front of the house and get out. Everyone is a little uncertain. Andriy breaks the ice. "Americans, meet the Ukrainians! *Ukrayintsi, zustrity amerykantsiv!*"

We laugh and shake hands. There are greetings in English and Ukrainian. I zero in on Julia. "Andriy says that you speak excellent English. I apologize for not speaking Ukrainian."

"I do not know about 'excellent,' but I study."

"My grandmother had your name. Julia."

"I was named after her; she was my great-grandmother. She went to America with her parents. Her brother, my great-grandfather Bohuslav stayed here."

"So that's how we are related. Your great-grandfather and my grandmother were siblings."

"Siblings?"

"Brother and sister. We are cousins."

"Welcome, cousin. Let us go inside. Dinner is ready."

Sasha was right. Lots of food. Lots of vodka.

Two hours later, we're still sitting around the table trying to ask and answer questions. Julia and Andriy and a couple of younger kids are kept busy acting as translators.

We've learned that Bohuslav corresponded with his sister until she died in the early nineteen-hundreds.

We've learned that the Bradoviches who didn't emigrate to America moved to Lviv, and then Kiev between the wars.

We've learned that the Bradovich farm became ruins and was destroyed during the Second World War. And we've learned that after the war, the land was divided up among neighboring farmers.

Lastly, we've learned that Bohuslav knows the location of the Bradovich burial grounds. It's getting dark now; he and Andriy will take us there in the morning.

It's late when the conversation winds down. It's been an emotionally draining evening and the vodka is doing its job. Andriy says, "I take you to hotel now? Farm starts early."

"Yes, Andriy. We are ready." After hugs all around – and one more toast – we say goodbye and pile into the car.

* * *

We're almost asleep by the time we get to the hotel. When we get upstairs, I lean on the wall next to my door. "I'll answer Kate's email tonight. Let's meet for breakfast about eight. We can work on the map until Andriy gets here. He said he'll be here after morning chores. About ten."

"Sounds good, Dad. See you at eight."

" Good night, son."

CHAPTER 64

Mike is already in the dining room when I get there. "Good morning, Dad."

"Morning' Mike. I need coffee."

"We have a new server this morning. Her name is Nastya, and her English is much better than my Ukrainian."

A twenty-something, chubby girl comes out of the kitchen. Mike waves at her. "Nastya. Coffee for my father, please."

"Thanks. I'm not ready to face the world yet."

"We've got two hours until Andriy shows up. I'd like to have the translations posted to Mitri's map by then. That way we'll be ready to go when we get back from the cemetery."

"Let's have breakfast then, and get on with it."

Nastya brings my coffee. Mike tells her we would like breakfast. "Ukrainian or Continental, Dad?"

"I'm still full from last night."

Mike tells Nastya that we are still full from dinner at our cousin's farm last night and asks her to just bring us some pampushky. "Perfect," she says, and scurries off.

* * *

We're quiet as we drink our very strong coffee and eat our very sweet pampushky. We're both thinking about Mitri's map and what today may bring. We're back in my room by eight thirty.

The notes on Mitri's map are different from those on Oleksandr's map. Oleksandr's notes were mainly landmarks to look for as we went upstream on the Uzh River. Mitri's notes are directions for a hike through the woods. Assuming the scales are about the same, it looks like about a four-mile hike from the river to the Red Diamonds.

I learned in Boy Scouts that day hikers cover about three miles per hour plus one hour for every 1000 feet of elevation climb. Backpackers cover about two miles per hour plus one hour for every 1000 feet of climb. So assuming we can follow the directions okay, we're probably looking at two hours at most.

The map is ready; we're antsy. We go down and tell Sasha we're going for a walk, and that we'll be back before Andriy gets here.

We walk to the old church, and then to the river. Then to the town center. Then to Saint Michael's Church. And back to the hotel. It's about ten to ten; we get to the hotel at the same time as Andriy.

Andriy's car is a Soviet era Lada. It's at least fifteen years old and a little dinged up, but it is a fairly roomy four door sedan, and it seems to run fine. Bohuslav rides shotgun, and Mike and I climb into the back seat. Andriy says, "It is not too far." He grinds the gears a little bit and we're off.

He drives past the Oparowski farmstead and continues on the same road. In about ten minutes, Bohuslav points out his window. "Tut. Tut!"

Andriy slows and turns right onto a grass covered dirt track between two fences. We go about two hundred yards and stop at an iron gate. The gate is open and a bicycle leans against it. Julia is sitting in the grass just inside the gate. She smiles, waves, and gets up.

We meet at the gate. "Hello. I knew the location of your family plot, but I have never been here."

I look at the small plot – and at the result of a hundred years of neglect. "It looks like no one else has been here either."

"There are no Bradoviches here to take care of it. Perhaps..."

"If we can borrow some garden tools, we might come back tomorrow and clean it up a little." There are about a dozen headstones in various states of disrepair.

"Good idea, Dad. For today, let's take pictures of each gravestone. Perhaps Julia can help us translate."

I look at Mike with an "I want to get out of here and go find the diamonds" look. He shrugs. And we proceed to pull weeds and take pictures.

With Julia and Andriy helping, and Bohuslav supervising in Ukrainian, it goes quickly, and we're done with our photos well before noon. The family plot looks much more respectable. "Julia, Andriy can we buy you lunch at the hotel?"

They look at each other. Julia answers. "We have to return to the farm, but if you give me the SD card from your camera, I will print your photos and transliterate the names. What are your plans for this afternoon?"

"We plan on exploring north of town. We may go up to Uzhansky National Park."

Andriy looks hard at Julia. Neither says anything. The silence becomes obvious.

Julia recovers first. "Well. I won't have the old Bradovich names transliterated until after dinner. I'll call the hotel..." She leaves something unsaid.

Andriy fills the momentary silence. "Let us return you to hotel."

We say goodbye to Julia and pile into the Lada.

.* * *

This morning, we asked Sasha if they could make us a couple of sandwiches to take exploring this afternoon. When we get out of the Lada at the hotel, we see our scooters sitting in the hotel parking lot. One has a plastic cooler bungeed in place behind the seat.

We go inside to thank Sasha. He asks how our explorations went this morning.

Mike answers. "We found our family plot and took lots of pictures. Julia is transliterating the names for us."

I take over. "We did lots of weeding; we may go back tomorrow and do some more. The plot looks like it has been neglected for a hundred years."

"I'm sure it has been. Family plots are the responsibility of the family. Your family left Velykyi Bereznyi long ago."

"I saw what looks like a cooler on one of the scooters."

"Your lunch. And snacks. And drinks. Enjoy."

Mike interrupts. "We shall. Thank you. But we need to get our maps first. I'll be right back."

Mike has been locking the folder of stuff I brought from the States in his room safe. I'm not convinced that it's secure, but he says he will be able to tell if anyone opens the safe while he's gone.

I got the impression this morning at the family plot that the "natives" suspect we're up to more than "discovering our roots." If they saw the maps by Oleksandr and Mitri, they would know. Our cover would be blown.

CHAPTER 65

We're on the road by noon and at the railroad bridge by twelve thirty. I keep looking over my shoulder to see if we're being followed. Paranoid? Perhaps.

We stash the scooters out of sight behind some bushes near the bridge. I put on a small backpack with the folder of maps and a few other odds and ends; Mike takes the cooler. We cross the bridge. There is a crude foot path along the east bank of the river. Not as nice as the one on the west bank, but good enough to make our walk fairly easy. We go upstream until we're directly across from the three tree stumps. It only takes a minute to find the small pile of white stones near the bank. That's landmark number one on Mitri's map.

The note next to landmark one is one of the longer ones. "Go two verstas east. Up the hill and down to the stream. Then go downstream to the pig-sized rock with the M carved on top."

I get out my lensatic compass and find due east. I mentally mark a tree at the top of the hill we're facing. The hill is not more than a hundred feet high, but there is no path and the going is rough. We're out of breath when we reach the summit. We find a downed tree and sit for a minute. "Two verstas is a little over a mile and a quarter. What do you think? Is this half way, Mike?"

"I think so. By the time we get down to the stream, we'll have covered about two verstas. Ready?"

"Let's do it." I mark a tree near the stream as due east and we head down the slope.

The stream is only a couple of feet wide. The banks are grass; there are no rocks. There is no sign of a "pig sized rock with the M". I break a fairly large branch on a tree to mark our spot, and we head down stream. We go about a hundred yards and start to see rocks along the stream. As they get bigger, we start to look for the "M."

"So what is pig-sized?"

"Beats me, Dad." We keep going. Another fifty yards. And then. "*This* is pig-sized, Dad!" Mike is kneeling in front of an odd pinkish rock that's about two feet high, two feet wide and three feet long. He traces the letter M for me. "Now what?"

There was a note that marked the top of the hill. The next note is here at the stream. It is similar to the note by the river, and at the same time more vague. "Go four verstas east. Up the hill and down to the stream. Go downstream to the next M."

We repeat the last trip. This time, up a steep hundred-foot slope and down a long gradual slope to another stream. I stop to rest. "Now what? The note just says go downstream to the next M. No mention of a 'pig-sized rock.' Not even any mention of the M being carved on a rock.

"My guess is that it has to be carved into a stone. He'd want it to be durable." Mike makes a small stack of flat stones to mark our spot. Then he starts downstream. I get up and follow. This stream is wider than the last one; it varies between six and ten feet wide. It flows over large flat stones. There are no pig-sized rocks. We go down stream a hundred yards. Nothing.

We go another hundred yards. Still nothing. Still no pig-sized rocks. Other than the flat ones that make up the stream bed, there no rocks of any size. We come to a small waterfall. And stop. "We missed it, Mike."

"How do you know?"

"I don't really know. I'm guessing. I think the note would mention this waterfall if we we're supposed to go beyond it." I'm getting tired. And frustrated.

"That makes sense. Kind of." He looks frustrated, too.

"We're getting low on water. We just passed a spring. Let's refill our water bottles, rest, and eat a sandwich. Then let's head back upstream and look more carefully. Somehow we must have missed the M."

The sandwiches Sasha provided are kind of like Italian panini. Small rolls sliced in half and filled with sliced meat and cheese. They're a little dry, but very good. Sasha packed six of them; we each eat one.

Sasha also packed two apples, two bottles of beer and a small bottle of what turns out to be vodka. We stick to ice cold spring water for now. Maybe after we find the Red Diamonds… If…

* * *

After we finish our snack, we slowly work our way back upstream. We get back to Mike's little rock pile. Nothing. Shit. We look at each other. "Now what?"

"There's got to be an M here somewhere, Dad. He did *not* say it's on a pig-sized rock. He did *not* say it's on a rock at all. What are we missing?"

"An M on a tree will be gone by now. He had to put it somewhere more durable."

"Let's work our way back down toward the water fall. You take one side; I'll take the other. Look at everything."

We go slowly. We have to find the M. If we don't, everything ends here.

After a while. "Anything, Mike?"

"No. You?"

"No. Maybe I was wrong about it being before the waterfall."

"I don't think so. It made sense. Kind of."

We keep going. I walk with my head down – part concentration, part dejection. I look at everything. I'm getting behind Mike. I don't care. We've got to find it.

I can hear the waterfall ahead. "Dad!"

Mike is standing in the middle of the stream at the top of the waterfall. He's looking at his feet.

"Dad! Come here!"

I jog down the bank and out into the stream. Mike points to the water in front of him. At the very edge, right where the water cascades over the falls are thirteen round flat stones, each about ten inches in diameter. They are arranged in the shape of an M. The stones are moss covered, but they are not randomly located. They definitely form an M.

I squat down. "Look." The middle rock, the rock at the center of the M is a little bigger. It is moss covered like the others, but it has a carving. I trace the M for Mike. "Wow."

CHAPTER 66

We sit on the west bank of the now twelve-foot-wide creek with our now wet hiking boots in the water. I get the map out to see what's next. "Mike, look here." I'm pointing to our present location.

"The waterfall!" There are two small squiggly lines across the stream where the stream and the dashed line cross. I've seen the squiggly lines before, but I didn't pay much attention to them. They are the waterfall.

From here, the map shows the line going roughly northeast. The note at the waterfall reads, "Go northeast by north two verstas up the slope to the meadow."

Northeast is 45 degrees and northeast by north is 33.75 degrees. The average hiker might not know that, but I'm a sailor. I know the compass rose. I face 33.75 degrees; I'm looking up a long gentle slope. I mentally mark a tree at the crest and we head up the mile plus slope.

When we reach the crest, we stop. We're facing a meadow full of blue wildflowers. I have no idea what they are, but they're beautiful. The meadow is about two hundred yards across. On the other side, the ground rises again toward mountain peaks in the distance.

Mike and I sit on a downed log and take a break. We get the map out again. We have seen the roughly circular line around what we think is the location of the Red Diamonds. We now know that it's the meadow.

The last note is at the edge of the meadow. Where we are sitting. "Find the highest peak on the horizon. Go toward the peak for fifty sazhen. You have arrived."

Fifty sazhen is three hundred fifty feet. "How good are you at guessing when we've come three hundred fifty feet?"

"Figure a little over a football field, Dad. It'll be a guestimate." We start moving in the direction of the highest peak. The map shows the details of what we should expect.

At three hundred fifty feet, we should see two or maybe three things in a row.

First, the map shows a rock with an **M** carved on it. We don't know how big of a rock. I'm hoping we can find it in the foot-high blue wildflowers.

In another three arshin (seven feet) the map shows a "Grave Cover." The map does not indicate its size or whether it's on the ground or below ground. It is the Grave Cover that has the **X** on it.

In another six arshin (fourteen feet) there should be another rock with a **Б** carved on it.

* * *

"This looks like a football field from the start of the meadow, Dad."

"Now what?"

"We've seen no rocks at all. With or without a letter. Let's start going ten feet farther, then twenty feet back, zigzagging away from our track. You work to the left of our track; I'll work to the right. Look for a rock. Any rock. A rock with an **M** or a **Б.**"

"Okay."

I start moving through the wild flowers, looking for a rock. I reflect on where this started and how far we've come. This is the culmination of a huge amount of work: months of research and planning; thousands of miles of travel. There has been a lot of guess work. But all of it has proven to be true. Unless Metodyj Bradovich retrieved the Red Diamonds himself or led somebody else here, we should be within feet of the treasure.

I stop. I look up at the sky. It's been almost four hours since we crossed the railroad bridge. We have maybe four hours of daylight left. I sigh. I look back down. And see a pink rock at my feet. A twelve inch round pink rock. A twelve inch round pink rock with a **Б** carved into its top.

Mike's twenty feet away. I almost whisper. "Mike."

He looks up. His expression says, "What?"

All I can say is, "**Б**."

He comes plowing through the wildflowers. I'm shaking. He looks down. "Oh, shit."

"I know. Twenty-one feet back that way should be another rock with an **M**. And fourteen feet back, there should be…"

"The Red Diamonds…"

* * *

It takes only a couple of minutes to find the other rock. We move slowly and carefully to where the Grave Cover should be. At first we see nothing. Then I see a small spot – maybe a foot square – where no flowers grow. It's covered with dead grass and leaves. I drop down on my knees. I brush the grass and leaves aside. And see a flat stone with **M Б** carved on it. The initials of Metodyj Bradovich. The Grave Cover.

We're both on our knees now. We lift up the Grave Cover and set it aside. I get a couple of small gardening tools – a rake and a shovel – out of my backpack. We dig.

Less than a foot down we come to a small box. It is wrapped in waxed cloth. I unwrap the box. It appears to be cedar; it's about eight inches wide by ten inches long by four inches deep. It looks like the lid was attached to the box with brass hinges and a brass clasp; all that's left of the brass is greenish blue powder.

I carefully remove the lid. There are two silk pouches inside. I take a silk pouch out. "Hold out your hand, Mike." I unfold the flap and let the Red Diamond slide into Mike's upturned palm.

The deep red Peruzzi-cut diamond gathers the light from the bright blue sky overhead. It seems to glow. I can't speak. Mike's breathing quickens. We just kneel there. Silent.

Mike breaks the silence. "I think I really didn't believe that this existed. I didn't think diamonds came this big. I…"

"They don't. This is ten times bigger than the largest known red diamond. And I think it's an even darker red than that one. Metodyj estimated it at fifty carats. This is worth millions of dollars; tens of millions; maybe hundreds of millions. Hold out your other hand."

Mike does as I ask. His hand is shaking a little. I open the other silk pouch. I slide the six red Mazarin-cut diamonds into his other palm. "There's another sixty carats for you.

CHAPTER 67

We've got to call the girls. Cell phone coverage here in the hills is non-existent. We'll have to wait until we're back in town.

The trek back to the scooters goes quickly. We feel refreshed. The hills are lower. The distances are shorter. We're back at the river before we know it.

We're almost giddy. We are rich. We are very rich. But we're rich in a country where private wealth is almost non-existent; where the government owns everything. We will be rich when we get the Red Diamonds back to the United States.

"Mike, before we get back to civilization, we need to talk."

"There's a stack of railroad ties at this end of the bridge. Let's have a picnic. Let's drink that vodka and those beers. And talk."

In a few minutes we're settled in at our makeshift picnic table. We unwrap the last two sandwiches and open the two beers. "Well. I said we need to talk. But I don't know what I want to talk about. What is our plan? Just for today, I mean. First item: do you really trust the hotel safe?"

"I know I said I will be able to tell if anyone gets into the safe. That's still true. So far, nobody has tried to get in. But, if somebody gets into the safe when the diamonds are in there, knowing that they did get in will be of no help. We will have lost the diamonds. I'm not willing to take that chance."

"What do you have in mind?"

"We'll put the cedar box in the safe, but I want to keep the Red Diamonds on my person. I have a fanny pack. They'll fit just fine. I don't think it'll happen, but anyone who tries to take them from me will have hell to pay."

"But you can't wear the fanny pack when you go through customs."

"No. I'll carry the diamonds until we get them hidden in the matryoshkas."

"Speaking of which, the matryoshkas are shrink wrapped. We'll have to open them to hide the diamonds. I'd like to reseal them, but I don't want to ask Sasha for shrink wrap or Saran wrap. It may cause questions. Any ideas?"

"Yes. When Sasha took us on a tour of the kitchen at the hotel, I noticed a food wrapping station of some sort. I think they use it for left overs. I'll sneak into the kitchen tonight and steal some wrap."

"What if you get caught?"

"I'll tell them I was hungry and looking for a snack."

"Yeah, right."

"Dad, I'm very nervous about Ukrainian airports and Ukrainian customs. I'd like to minimize our exposure. What do you think about taking the train from Lviv to Kiev?"

"I think it's a great idea! That will leave us with one non-stop flight from Kiev to Venice. They will search our bags in Kiev. I'm hoping the hunting knives will divert attention from the matryoshkas."

"And Italian customs won't care. They'll just smile and say 'Welcome.'"

We laugh a little. It breaks the tension that has built. "Let's get back to the hotel before dark."

* * *

Sasha is at the front desk when we get back to the hotel. "Mike, why don't you go up and do what you need to do. I want to talk to Sasha about our change in plans."

"Okay, Dad. Call me when you're ready to go to dinner."

"You want to change your plans? How? And why, may I ask?"

"Well… We enjoyed today very much. The hill country is beautiful. But we feel we've gone as far as we can here. The family plot was very interesting; Julia is going to transliterate the names from the tombstones. We'll be able to construct a family tree."

"And that is why you came, right?"

"Yes. That is why we came. This has been my opportunity to find my past. And I have done that. My children and their children will know their past. But the Bradoviches are gone from Velykyi Bereznyi. We learned from the Oparowskis that the Bradoviches who didn't immigrate to the United States before World War One moved to Lviv and then Kiev between the wars."

"And so now you are finished?"

"Finished here. We want to explore Lviv a little. And Kiev. Maybe we can find more traces of our ancestors."

"We will be unhappy to see you leave. This has been a memorable visit for many of us."

"And for us as well."

"Julia told me that she saw Bohuslav cry for the first time in her remembrance. When she asked him what was wrong, he said, 'Nothing. I am just remembering.'"

"I know how he must feel. I am his sister's grandchild. A relative he didn't know existed."

"And now Julia wants to see America."

"Really? We would love that. My daughter lives in Chicago. She has a Ukrainian nanny."

"What is her name? Where is she from?"

"I only know her as Anna. I will have to ask when we get back to the United States. But for now we need your help in changing some reservations."

"If you must. What needs changed?"

"First is our car and driver. They were supposed to come the day after tomorrow; we need them tomorrow instead."

"I have a better plan. I will cancel your car and driver from Lviv. I can arrange for a car and driver from our town to take you to Lviv."

"The same price?"

"Cheaper."

"Perfect.

"Next, we need to change our reservation at the Leopolis Hotel in Lviv to tomorrow night."

"That's easy. I will have my daughter do it tonight. Have you met Anastasia?"

"No, it seems like you are always here."

"I *am* always here, but she is here as well in the evenings after school and dinner."

"She is a student?"

"No, no. A teacher. A very good one. I am proud of her. I will introduce you to her tonight. What else do we have to change for you?"

"Two more things. We will need a hotel in Kiev for one night. We would like a nice place near the city center."

"I know just the place. You will have reservations at the Premier Palace Hotel. It is marvelous. And what is the last thing?"

"Well, the last thing we haven't decided for sure. We have airline tickets from Lviv to Kiev. But we're thinking of taking the train instead. It's not too much longer, and we'll see Ukraine instead of clouds."

"That one is more difficult. Give me your tickets. I will have Anastasia try to get you a refund. If she can do that, I'll have her book a first class roomette on the train. It is a very nice ride through the heart of western Ukraine. You will enjoy the trip."

"I will bring the tickets down. I bought them using my American Express card; perhaps she can arrange a credit to my account."

"She will try."

"Thank you for all of your help, Sasha. I am amazed at how many Ukrainians speak English, and speak it very well. But to have an American expatriate as our host here in Velykyi Bereznyi has been an unexpected blessing."

"And it has been a blessing for me as well. I love it here. This is my home. But I miss America. It has been good to be with Americans for a while. Perhaps, if I ever visit America…"

"We would love it if we could show you our part of the United States. I live near Cleveland right on Lake Erie. Mike lives in Colorado, in the mountains. Perhaps…"

"Perhaps…"

"I need to go get cleaned up for dinner."

"Will you eat here?"

"Of course. It will be our last night in Velykyi Bereznyi."

CHAPTER 68

I knock on Mike's door. I'm always amazed at how quickly he answers. It's like he's always standing at the door waiting for a knock. "How do you do that?"

"Do what?"

"Answer the door so quickly. It is like you are standing at the door waiting for someone to knock."

"It's just that I know you're coming and I'm prepared to let you in."

"Well anyway, now what?"

"Now what, what?"

"What do we do with the Red Diamonds? Put then in the safe? Hide them?"

"As I said, we put the cedar box in the safe, but not the diamonds. The diamonds stay with me. I hate fanny packs, but I do own one. The diamonds go in my fanny pack, and we go to our last dinner in Velykyi Bereznyi."

* * *

When we get down to the lobby, Sasha is deep in conversation with a twenty something light eyes.

When Mike and I approach the counter, they booth look up.

"Aha. Gentlemen, let me introduce you to my daughter, Anastasia. Anastasia, meet our American guests Peter and his son Michael."

Anastasia comes out from behind the counter. She is a very attractive twenty something, but she has a slightly hard look about her. Anastasia shakes hands with each of us, and says in almost perfectly accent-less English, "I am very happy to finally meet you."

I answer for both of us. "And we are very happy to meet you, as well."

"My father has told me of the arrangements I must change. Did you bring your airline tickets down?"

"Yes. Here are both of them."

"I will need the credit card to which you charged the tickets. At the very least, I will need the number on the card."

I pull out my Amex Gold Card and give it to her. "This is the card I used to buy the tickets. I will also be paying my bill with it in the morning. Take as long as you need; we are not going anywhere this evening."

Mike adds, "Except to dinner here. And soon, I hope. I'm hungry."

Anastasia smiles. "My father has asked our chef to make you something very special. Enjoy your meal."

Anastasia's lack of an accent is a little unnerving. Everyone speaks with some accent. Everyone makes some grammar errors. Not her. Her English is as perfect as I have ever heard. It's almost computer-like. If I get a chance, I'll have to ask Sasha where she learned English.

Sasha walks us into the dining room and seats us at what has become our favorite table. He bows deeply. "I think I told you that our chef is a cousin. I have asked Dima to prepare a very special meal for you. It is our going away gift to you. Let me go get him."

Sasha walks into the kitchen and comes back out in less than a minute. He is followed by a rather rotund middle aged gentleman who is wearing a very tall chef's hat. They approach our table. "Dima speaks no English. I will act as translator. Peter, Michael, this is

Dima." We stand to shake hands as he says something in Ukrainian to Dima. We shake hands all around, and Sasha tells us to please sit down. Dima says something to Sasha and leaves. Sasha turns to us and says, "Either I or Anastasia will come to tell you of each course as you are served. Your first course is kapusniak: pork soup with sauerkraut and sour cream. I will be back. Enjoy."

The soup is followed by studenetz, a kind of fish aspic that neither Mike nor I are very impressed with.

Next comes the main course: kruchenyky, beef rolls, served with kasha, buckwheat cereal, and mushroom sauce.

And finally dessert: symyky, fried quark fritters with sour cream and honey sauce.

All of this is washed down with large quantities of nalyvka, a strong berry wine.

And thankfully, some American coffee.

At the end of the meal Sasha and Dima come out of the kitchen. Sasha asks, "Well? Did you enjoy?'

I answer for both of us. "Yes, very much. I am absolutely stuffed."

Mike adds, "Me, too. I can hardly breathe."

Sasha says a few words to Dima. He beams, bows, and heads for the kitchen; one very happy chef.

Sasha watches him go, and then turns to us. "I know that many Ukrainian dishes are somewhat alien for the American palate. I wanted Dima to give you a wide variety of dishes. I hope that nothing was too 'unusual.'" He laughs.

"No. No. Everything was fine."

"I'm glad. Remember us well."

"We will, Sasha. We will. This has been a truly unforgettable visit. Thank you."

We say good night and head up the stairs to our rooms. When we're safely out of earshot, I turn to Mike. "I will be glad to get back to Venice and more familiar food."

"Me, too, Dad. Me, too."

CHAPTER 69

It's a little before eight a.m. I knock on Mike's door.

He takes less than a minute to answer. "I just finished with the matryoshkas. Come see."

The three matryoshkas are sitting on his desk. The fresh shrink wrap is not quite as smooth as the original, but it is close. "What is where?"

"I put the red diamond in the big matryoshka; I had to eliminate two of the inner dolls. Each of the small matryoshkas has three small red diamonds; again, I had to eliminate two of the inner dolls. Everything is packed with tissues. Nothing rattles."

"This may be a premature question. Are you thinking checked bag or carryon?"

"I'm not letting the matryoshkas out of my sight until we're home. The matryoshkas will go in my carryon and the knives will go in my checked bag. I'm hoping the knives shift interest away from the matryoshkas when we go through security."

"Makes sense. Let's pray it works. Question: I do not remember seeing any x-ray machines in the secure check in area at Boryspil Airport, do you?"

"There were none. My guess is that they x-ray the checked bags before they go on the aircraft. The carryon bags do not get x-rayed; they get searched by hand. That's another reason to put the matryoshkas in my carryon valise. I don't know how the matryoshkas will x-ray."

"I appreciate you taking over on this. I would be a wreck if I had to do it."

"Well, you need to remember my background. It only makes sense that I do it. Besides, my 'Official' passport can intimidate some border personnel. I often get a pass and a wave-through when they see the maroon cover."

"Let's hope it works for us this time."

"I agree. What time does our car get here?"

"Around eleven. Let's go have breakfast."

"I've still got some last minute packing to do. I can do it after we eat."

"Me, too."

* * *

After breakfast we finish packing and drag our stuff downstairs.

We just finish settling our bills with Sasha when a small, slightly shabby white van pulls up outside. The driver hops out and comes into the lobby. He looks to be in his mid-twenties. I have to ask Sasha. "Another cousin?"

He laughs. "No, better. Anastasia's boyfriend. His English is very good, and he has a great first name. Peter, Michael, meet Sasha!"

Sasha, the driver, laughs and says something to Sasha, the hotelier. They both laugh. Sasha, the driver, comes over to us with his hand outstretched. "I am happy to meet you. I will get you to the Hotel Leopolis quickly and safely. Anastasia will have my head if I do not."

"Perfect."

"Is it okay if Anastasia accompanies us? I would like her company on my way back to Velykyi Bereznyi. We can pick her up at her school."

"Of course, it is okay."

"I will put your bags in the van while you say goodbye to the old Sasha." He laughs again.

I hold my hand out to the old Sasha. He grabs me, gives me a huge bear hug, pats my back, and then holds me at arms length. "When the girl from the Leopolis called to make reservations for two Americans, I was pleased. I never dreamed that it would be such a memorable occurrence. We will not forget you. Safe travels, my friends."

He moves on to Mike. Another big hug and pat on the back. Mike looks a little nonplussed. I interrupt to save him. "Her name was Oksana. The girl at the Leopolis. If she is there tonight, I will thank her for the wonderful arrangements. You should thank her, as well, Sasha."

"I will. I will. Godspeed. And make sure Anastasia comes back to Velykyi Bereznyi. She wants very much to go to America. I'm afraid she won't return."

Sasha, the driver chimes in. "I will bring her back! The only way she will go to America is with me. As my wife!"

Sasha, the hotelier laughs. "*My pobachymo.* We shall see."

We pile into the van, and I check to make sure that all of our luggage is aboard. I count four pieces: two suitcases and two valises. Sasha starts the van and pulls out into the light traffic. He clips an earpiece on and speed dials a number. In a moment he starts talking. *"My znakhodymosya na nashomu shlyakhu"*. A pause. *"P'yat' khvylyn."* Another pause. *"Do pobachennya."* He taps his earpiece to hang up.

He looks at us over his shoulder. "Anastasia is ready. We will be at her school in five minutes."

* * *

Ten minutes later, Anastasia is riding shotgun and we're on our way. Sasha makes good time through the hills, and Anastasia plays tour guide. It seems like she has something to say about every building we pass. And there are lots of them.

After about an hour, Sasha, pulls into the parking lot of a small building with gas pumps outside. "We shall go in for refreshments before we go onto the Federal Highway."

We go in the front door and out the back door onto a small patio. A waiter comes over with four water glasses, a bottle of water, and four shot glasses that he fills with vodka. No words have been exchanged. This must be the standard "refreshment" before going onto the Federal Highway.

Anastasia holds up her shot glass, says, *Khoroshe zdorov'ya*, and downs her vodka! Mike and I say, *Ura*, the only Ukrainian toast we've learned, and down our vodka. I think *Ura* means "Cheers," or something like it.

In about ten minutes, Sasha gets up and points to the restrooms. There are two, and they are not labelled by sex. We all head in that direction. Sasha and Mike let me and Anastasia go first; age and beauty first. We're treated to old style squat toilets, so it's a quick trip for everyone.

Our break is over; we're back on the road. Sasha turns onto the M06. Traffic is heavy. The van has a bad shimmy at ninety. He has to hold it down to about eighty-five. I'm glad. We get passed and honked at a lot, but we'll probably get to Lviv alive.

CHAPTER 70

A little over an hour later, Sasha parks in front of the Hotel Leopolis. We made it. Alive.

We all go into the lobby. It is old, but very elegant. Anastasia does a slow 360-degree spin. "Very nice. *Very* nice." Mike and I go up to the front desk to check in. The clerk's name tag says "Саша – Sasha." I can't help but laugh a little. Sasha, the clerk looks miffed. "Sir?"

I smile. "Do you speak English?"

"Yes, sir. I do."

"I meant no offense. The owner of our hotel in Velykyi Bereznyi is Sasha. Our driver is Sasha. And now you are Sasha. It seemed a funny coincidence. That is all. I apologize if I offended you." We hand him our passports. "We have reservations."

He looks pointedly at Sasha and Anastasia. "And that Sasha and the girl?"

"They are returning to Velykyi Bereznyi. It is only us two who are staying."

He gets busy with his computer. We have not made a good first impression.

In a couple of minutes Sasha, the desk clerk is finished. He has a small silver whistle on a silver chain hanging around his neck. He puts it to his lips and blows a short note. A bellman appears from a room off to the side of the elevators. He is pushing a four wheeled cart.

Sasha, the desk clerk fights a smile. "Yet another Sasha will escort you to your rooms." He hands Sasha the bellman two keys. "I will return your passports when you first come down from your rooms."

When I lived in Europe many years ago, hotels kept your passport for your entire stay. That always left me feeling a little uneasy. I did what many savvy travelers did then; I carried a copy of the ID page of my passport with me at all times.

At least now they give your passport back to you rather quickly. *After* they've copied it or scanned it, so they can give it to some government agency, I'm sure.

Sasha, the desk clerk looks pointedly at Sasha, the driver and Anastasia. He says something in Ukrainian. I look at Anastasia for a translation. "He said that for security reasons, we are not permitted to go beyond the lobby. We will wait for you here. We can stay in Lviv for a little while before we must return home."

"Great. We won't be long."

We follow Sasha, the bellman up to our third floor rooms. They're the same rooms we had last time. Coincidence? Or design?

* * *

It's still early afternoon. We have time for lunch and a quick walking tour of Lviv's old city center before Anastasia and Sasha have to return to Velykyi Bereznyi. We try to convince them to stay for dinner, but Sasha says the mountain roads are not good after dark. He wants to be home by then.

We go back to the lobby of the Hotel Leopolis. Our goodbyes are long and tearful. We all hope to see each other again, but we all know that it's unlikely.

Sasha, the desk clerk watches from his post at the front desk. After we part, and after we've composed ourselves, I walk across the lobby to the front desk. "My grandparents lived in Velykyi Bereznyi. During the revolution, they emigrated and settled in America. Michael is my son; we spent a week in Velykyi Bereznyi learning about our ancestors' home. Your coworker, Oksana, booked us into the Hotel Gold, and during our week there, we became close friends with its owner, Sasha, and his daughter, Anastasia."

"I see. That explains much."

"I would like to thank Oksana for her marvelous choice of hotels. Will she be on duty?"

"She will be on duty in the morning. I'm sure she will be pleased that you were so happy with her booking."

"We were. Very much. Do you have a recommendation for dinner?"

"Our own restaurant is as good as any you will find in the city. I heartily recommend it. Can I make you a reservation?"

"Yes, for seven o'clock, please."

CHAPTER 71

Mike takes a hard look at the safe in his room. It is newer than what was in our rooms in Velykyi Bereznyi. These have a digital electronic lock, the kind that takes a five-digit combination that you can set yourself. "What do you think, Mike?"

"These are no better than what we had in Velykyi Bereznyi. They invariably have a house code so the hotel can open the safe when some guest screws up his combination. I will keep the matryoshkas in my fanny pack."

"As long as it works..."

"Meet you down stairs a little before seven?"

"Sounds good."

* * *

As we are coming down for dinner, Mike and I have a moment alone in the elevator. "What did you think of Anastasia?"

"What do you mean, Dad?"

"I thought her near perfect and accent-less English was a little – well, odd"

"I noticed."

"I asked Sasha where she learned to speak English so well."

"What did he say?"

"He said that she learned English from him."

"Then she should have a New York City accent."

"Sasha also told me that when Ukraine was part of the Soviet Union, Anastasia had the opportunity to go to an English language school in Moscow."

Mike looks at me rather intently

"What?"

"Dad, during the Cold War, there were English language and culture schools in Moscow."

"So?"

"They were run by the KGB…"

* * *

We get seated immediately in the very elegant dining room. They are quite busy for a Wednesday evening. I did a little research in Lviv before we came. This quote from the Lonely Planet web site sums it up pretty well: "Mysterious and architecturally lovely, this Unesco World Heritage Site is the country's least Soviet and exudes the same authentic Central European charm as pre-tourism Prague or Kraków once did."

The city seems to be thriving. And the Hotel Leopolis bears witness.

Though most of the diners seem to be Ukrainian, the menu is multilingual, and we each select an entrée that sounds a little more American than what we had in Velykyi Bereznyi last night. Sasha and his cousin, the chef had their hearts in the right place; they wanted to give us an unforgettable meal. Unfortunately, it was unforgettable for the wrong reasons. Tonight will be more normal.

"I called Kate. I told her that we were in Lviv and that we were taking the train to Kiev tomorrow."

"And I called Lauri. Same discussion. She wanted to know why the train, and I told her it eliminates one confrontation with airport security people. It made sense to her. She said to say hi and to take care."

"Sounds like we had the same discussion. Kate said hi as well."

Our appetizers arrive; we concentrate on eating and keep the conversation light.

As we finish with dessert and coffee, Mike looks at his watch. "What time is our train?"

"Ten o'clock."

"Meet for breakfast at eight?"

"Before we go up, let's check with Sasha at the front desk to make sure that allows us ample time."

Sasha says we should allow more time because traffic is very heavy in the morning. We agree on seven thirty.

"Mike, I'm going to take a little walk before I turn in. Care to join me?"

"I don't think so. See you in the morning."

* * *

Lviv at night reminds me of the Europe I fell in love with forty years ago. Most of the tourists are gone. There are only a few strollers – mostly couples. A light mist is falling; it makes halos around the street lamps. There is something almost mysterious about Lviv at night. I just wander for an hour. I imagine my great grandparents here a hundred years ago. Our western world has lost much of its magic in the last hundred years. Lviv has managed to hang on to some.

Venice is my favorite city in the whole world. Lviv could become my second favorite.

CHAPTER 72

Six a.m. comes early. I'm a little tired from my wanders last night. But it was worth it. I know Lviv better now. And no matter what happens, I will remember it always.

At seven fifteen, there is a knock at my door. Or rather, three knocks, twice. It's Mike. "I thought we could take our bags down now. Save us a trip back up after breakfast."

"Good idea. Let me get mine together."

When we get down to the lobby, we're greeted by Oksana. She remembers us, of course. "You did a great job with the hotel in Velykyi Bereznyi. The proprietor was raised in America. We got to know him and his family very well. They helped us find the area where my great grandparents lived. And the place where my ancestors are buried. They even found some distant relatives. It was a marvelous week. Thank you, again, Oksana!"

"I'm very happy that you were pleased. I knew that the proprietor was American. I thought it would be a good place for you. But what can I do for you now?"

"We are checking out right after breakfast. We will need a taxi to the train station."

"To the train station? But you flew in, no."

"We flew in, yes, but we've decided to take the train back to Kiev. We look forward to seeing western Ukraine instead of clouds."

"That is an excellent plan. I will arrange a taxi."

"May we leave our suitcases here until we check out?"

"Yes. Of course. Go enjoy your breakfast. I shall ready your bills."

* * *

Breakfast is uneventful. We're a little anxious to get going. We're back at the front desk by eight. Oksana has our bills ready, and a taxi waiting. The driver has already loaded our luggage. We pay our bills, and say goodbye and thank you again to Oksana. She reciprocates with hugs and kisses for both of us. We go outside and I check to make sure we have all four pieces of luggage. Mike has his fanny pack on. At last, we're in the taxi and on our way.

It's only a mile or two from the Leopolis Hotel to the train station, but traffic is heavy and it seems to take forever. The taxi driver speaks no English. We listen to him mumble what are probably obscenities for the whole ride. He pulls up in front of the large stone station; my guess is communist era architecture. The taxi driver sets our luggage on the curb, takes our money, tips his hat, and leaves. He shows no interest in helping us inside.

We stand there for about two minutes deciding what to do next when a gentleman in his sixties comes up with an old wooden luggage cart. "Amerykantsi?" How do they now?

Mike recovers before I do. "Yes. Amerykantsi. The train to Kiev?"

"*U vas ye kvytky?* Tickets?"

Mike shows him our tickets.

"*Pershyy klas.* You come."

We follow him into the station; he turns left and passes a few platforms. He stops to have a brief conversation with a uniformed railway employee. We wait nearby. He waves to us. "*Pershyy klas.* You come."

Our porter starts down the platform. We walk past coaches with a 3 on the doors, then past several with a 2 on the doors. The porter stops when he gets to the first coach with a 1. "Tickets?"

He takes a quick look. "You come." And he's off again.

At the third coach with a 1 on the doors, he stops, grabs our two suitcases and climbs aboard. He has to be in his sixties, but he is hard for us to keep up with. Mike and I grab our valises, and follow him aboard.

He turns into a compartment and puts our suitcases up on the overhead rack. "*Pershyy klas!*"

We do the same with our valises. Our porter smiles and waits for his tip. I have no idea what to give him. I pull my wad of hryvnia bills out of my pocket. On top of the pile is a 50 hryvnia note; I think it's about five dollars. I hand him the note. "Enough?"

He breaks into a huge grin. "Yes. Yes. Thank you. Thank you." He backs out the door.

The compartment is designed to hold six passengers. There are two upholstered bench seats facing each other – kind of like a restaurant booth, but with no table in the middle. Our companions are a young family: husband, wife, two pre-teen age boys. The boys had been sitting on the seat opposite their parents. When we entered, they moved to sit beside their parents. Mike and I sit on the now empty seat. Mike slides a little away from the window, points to the older boy and pats the seat next to him. The boy doesn't move. His father laughs a little. "They will both be over there soon enough."

Mike smiles. "And that is no problem. We are Americans. I assume you are Ukrainian?"

"Yes. We go to visit the old folks in Kiev. You just gave that porter two days' wages. You made him very happy."

"He earned it…" There is a lurch and the train starts moving. We pull out of the station and almost immediately are into suburban Lviv. The train picks up speed as it moves into farm land. Our train is listed as "fast," but it's not like the high speed trains of Western Europe. It will cover the three hundred miles from Lviv to Kiev in about five hours. We'll be in Kiev in the afternoon.

* * *

As it turns out, the train trip is only a little more interesting that the clouds we would have seen had we made the trip by air. After a while the farm lands interspersed with tracts of forest all begin to look the same. We roar through small town stations so fast that we can see very little. Both Mike and I take a couple of walks along the train, but that gets boring, too. We try snoozing, but the bench seats don't recline. They are designed for sitting not snoozing. The train does make a couple of stops, but a train station is a train station is a train station.

I think we just want to get on with what we have to do. Tomorrow we fly from Kiev to Venice. Tomorrow we smuggle the Red Diamonds out of Ukraine. Or tomorrow we go to prison.

CHAPTER 73

The train starts to slow as we move through the suburbs of Kiev. The first things of note are the truly ugly high rise apartment blocks -- a left over from the communist era. Thankfully, they disappear as we approach the old city.

The train stops. We're on a wye branch used to turn the train around so that it can back in to the station. Another slight lurch and we're moving backwards. Our young traveling companions – Danilo and Dmytro – have the widows open and are leaning out to see what can be seen. Their mother says something in Ukrainian and they both pull back – a little.

Another lurch and we stop. We are in Kiev. We gather up our luggage, and follow the crowd off of the train and down the platform to the central station. The station is immense. The crowd is huge. I read that this station handles 200,000 people per day! I believe it. We make our way to the main entrance. We go through the gigantic front doors, and down the well-worn marble stairs. We stop and turn around to check out the facade. A guide book called the architecture Cossack Baroque; all I can say is that Cossack Baroque appears to be only a little less baroque than typical Western European Baroque. We're not impressed.

We continue down the broad stairs to the taxi stand. The first taxi in the queue is a small van. The driver puts our luggage in the back; we slide into the second row seats; we tell the driver Premier Palace Hotel; he pulls out into the very heavy afternoon traffic.

It takes us a half hour to cover the less than two miles from the train station to the hotel. I think we could have walked it faster.

We finally arrive; the Premier Palace Hotel looks magnificent. Sasha and Anastasia chose well. Our driver hands our luggage off to a liveried hotel porter. We pay the driver and follow the porter in to the hotel. The lobby is as magnificent as the entrance.

We lay our passports on the check in desk. A lovely light eyes whose nametag says "Марина – Marina" comes over. "Good afternoon gentlemen. You have a reservation?"

We each hand her an American Express Card; mine is a Gold Card; Mike's is a Platinum Card. "Yes, we do. For two rooms."

"Of course. One moment." She swipes our credit cards and scans the ID pages of our passports.

She hands everything back to us. "Vladislav will take you and your luggage to your rooms. Is there anything I can do for you before you go up?"

"We'd like a reservation for the two of us at the Atmosfera Restaurant."

"Of course. And the time?"

"Seven o'clock."

"Perfect. The roof top views are very nice."

Marina hands two key cards to the porter who has been patiently waiting. "Follow Vladislav, please. Enjoy your afternoon and evening."

As we follow Vladislav to the elevators, I turn to Mike. "I need to stretch out for an hour. Then if you're up to it, let's go explore."

"Sounds good, Dad."

* * *

An hour later I feel a little refreshed and ready to tackle Kiev. I rinse off my face, put on a clean shirt, and knock on Mike's door. He opens the door almost immediately. He has changed clothes, too. "Dad, I found two Bradoviches in the on-line phone book. Actually,

I had to look up the Ukrainian spelling: Бродович. Do you want to try to contact them?"

"Quite frankly, no. I've had about all I can take of relatives. And of Ukraine. All I really want to do is get through the night, get through customs in the morning, and get back to Venice and the girls. I want this part of our adventure to be over."

"I kind of agree with you. I'm worried about clearing customs tomorrow."

"Let's go for a walk."

* * *

Neither Mike nor I have done our homework on places to see in Kiev. And the city is just too big to tackle in an afternoon. We wander aimlessly for a couple of hours. And we lose interest.

We stop at a sidewalk café overlooking the Dnieper River. The Dnieper is one of Eastern Europe's grand rivers. It's over 1300 miles long, and it wanders through Kiev on its way to the Black Sea. We watch the river traffic as we drink our coffee.

Mike checks Trip Advisor on his tablet, and we decide to visit Saint Sophia Cathedral. We decide to visit for three reasons: it's number one on the list, it's an easy walk from the café, it's something to do to kill some time. The desire to just "kill time" sounds jaded, but both of us are anxious to get on with our quest, to get out of Kiev, to get through customs, to get out of Ukraine.

We're both very nervous about Ukrainian Customs. It is one of the scariest encounters of the whole trip. And it is tomorrow morning.

Actually, Saint Sophia Cathedral is well worth the trip. It's over a thousand years old and it's in amazing condition. The mosaics are awesome. Outside it's patterned after the Hagia Sophia in Istanbul. Inside, it has five naves, five apses, and thirteen copulas. We get lost several times just looking. Saint Sophia was once the central church of the Kievan Rus empire, of the Rusyn people. My grandmother talked about being Rusyn. I thought she was mispronouncing Russian. Now I know differently.

We wander out of the Cathedral and make our way back to the hotel. We each call our wives. We each express our fears about tomorrow, and promise to call as soon as we're through customs.

A little before seven, we take the elevator up to the Atmosfera Restaurant, the rooftop restaurant. The menu has what sounds like an American style filet. We both order one. We sip our very good red house wine as we eat our salads and wait for the main course. We're not disappointed. The filets are great and are accompanied by baked sweet potatoes and a variety of strange vegetables. This is as close to American food as we've had since we left the United States. We finish with cheesecake, expresso, and cognac. A truly great meal.

As we stroll back to our rooms, we agree to meet for breakfast at eight.

CHAPTER 74

I'm still full from dinner last night, but it was a great meal – one of the best I've had in Europe. But a good breakfast is prudent. We don't know what the day will hold. We decide to head for the airport at about ten.

Marina is at the front desk again. We stop to tell her that we will be checking out about ten, and that we'll need a taxi to Boryspil Airport.

* * *

I meet Mike at the front desk at about five to ten. I immediately notice the absence of his fanny pack. "No fanny pack?"

"Everything's stowed where it needs to be."

As we check out, we notice a young man standing near the door. Marina calls him over. "Anton will take you to the airport. Where do you go?"

"We are meeting our wives in Venice, Italy. Thanks you for everything. Your hotel is beautiful. Last night's dinner was the best we've had in the Ukraine."

"Thank you. God speed you on your journey. Stay well."

* * *

The ten-mile ride to the airport is quiet. We're both deep in thought.

Anton stops the van and breaks the silence. "*Mizhnarodni vyl'oty.*"

We have no idea what that means, but the sign over the building entrance says "International Departures" in several languages. Here we go.

We pay Anton, gather up our stuff and head inside. We see no porters so we follow the signs to the Customs Hall. The crowd is light. We go in and put our bags up on the long, low table for inspection. Mike puts his ticket and his dark red Official Passport on top of his suitcase. I do the same with my ticket and my dark blue regular passport. A uniformed and armed inspector comes over. He starts with Mike. He opens the passport and compares the photo to Mike. He nods, and holds the ID page under a scanner. The scanner beeps. The inspector stamps the passport, and hands it to Mike.

He enters some information from the ticket into his computer and turns to Mike. "Check or carry on?"

Mike points to his valise. "Carry on." Then he points to his suitcase. "Check."

The inspector enters a couple of key strokes and hands Mike's ticket back to him. Then he opens Mike's suitcase and starts digging through the contents. Almost immediately he finds the hand towel containing the three hunting knives. He unwraps the towel and lays the knives on the table. He shakes his head no. "Nee. Nee. Not allowed."

Mike looks unflappable. He smiles. "Knives for my sons. Gifts." He holds his hand out, palm down, and gestures to show the heights of his sons.

Again, the inspector shakes his head. "Not allowed to export."

Mike pulls an envelope out of the top of the suitcase. He removes a Ukrainian Certificate of Origin. Folded into it is a fifty Euro note. The inspector looks at the Certificate of Origin, pockets the fifty Euro note, and hands the certificate back to Mike. "Very good. Okay." He closes the suitcase, put a small sticker on it, and attaches the baggage tag that got printed while he was searching the suitcase.

Then he turns to Mike's valise. He digs around for a little while and then pulls out the matryoshka dolls. All three of them. "Russian junk." He starts to unwrap the largest – the one with the Red Diamond. I panic. "No! Don't unwrap them. They are gifts for my granddaughters!"

He reacts in a way I never expected. "Russian junk! No export! Trash!" And he throws all three dolls into a cardboard box behind him.

I almost go over the table. I yell, "No! Give them back! They are for my granddaughters! Please!"

Mike grabs my arm. "Dad."

Movement in the Customs Hall stops. Nobody talks. Then another official strides over. This one is in civilian clothes. He has a very short conversation with the customs inspector, and then turns to us. "What is wrong? Why did you yell?"

I'm shaking. Anger? Fear? I point to the cardboard box behind them. "He threw away my three matryoshkas! They are gifts for my granddaughters. I want them back!"

He has another very short conversation with the customs inspector. "He says that they are Russian junk. That allowing you to export them will reflect badly on Ukraine."

"He may think that they are Russian junk." I point to Mike. "But his daughters, my granddaughters, will love them. Please give them back."

"I am the supervisor, but he is the inspector. His decision is final." He starts to turn away.

I'm desperate now. "Ask him about Mike's hunting knives. And the fifty Euro note he pocketed."

The supervisor stops dead. "Fifty Euro note?"

I look at him very seriously, almost coldly. "It was with the Certificate of Origin. He put it in his pocket."

He turns to the inspector. Their conversation starts quietly, then gets more heated. A dozen other passengers are now listening. Finally, the supervisor slams his fist on the table. "*Dosyt'*." The inspector stands rigid. Almost at attention. The supervisor digs through the box, retrieves the matryoshkas, and almost throws them into Mike's valise. He affixes a small sticker. "*Yty*! Go!"

As Mike gathers up his stuff, the supervisor grabs my passport and ticket. He glares at me for what seems forever, then turns to the computer. In a few seconds, the printer cranks out a baggage tag. He scans my passport, stamps it, and hands it back. He doesn't even open either of my bags. He puts stickers on both my suitcase and valise; he attaches the baggage tag to the suitcase. He glares at me again; longer this time. "*Yty*! Go!"

"Thank you. *Dyakuyu.*" I gather up my stuff and follow Mike.

Near the exit from the room, another uniformed inspector stands in front of a row of luggage buggies. Like everybody else in the room, he has watched the drama. As we approach, a slight smile reveals his feelings. "Checked baggage?"

Both Mike and I hand him our suitcases. We hang onto our valises and go through the exit doors. After the doors close, I stop and lean against the wall. I take deep breaths for a couple of minutes. I lean forward and put my hands on my knees. Then I stand up straight. "God. That was scary. I didn't know if we were going to get arrested. Or shot."

Other passengers are now starting to exit the Customs Hall. Some smile and nod. Some studiously ignore us. One guy gives us the thumbs up.

"Dad, you done good. I was still trying to figure out what to do when you yelled at the inspector."

"I'm a wreck."

"But we still have the matryoshkas -- and what they contain. Let's go find our gate."

CHAPTER 75

I'm starting to unwind by the time we get to the Lufthansa gate. Mike has been reassuring me. He says that we did the hard part. Now we have an easy flight to Venice. If the past is any indication, Italian customs will be easy. They won't even open our suitcases.

We get to our gate. The waiting area is sparsely populated; there are only a few early arrivers like us. It's almost an hour before our flight boards. There is a bar just down the concourse from our gate. Mike suggests a last drink in Ukraine before we embark. I agree. Two large shots of vodka later, I've unwound even more. We slowly make or way back to our gate. Our flight should be boarding soon.

When we get to the waiting area, we find that things have changed. When we left for the bar, the small crowd was a typical tourist crowd. Lots of talking; lots of milling about; lots of noise; lots of confusion.

Now the crowd is dead quiet. People are visibly worried. Eight military types surround the small crowd. They hold their Kalashnikovs across their chests. They look ready to shoot. Two more military types work their way through the crowd, checking documents and tickets. I notice that they are concentrating on men my age. This is not good.

They approach a white haired, rotund gentleman. He bolts. He gets no more than six feet when one of the guards surrounding the crowd tackles him. Almost before we realize what's happening, they have him handcuffed and they are leading him away. A murmur and then a collective sigh of relief goes through the crowd. It's unlikely that we'll ever know who the white-haired gentleman is or what he did. But there are obviously many people who look like I feel -- relieved that they weren't after me.

Mike looks at me hard, but says nothing. I look back at him. And say nothing. Right now, silence is the safest measure.

I consider asking Mike if he wants to get another drink, but the Lufthansa agent at the gate announces that we will be boarding in a few minutes. She does not mention what we all just witnessed. She asks that we turn off our mobile telephones before we board. Neither Mike nor I have thought about calling the girls since our little adventure at the Customs Hall. Mike looks at me. "I'm going to text Lauri that we made it through customs and are boarding. I'll save the ugly details for our rendezvous in Venice."

"Good idea. I'll text Kate."

We're still texting as our fellow passengers start to board. We finish our texts and join the line. In fifteen minutes, we're in our seats and settling in for the two-and-a-half-hour flight. We each order a vodka, and are already anticipating the next one. We've had enough excitement to last us for a very long while.

* * *

I awake to the sound of the landing gear going down. We're almost to Venice. Mike looks like he just woke up, too. We've both been snoozing. Four vodkas will do that to you.

In a few minutes, we feel the reassuring thump of the wheels hitting the runway. After a short burst of reverse thrust, we turn off the runway and taxi to the apron surrounding the terminal at Venice's Marco Polo Airport.

Customs turns out to be the non-event we expected. We get our passports stamped by a disinterested looking immigration agent, and retrieve our suitcases from the luggage carousel.

We carry them to the inspection area. We unzip our suitcases and set our passports on top.

The agent comes over, smiles, stamps our passports, and hands them back to us. He does open our suitcases, but he just looks without rummaging around. He peers into our valises, but does nothing more. He smiles again, and waives us away with a "*Benvenuti in Italia.*" We don't hesitate. We go.

As soon as we get out of the terminal, we'll take the shuttle bus to Santa Lucia Train Station in Venice, and then take the vaporetto to the hotel. We head out the Customs Hall door – and almost run into a large sign held by two girls. The sign says "OUR HEROES! WELCOME BACK!" The two girls are Kate and Lauri!

PART FOUR:

HOME AGAIN

CHAPTER 76

The girls were not supposed to be here at the airport. It's a very pleasant surprise; we're glad to see them.

After lots of hugs and kisses, Lauri looks at Mike. "Well?"

"Well, what?"

"We want to see the..."

Mike interrupts her; "At the hotel. They're inside of shrink wrapped matryoshka dolls. I don't want to unwrap them in public."

"Shite!" And she scowls at Mike. She knows that Mike is right, but she doesn't like it.

I try to smooth her ruffled feathers. "We planned on taking the vaporetto to the hotel. We can cut the travel time way down if we take a water taxi. What do you think?"

Mike is very aware of the need to be circumspect. "Great idea, Dad. I was going to suggest lunch, but we'll get no rest until the girls see our souvenirs."

"Let's do it then." Mike and I each grab a suitcase. Kate and Lauri each take a carry on valise.

Mike considers whether or not to take his valise from Lauri. He quickly decides. And he's still circumspect. "You've got all of the souvenirs, Lauri." He looks at her hard. She gets the message.

It's only a two hundred yard walk to the water taxi docks. As we leave the building, the usual horde of locals descends on us offering taxis, buses, lunch, souvenirs, hotels, tours, about anything we could want. We do our best to ignore them.

When we get to the dock, we find a line of water taxis waiting. The third one in line is owned by Luciano, the driver who took us to the Londra Palace when we first arrived almost two weeks ago. It's a happy coincidence.

I walk over to his boat. "Ciao, Luciano." I can see that we look familiar to him, but he's not sure why.

I explain to him in Italian that he took us to our hotel when we first arrived, almost two weeks ago. I tell him that though he is not the first boat in line we would like him to take us there again. I ask if that is possible.

He looks at the two boats ahead of him. His mix of Italian and English is odd but effective. "*No problema.* I fix. *Aspettare.*"

He walks up to the head of the line of boats and has a short conversation with the two drivers in front of us. He's back in a minute. "Okay. It is fixed. *Imbarcarsi.*"

He puts the suitcases and valises on board and then holds out a hand to help Lauri. Then Kate. Then Mike. And finally me. As I board, I remind him of our destination. "Londra Palace."

He nods vigorously. "Si. Si I remember." I'm not sure he really remembers. But it's good salesmanship, so I thank him. He throws off the lines, and with a little help from the driver in front of us, shoves off.

Almost as soon as Luciano gets us up on a plane, Lauri looks at Mike. "Now? In the cabin?"

"No. Hotel."

And we start a very quiet ride to the Londra Palace.

* * *

The quickest way to the Londra Palace is to go to the east of Venice, and then south and west to the entrance of the Canale Grande.

After a week in Venice, everyone has a pretty good idea of where Luciano is taking us, so we all sit back and enjoy the ride. Well, some of us more than others…

In what seems to be just a few minutes – for some of us -- Luciano brings us in to the dock at San Zaccaria.

Lauri is out of the boat as soon as Luciano stops. "We have the same rooms as before. Let's go up and freshen up." And she is gone.

Mike just shrugs. "She'll get over it."

Luciano unloads our luggage, and offers to help us to the hotel. I tell him that we can manage and pay him the going rate plus a generous tip. He gives me a business card and tells me to call him whenever we need a water taxi.

The remaining three of us say goodbye, gather up our luggage and walk the twenty or so yards to the hotel. We go into the lobby and are greeted by our friend from last time, Paolo. "*Ciao signori.* Welcome back."

"Thank you. It's good to be back. Ukraine was interesting and I'm glad we went, but coming back here is almost like coming home."

"Bene. Bene. What did you do in Ukraine?"

"My grandparents were from Ukraine. We flew to Kiev and then to Lviv in the west. We drove about 150 kilometers to Velykyi Bereznyi, the village of my grandparents."

"It was good?"

"Yes, the owner of our hotel was a Ukrainian who was raised in America and then moved back to Velykyi Bereznyi, the town of his birth. He helped us find our ancestor's farm and the family burial plot. He even found some of our relatives who still lived in the area. It was amazing, but we're glad to be back here. Ukraine is very – different."

Paolo turns to Mike. "Your wife is waiting in the bar. She asked that I tell you."

The bar is just a few feet from the front desk. Lauri is nursing an expresso. I ask the barman to send a bottle of Asti Spumanti and four glasses up to our room. We gather up Lauri and head for the elevator.

CHAPTER 77

The girls are almost bouncing off the walls. Mike spreads a towel on the desk, and carefully removes the shrink-wrap from the three matryoshka dolls.

Matryoshkas typically have at least five nesting dolls, each one smaller than the previous one. He starts disassembling one of the small dolls. He opens the first doll to reveal the second one. He opens the second one to reveal the third one. He starts to open the third doll. Lauri can't stand it any longer. "How many are there?"

"There were seven. But not now. Hold out your hand."

Lauri does as she is told. Mike opens the third doll to reveal a wad of tissue paper inside. He slides it into Lauri's open palm. "Open it carefully."

Again, Lauri does as she is told. She peels off several layers of tissue. And she carefully lays three light red, almost dark pink Mazarin cut diamonds on the towel. "Oh, shite."

Each diamond is about ten carats. They are perfect. The girls just stare at them. Mike opens the second of the smaller matryoshkas. When he gets to the third doll he stops. "Kate?"

She holds out a hand; he opens the third doll; he drops another wad of tissue paper into her hand. Her fingers are shaking as she unwraps three more diamonds and lays them beside the first three. Mike grins at Lauri. "Those are for your bracelet…"

Just then, there is a knock on the door. I go to open it. Mike stops me. "Wait."

He spreads another towel over the first one and puts the large matryoshka in the desk drawer. "Okay, Dad."

I open the door. A waiter stands behind a small cart. The cart has an ice bucket with a bottle of Asti Spumanti in it. It also has four wineglasses, and a tray of small pastries. "Come in."

The waiter wheels his cart in and stops near the desk. He looks at the towels spread out on the desk. Before he can touch them, I point to the French doors. "Out on the terrace, please." I don't think he understands much English, but he understands my gesture. I open the terrace doors and he wheels the cart out. He opens the bottle of Asti Spumanti, pours a small amount into a glass, and holds it out to me. I taste it and nod. He starts to turn the other glasses over. I put my hand on his shoulder. "*Lo farò più tardi.*" I will do it later.

He sets the glass back down. "Si, signore." He corks the wine and looks expectantly at me. I give him a tip, and start towards the door. He gets the idea. He does the small bow that service people do here in Italy, opens the door, and closes it behind him.

Mike is heading for the desk as the waiter leaves. He waits for me to lock the door, and then retrieves the large matryoshka from the desk drawer. He pulls the top towel off the desk and tosses it on the bed.

Everybody watches intently as he opens the first doll, then the second. "Dad?"

I hold my hand out. He slides the tissue wrapped diamond into my upturned palm. I've seen it before, but my hands still shake as I unwrap the Red Diamond. I lay the fifty carat Peruzzi cut fiery red diamond next to the six smaller diamonds.

I'm expecting another "Oh, Shite," but there is nothing. Just silence. Kate and Lauri are not breathing. They stand open mouthed, just looking. Just looking at over a hundred carats of diamonds. Amazing diamonds. Diamonds that have gone unseen for a hundred years. Diamonds that were once held by Tsarina Alexandra.

Finally, Kate breaks the silence. "They are absolutely breathtaking. Is there anything else like them anywhere in the world?"

"Up until now, the biggest red diamond was the Moussaieff. It weighs a little over five carats. It last sold for seven million dollars. This stone, our Red Diamond, is a deeper, more vibrant red. Metodyj estimated its weight at fifty carats."

Mike sets a magnifying glass and an eye loupe on the towel. "Neither of us are experts, but we could find no sign of any flaws or inclusions in any of the diamonds. Check them out."

Lauri is just shaking her head slowly from side to side. I think she doesn't want to acknowledge what she's looking at. She can't admit that they're real. Finally: "Are these really diamonds? Are there other diamonds this big? Is this even possible?"

"The Hope Diamond is a little smaller; about forty-five carats. It's blue, not red, and it's valued at three hundred fifty million dollars. There are several bigger diamonds than the Hope, but they're listed simply as "priceless."

Now we get what I've been expecting: "Shite. Shite. Shite!"

* * *

We spend over an hour taking turns with the magnifier and the loupe.

Lauri gets out her gold costume jewelry. We compare the sizes of the glass stones and the diamonds. They're close; very close.

Tomorrow we pop out the glass and put in the diamonds. One thing that is very obvious to me is that even though the red diamonds are not modern brilliant cut diamonds, they have a lot more sparkle than the glass stones. This is especially true of the big Red Diamond. It just seems to suck in the light. It almost glows. I wonder out loud. "What can we do to make the diamonds sparkle less?"

Kate has an idea. "Hair spray. Too much spray can dull your hair. Maybe it'll work on diamonds."

Mike's turn. "Maybe. We'll try tomorrow. Right now, I'm hungry."

We help Mike wrap up the diamonds and stash them in his money belt. By the time we're done, his belt is a little lumpy, but acceptable.

CHAPTER 78

Before we go to dinner, I've got to text my younger son, Gabriel. It's early afternoon in Charlottesville. I keep the text vague. "Having a great time. Got lots of souvenirs. Be home Monday."

Almost immediately, I get a text back. "Are the souvenirs nice?"

"You will love what we found in Ukraine."

"Can't wait. Where's home?"

"The Lakehouse. We leave VCE late Mon AM. Land CLE late Mon PM."

"Great. Can I call you back in about an hour?"

The "Can I call you back in about an hour?" is a prearranged code for "I'll call you as soon as I can get to a private location."

I've been reading the texts to the gang. Hmm. "Gang" just sort of came out. But I guess we are a gang. A gang of diamond thieves. If word of our heist ever slips out, I'm sure that that's how the press will refer to us.

While I'm contemplating this, Kate speaks out. "Now what? Do we wait for a call? Do we go eat supper?"

"Let's give him a few minutes." While we're waiting, I tell them about my thoughts of us as a gang.

Kate Smiles broadly. "The Red Diamond Gang. I *like* that."

Mike snorts. "As long as they don't use that to refer to us in prison."

"Point."

And my cell phone rings. "*Pronto.*"

"It's Gabe, Dad. English, please."

"Okay." I put him on speaker. "The whole gang is here."

We assume that our phone conversations are not being monitored. The odds are very slim that they are, but there is always the possibility. We continue to be a little circumspect. "Give me the one-minute version."

"The maps were relatively easy to follow. We met some distant relatives. We visited the family burial plot. We wandered all over the place."

"And the knives?"

"We… got… them… And they… are… amazing… Unlike anything you've ever seen."

"Cool."

"We had a few dicey minutes coming back to Italy, but we are here."

"You had problems?"

"Ukrainian Customs was scary. They almost confiscated our souvenirs. And I almost got arrested for yelling at a Customs Official. We came very close to being discovered. We will tell you all about it when we get home."

"And you're coming home Monday?"

"Yes. Venice to New York City to Cleveland.

"The bracelet and pendant will work?"

"Yes. They're a good fit. Can you meet us in Cleveland Monday night? We won't be in until late, but you can stay at our place."

"Not Monday night. Tuesday afternoon works, though."

"Bring Karen if you can."

"Depends on if the nanny can stay over. We'll see. What do you do between now and Monday?"

"Play tourist. And repair some broken jewelry."

"Sounds like fun. I wish I could have been there. Love you all. Safe travels."

"Thanks, Gabe. See you soon."

CHAPTER 79

We decide to go back to the Ristorante All'Angelo for dinner. It's kind of where we started our quest here in Italy.

The multi-lingual menu is still posted outside, and a multi-lingual waiter is still standing next to it inviting us in. We turn toward the door and the waiter smiles broadly; he recognizes us as Americans. He starts to go into his standard script. "Welcome. You are ..."

He stops and bows a little. "But you have been here before. Welcome back."

I laugh a little. "*Sono stato qui prima che tu nascessi, ma questa è una storia lunga.*" He looks a little surprised. I translate for my companions. "I told him that I was here before he was born, but that it was a long story."

The waiter nods. "My name is Georgio. I understood. Your Italian is excellent. And your dialect is local."

"I learned to speak Italian in the Veneto. Many years ago, I lived near Padova. I came here often. The owner of the ristorante befriended me and made me feel welcome. I have never forgotten him."

"Well, then, welcome back, and welcome to your companions."

"This is my wife, Kate, my son, Mike, and his wife, Lauri. We have been here several times over the last two weeks."

"*Piacere*. Let me show you to a nice table, with a view. I will be your waiter." He stops to have a quick word with another waiter. Then he takes us to a table overlooking the Calle Larga San Marco. It had a small RISERVATO sign on it, but he pockets that and pulls out a chair for Kate. After he seats us all, he passes out menus and asks if we would like to start with drinks.

I look at Kate and Mike and Lauri. "White or red?" The vote is unanimous. "A carafe of your house red, Georgio, and a bottle of *acqua minerale con gas*."

"*Si signore. Subito.*"

As we wait for our drinks, I tell a quick anecdote. "I told Georgio that the owner befriended me. I didn't feel that I needed to tell him that we also had a little deal going. About once a month, we traded wares: A carton of American cigarettes – Marlboros -- for a case of Chianti Ruffino."

Kate reacts first. "A case of wine for a carton of cigarettes?"

"Well, a case was just four raffia covered one liter bottles. You've seen them, I think."

"For a carton of cigarettes?"

"I could get up to four cartons a month at the Army Post in Vicenza. They cost me eighteen cents a pack."

Mike reacts next. "My father, the black marketeer!"

"Zippo lighters were big, too. I don't remember what our ration cards allowed, but everybody maxed them out. Whether they smoked or not."

As we're laughing about that, a fifty-some year-old gentleman comes to our table with a bottle of San Pellegrino and a carafe of red wine. He sets the carafe down and pours four glasses of San Pellegrino. He starts to do the same with the wine. He stops and looks at me. Hard. "I think you knew my father. May I ask when?"

I stand. He sets the carafe down. "Nineteen-sixty-five. My name is Peter -- Pietro. And you are?"

"I am Marco. The same as my father. He is in Heaven now, and Ristorante All'Angelo is mine." We shake hands.

"I remember your father well. I was in the U. S. Air Force, and stationed on a small radio site in the Colli Euganei. I had few friends here, so I came to Venice often, and stayed at the Albergo All'Angelo; I ate most of my meals here. Your father befriended me; he made me feel welcome in his beloved Venezia. He taught me much about the city and about Italy."

"I was young, but I think I remember. He smoked American cigarettes – Marlboros – from you, I think. And you and your friends drank Chianti Ruffino!"

All I can do is smile. And swallow hard. "It was a long time ago…"

"Si, signore. It was."

"It is good to be back."

"And it is good to have you back. *Un momento.*" He picks up the carafe of red wine and hands it to Georgio. He says something that I don't catch and Georgio scurries off to the back.

Mario asks about my companions. "This is my wife, Kate, my son, Mike, and his wife, Lauri."

Mike stands and shakes Mario's hand. "Nice to meet you. My father has told many stories of living in Italy long ago."

Just then, Georgio scurries back with a bottle of Chianti Ruffino. He hands it to Mario. As Mario opens the Chianti, I think I see a tear. "The wine is for the remembrance of earlier times. Dinner is my gift to all of you."

"No. We can't…"

"For my father. And for times remembered."

We hug. "Thank you." I sit down. Shaken.

Marco uncorks the wine, and pours me a taste.

I nod. He fills our glasses. And leaves. Before we both start crying.

* * *

Dinner is marvelous. Too many courses to remember.

We try very hard not to talk about the Red Diamonds. We chat about everything else. But we're thinking Red Diamonds.

Over coffee, we finally give in. Mike starts. "What do we do when we get home, Dad?"

That breaks the ice. Kate speaks up. "What is Gabe up to? What does he know?"

Lauri chimes in. "I'm scared shiteless about wearing them. They're worth…"

I interrupt her. "Easy gang. In due time."

I get some sheepish nods. "Let's talk tomorrow."

We finish our coffee, and ask Georgio to get Marco for us.

In a few minutes, Marco comes out of the back room.

After many hugs and thanks all around, we promise to come back tomorrow night. But only if we are allowed to pay.

* * *

We're all very full. No gelato tonight.

As we walk slowly back to our hotel, I bring up the subject again. "Just so you can sleep. Gabe knows everything. He is talking to Sotheby's and Christie's. He will be in Cleveland on Tuesday. We can formulate a plan then."

I get some nods. But no comments. As we walk side by side, I hug Lauri. "I'm scared, too..."

CHAPTER 80

After breakfast, we're back in our room with the diamonds again spread out on a towel. Except this time, we have Lauri's pendant and bracelet.

And we have the small jeweler's toolkit I brought from the States.

We start with the bracelet. Mike holds it down on the towel while I bend back the six metal tabs holding one of the glass stones in place. The stone lifts out easily. The rectangular frame waits for its new stone. I set the first diamond in the frame. It doesn't fit quite right; the circumferences of the frame and diamond are virtually identical, but the frame is more rectangular; the diamond more square. I use the round tipped, needle nose pliers to carefully change the shape of the frame to fit the shape of the diamond. They now match perfectly. I drop the diamond in place and bend the six tabs tightly up against the stone. Done!

While Mike and I have been mounting the first stone, Kate and Lauri have been experimenting with hair spray. While Mazarin cut diamonds are fairly dull compared to today's brilliant cut diamonds, they are still lot more brilliant than glass.

It turns out that Kate's Redken Hairspray works better than Lauri's Aussi Hairspray. Two coats dull a Mazarin just enough to make it virtually identical to glass. The girls spray all of the diamonds.

While the diamonds are drying, we discuss another issue. The glass stones have a large culet – flat bottom. The diamonds have no culets – their bottoms come to a point. This makes the diamonds much deeper than the glass stones. This causes two problems: the finished bracelet won't lie flat against Lauri's wrist; the points of the diamonds will dig into her wrist. My suggested solution: don't wear the bracelet until right before customs; take it off as soon as you get through. For a few million dollars, you can endure a little pain.

After the diamonds dry, Mike and I take turns swapping the glass for the diamonds. When we get done, we have a bracelet that looks like a slightly mistreated piece of costume jewelry. Exactly the look we want.

Next comes the pendant. Again we pop the glass stone out, and again the diamond doesn't quite fit. But this time, the circumference of the frame is off; it's a hair too small. We're stymied. We consider cutting the frame, and adding a small piece of metal, but we have nothing to add and no way to bond it back together.

Kate has an idea. "The frame is probably gold plated brass. Brass is pretty malleable. Can we stretch it by working it against a hard surface?"

"You mean hammer it thinner and therefore longer?"

"Yes."

That sounds like the best idea so far. Actually, it's the only idea so far. Hard surface? Mike and I move to the bathroom. The sink is set in a granite countertop. Mike holds the frame. I use the blunt end of a small drill bit from my toolkit as a punch. I tap lightly for what seems like forever, but the frame slowly stretches and eventually the Red Diamond fits. I set the diamond in place and bend the eight tabs over to hold it there. The frame looks fragile; ready to break. But it's as good as we can do.

The pendant has the same slightly mistreated piece of costume jewelry look as the bracelet. But even with two coats of hairspray, the Peruzzi cut Red Diamond sparkles too much. It takes two more coats of hair spray to make it look like glass. We're ready for customs.

* * *

We have the afternoon free. We decide to take a vaporetto ride to unwind. We take the number 2 semi-express boat to the Santa Lucia Train Station. We stop at a local café for coffee and a snack.

We walk across the Calatrava Bridge over the Canale Grande to Piazzale Roma. The Calatrava Bridge has been a source of controversy since it was installed in 2008. Most Venetians think its modernist-minimalist style is completely incompatible with Venice's decorative medieval architecture. And I think that they're right.

At Piazzale Roma we catch the number 1 vaporetto. It's the local that zig zags between twenty stations along the Canale Grande. It's a long ride, but worth it; we get to see the entire canal, and then the boat goes across the lagoon to the Lido, Venice's beach on the Adriatic Sea. The beach is deserted; it's too early in the season for even the hardiest tourists. We enjoy the walk, though, and stop at another café before heading back to the Londra Palace.

We all agree that a nap is in order before dinner. At the Ristorante All'Angelo again.

CHAPTER 81

We're all ready to go home; to be done with this adventure. We know that if we get the Red Diamonds home, we will be fabulously wealthy. But we also know that if we get caught, we may well go to prison. I'm not sure what crime we'd be accused of committing, but I'm sure the feds would think of something. We would probably also be charged by the Ukrainian government. That is just plain scary.

Gabe has done his research, and piqued the interest of both Sotheby's and Christie's. They both have expressed extreme interest in seeing the Red Diamonds. One of them stands to make a very nice commission.

Mike and I told the girls all about our near disaster at Ukrainian Customs. They were horrified. U. S. Customs is our next – and last -- really difficult test.

Maybe we're being paranoid, but even though we're ready to go home, we all believe that we must act like tourists and stay a reasonable amount of time. And another dinner with our new found friends at the Ristorante All'Angelo fits our desired image perfectly.

* * *

We arrive at the Ristorante All'Angelo at seven o'clock, the time Marco asked us to arrive. Georgio is at his station next to the multi-lingual menu. His face lights up when he sees us coming. "*Buona sera.* Welcome back!"

Several other groups of diners check us out to see if we are somebody well known. They satisfy themselves that we are not movie stars or some other kind of notables. They go back to their meals. Georgio takes us to the same table we had yesterday evening. Again, he pockets the RISERVATO sign before he seats us. I'm beginning to suspect that this table is always reserved. Just in case.

After he gets us seated, Georgio asks if we want our usual -- a carafe of the house red, and a bottle of *acqua minerale con gas*. When I say that we do, he tells us that signore Marco will be out to greet us in a few minutes, and he scurries off.

We sit for about five minutes, still getting an occasional surreptitious look from a neighboring diner who is still trying to figure out if he should know us.

And then from the kitchen, out comes Georgio, followed by Marco. Georgio is carrying a platter with some awesome looking bruschetta. Marco has a bottle of San Pellegrino sparkling water and a bottle of Chianti Ruffino. Georgio sets the platter of bruschetta on the table and steps aside for Marco. Marco does a little bow. "For old times, you must allow me to gift you with a bottle of Chianti Ruffino. My father would have wanted it so."

I know better than to argue with an Italian on his home turf. "Thank you, Marco."

"I have asked our chef to prepare a special meal for your last night with us. I hope that is acceptable."

"Of course it is acceptable. We are honored. But last night we agreed to come back tonight only if you allowed us to pay."

"Si. Si. If you insist, I will prepare a bill. *Dopo*."

This exchange really gets the attention of the guy at the next table who has been trying to figure out who we are. He leans over and says something to his female companion. She nods vigorously and they both smile knowingly. It appears that they think they have figured out who we are. I can't resist. I slide my chair back, get up and make my way to his table. I stoop down between him and his companion. "Thank you for not blowing our cover. It is difficult for us to get out without attracting attention. And by the way, you have chosen a very good restaurant. Enjoy." The look I get is priceless. I really wonder who they think we are...

We spend the next two hours slowly stuffing ourselves with all kinds of great food. I, for one, am happy that the main course is roast pork. And it's very good roast pork; it's infused with grapes and ricotta. I was afraid that we might have been treated with a Venetian favorite, *Frutta del Mare.* Literally, Fruit of the Sea, it has all kinds of exciting things like squid and octopus and sea urchins... I am much happier with pork.

It's nearly ten o'clock as we finish our desert and coffee.

I catch Georgio's eye as he walks by with a tray for another table. After he serves them, he comes over. "Signore?"

I ask for our bill. "*Il conto per favore.*"

"I will ask Signore Marco to prepare it." And he heads for the kitchen.

In a few minutes, Georgio comes back out. He is accompanied by Marco. Marco sets the bill down in front of me. "If you insist Signore Peter."

"I do. It is only fair." I look at the bill. The writing is pretty much unreadable. The bottom line amount is fifty Euros; a reasonable amount for a modest meal for four at a modest restaurant in Venice, but certainly not enough for this restaurant or for the feast we just enjoyed. However, I know that it will be futile to argue about the amount.

I lay a fifty Euro note on top of the bill. "For the restaurant."

I hand Georgio a twenty Euro note. "For you."

I stand to shake hands. My companions all do the same. Handshakes turn into hugs. Hugs turn into tears. "Marco, your father trained you well. Or perhaps it is not training, but rather genes. You have made us feel welcome. You have treated us like old friends. Our experiences here at Ristorante All'Angelo will become memories that we will never forget. I thank you. We all thank you."

"Return to Venezia soon. We will be here and waiting."

"We will return. I promise." And I mean that. I suspect that we will be doing lots of traveling in the future.

CHAPTER 82

As we're walking back to the hotel, my cell phone dings. Incoming text message. I take a quick look. It's from Gabe; it's early evening there. I'll answer him after we get to our room.

Another ding. Another text message from Gabe. I stop and send him a quick text back: "Will answer soon."

Another ding. A response from Gabe. "K"

We get to our room. We all spread out in various attempts to be comfortable.

Mike raises a question. "Do I remember correctly? Did Marco say something about this being our last night here?"

"You remember correctly. I'm not sure how they got the idea, but they think we're leaving tomorrow. I didn't think it was necessary to tell them otherwise. We'll just have to not walk past the All'Angelo tomorrow."

"What did Gabe have to say?"

My phone kept dinging away as we walked home. "Let me look."

I pull up the first message. I read it aloud. "Christie's wants to know when we can bring the Red Diamonds to New York City."

The next message continues. "Sotheby's wants to know if they can send someone to Cleveland."

The next one is troubling. "Both auction houses are taking this very seriously. Their interest surprises me."

Another text continues the thought. "I told them about great-great-grandfather Metodyj. I think that they might have done some research and decided that we might be for real."

And his last text sums it up. "NOW WHAT???"

I look around the room. What I see is three more "Now what?" faces. "Well. I think the answer to 'Now what?' is that we stay the course. Tomorrow, we play tourist as planned. Monday, we fly home. Tuesday, we are rich. Very rich. Filthy rich."

Lauri scowls. "Or in jail."

"Yeah, that is a possibility. But we've come this far. We can not back up. I think it's too late to do anything except finish the quest, whatever the outcome."

I get three nods. Not very enthusiastic nods, but we all agree. We have to finish this.

* * *

We move out onto the terrace. It is late. We are full. We are tired.

It's a cool but pleasant night. The city is quiet now. All the tourists have gone back to their hotels or to their ships. The Veneziani who are still out, walk quietly. Most are going home after a long day of catering to the whims of the tourists. The sky is clear. Venezia is not brightly lit. We can see lots of stars.

After a while I break the silence. "There are two things we need to talk about tomorrow. I want to give you some time to think about them. We don't need to decide tonight, or even tomorrow, but we will have to decide soon."

Kate sits up. "One of them has to be 'What's our cover story?'"

"Exactly. Assuming we smuggle the Red Diamonds into the States successfully, at some point we'll have to explain where they came from. When we auction them off, no matter how discrete Christie's and/or Sotheby's are, the IRS will probably get involved.

And somebody will leak something to the press. It's too big a deal to keep secret."

Though his eyes are almost closed, Mike has been listening intently. "I think the only plausible story is that you found the Red Diamonds in Uncle John's safe."

We're thinking along similar lines. "Go on."

"You had Uncle John's safe drilled; that's verifiable. You have the packet of hundred-year-old letters and maps; that's a fact. You might even get Rudy from Rudy's Righteous Restaurant – love that name – to attest to the fact that you sat in his place reading old documents. And you have the Red Diamonds; millions of dollars' worth of red diamonds."

"Go on."

"You found the packet of documents in his safe, and you found the Red Diamonds there as well. You have no idea how they got there."

"I like it. I showed you the Red Diamonds, and we decided that since everyone here in the States who might know anything about them is long dead, we should go to Italy and Ukraine to try to figure out how the Red Diamonds got from Velykyi Bereznyi, Ukraine, to Sharpsville, Pa."

"That works. It pretty much explains everything we have done since you looked in the safe and found the Red Diamonds. And we have not figured it out. Nobody in Velykyi Bereznyi knew anything. We even went to the spot where they were supposed to be buried and found nothing. Obviously somebody dug them up and brought them to the Unites States. We just don't know who or when."

"So. I found the Red Diamonds in Uncle John's safe. His will says that I should auction off all of his assets and split everything evenly between Beth, George, and me. My expectation is that his will should apply to any assets: guns, or moose heads, or diamonds."

"We might have an issue there, Dad. House full of guns and moose heads, yes. Red Diamonds, I'm not so sure."

"What do you mean?"

"It won't take too much work to figure out that the Red Diamonds were once owned by Tsar Nicholas and Tsarina Alexandra, that they were part of the Russian Empire's Crown Jewels. How does the law deal with re-discovered lost treasures? I'm remembering the reclaiming of the treasures the Nazis confiscated during the Second World War. Some of that stuff took years to resolve. They even made a movie about one incident, *Woman in Gold*."

Kate is now awake and alert. "And that's why we need Christie's or Sotheby's to sell the Red Diamonds quickly and discreetly."

And Laurie agrees with Kate. "I agree. Also, I wonder about the tax liability."

"I've been wondering about that, as well. Uncle John's will states that Beth and George and I are to split the proceeds. I have no idea whether or not the proceeds are taxable income. I figured I'd ask the CPA who does our taxes. I'll give him a small number; a few thousand dollars. See what he has to say."

Kate has another idea. "Let's ask Devin, too. I know he's a defense attorney, but he's got to have friends who deal with inheritances. They've got to have a thriving business in inheritance law in Miami."

Devin is my youngest son. Stepson actually, but I raised him from about age four; he's my son. He and his wife who is also an attorney live in Pompano Beach. "Good idea. I'll text him right now and ask him to call me tomorrow at his convenience."

Kate continues. "Now that you have woken us all up, what's the second thing?"

"How do we split up the money?"

"Uncle John's will is very clear. The money gets split three ways: you, Beth, and George."

"When he wrote that, I doubt that he was thinking of the Red Diamonds. Besides, Mike and Kate, you should get a cut, a big cut. We wouldn't have the Red Diamonds if it weren't for you."

"True…"

"And Beth has never married. She has no heirs. What happens to her share?"

"Point."

"George and his wife never had kids. They have no heirs either."

"Point, again. But they should get to decide what happens to their share. I think there will be more than enough money to go around."

Lauri interrupts. "Or there will be no money. Or we'll all be in jail."

"On that happy note, let's end this. It's after midnight. We can continue tomorrow."

Mike and Lauri get up to go next door. "I'm glad you brought up these issues, Dad. We have some hard decisions to make."

"But not tonight. Or even tomorrow. Don't lose any sleep over it."

"Goodnight, guys."

CHAPTER 83

We meet for a light breakfast at Do Leoni. We've decided to go to Murano and back to Burano today. And maybe even Torcello. While we wait for our breakfast, we make tourist chatter about the coming day.

Mike looks around to make sure nobody is listening, and then drops the bomb. "The frame around the Red Diamond broke."

"What?"

"I was packing the stuff into my money belt and it just broke. We knew it was fragile. We thinned it too much by hammering it to stretch it to fit around the diamond."

Kate looks ready to cry. "Now what?"

"I've been thinking about it all morning. It may not be a tragedy. We buy some costume jewelry with a similar frame. We buy some glue for metals, and we fabricate a new frame. We can make it fit well; it'll be better than what Breeze made for us."

"So where do we get glue for metals?"

"Paolo will know. I'll tell him I need it to repair a broken camera."

Our breakfast arrives. "Sounds like a plan, son. After breakfast, let's talk to Paolo about the glue and then head for Murano."

* * *

The glue turned out to be easy. Paolo had a tube that he gave us. He said he bought it a week ago to repair a guest's broken brooch.

Instead of catching the vaporetto at San Zaccaria, we walk along the Riva degli Schiavoni and through the Piazza San Marco to the Merceria Orologia. It's a street filled with all kinds of shops that cater to tourists. There is probably more tourist money spent here than any place in Venice. It's the perfect place for the girls to shop for costume jewelry to repair the mount for the Red Diamond. In less than an hour they've purchased four pieces that will probably work.

The shortest way back to San Zaccaria will take us past the Ristorante All'Angelo. We avoid it and some potential embarrassment by returning the way we came. By late morning, we're on the vaporetto and heading for Murano.

Murano is actually a clump of small islands. In total, it's about a mile long by half a mile wide. It's not big, but it's jammed with houses and shops and glass factories. Few tourists come here, except to visit the glass factories, and they're on tours that allow little freedom to explore. This is Venice as it's been for hundreds of years.

You could spend all day here and not see everything. But we're all preoccupied. We leave tomorrow. And we need to fix the necklace that holds the Red Diamond. It has got to be wearable when Lauri goes through customs.

We decide to have lunch here in Murano, and then head back to the hotel. We find a little trattoria. I think the name translates to "The Old Fisherman." Or maybe it is "The Old Fish Market." Anyway, it has two tables outside, so we take one of them. A waiter comes out to greet us. He might be "The Old Fisherman" himself. He brings no menus. He introduces himself as Carmine, and asks, in Italian, what we would like. I tell him that we would like lunch. He says the special is – fish. I ask him how it is prepared, and he answers – cooked. This is not going well. I ask him to wait a minute while we decide. And we decide to leave. I offer my apologies to Carmine as we get up to go. He shrugs and says, "*Buon pomeriggio.*"

As we're walking back to the vaporetto stop, we pass another trattoria. This one has four tables outside and an actual menu posted. We decide that this one looks a little better. We sit and a waiter brings us menus. His name is also Carmine, but he speaks a little

English. We order a light lunch; first prosciutto with melon, followed by paninis washed down with a carafe of good local white wine.

* * *

After lunch, it's back on the vaporetto, and back to the hotel. And to our jewelry repair job.

CHAPTER 84

We're back on our terrace with a bottle of Asti Spumanti, the costume jewelry the girls bought, and the large diamond. The costume jewelry looks like what it is: inexpensive and very flashy. Even with four coats of hair spray, the diamond looks like what it is: an amazing, almost impossible, extremely precious stone.

One of the pieces the girls bought has a really ugly blue stone that is almost exactly the same size as the Red Diamond. We make the swap. The Red Diamond nestles into its new home perfectly. I put a couple of drops of glue between the band and the diamond to make sure it stays put. "Kate, do you think another coat of hair spray will help."

"Yes I do." She goes inside to get the Redken #18 can.

Meanwhile, Mike has an idea. "Why don't we put a couple of drops of glue on the small stones, too?"

"Good idea. Do you want to do it?"

"Sure."

While he busies himself with that project, I relax in the sun. This could be our future.

* * *

The Red Diamonds are ready. We're ready. Tomorrow is the day.

We decide to have a last really nice dinner. TripAdvisor lists over twelve hundred restaurants in Venice. The choice is difficult. Ristorante Alle Corone is consistently top rated by many reviewers. Antiche Carampane near the Rialto Bridge has been famous for its seafood for a hundred years. Osteria Alle Testiere claims to have been in business since 1452. Locanda Cipriani on the island of Torcello is supposed to be well worth the half hour boat ride.

Finally, we decide. The Londra Palace's own Do Leoni. We've eaten outside on the patio many times, and inside in the casual breakfast area, but never in the formal dining rooms. We've peeked in to them; they have several. They look as elegant as any dining rooms we've seen: original renaissance oil paintings, very old oriental rugs, obviously fine crystal and cutlery, soft music in the background, and formally clad waiters. Tonight we'll dine in style.

I've made our reservation for a fashionable seven pm. The Venetians eat a little earlier than most Europeans. I'm not sure why, but we've noticed it. We've decided to "dress for dinner." Mike and I are wearing coats and ties and the girls both have stunning long dresses. The maître d' escorts us past a serving table with a huge bone-in ham mounted on a sort of rotisserie – *prosciutto crudo* – to our corner table. The dining rooms can accommodate perhaps sixty people but there are fewer than fifteen other diners. I notice that we are dressed quite appropriately. I comment to Mike, "Glad I didn't wear jeans."

In a few minutes, our waiter comes to our table. He introduces himself as Bernardo and leaves the wine lists and menus. I ask him to bring a bottle of *acqua minerale con gas* while we are deciding. He nods and quietly disappears. In a moment he is back with a large bottle of San Pellegrino. He shows me the label; I nod; he pours four glasses, and disappears again. He'll watch from his corner of the room, and return when he thinks we have made a decision.

Walking past the big chunk of *prosciutto crudo* helps us decide on our first course: we all want *Prosciutto con Melone.* The second course is more problematic: Mike wants the *Frutta del Mare*; Lauri wants a veal dish but doesn't know which one of the several that are on the menu. Kate and I have no idea what we want.

As if by magic, Bernardo reappears. I tell him that we all want *Prosciutto con Melone* for our first course. And I ask him to bring an appropriate house wine.

We each tell him our thoughts on our main courses. Mike is easy; Bernardo says that Do Leoni is known for its *Frutta del Mare*. Lauri almost as easy; Bernado recommends their special for today; I don't catch its name. Kate says she is thinking maybe chicken; Bernado chooses a dish for her. I tell him that I'd like beef, perhaps a filet; he recommends the *Filetto di Manzo*. Interestingly, that's something I often order at Brio in the States. Again, I ask him to bring appropriate house wines.

He collects the menus and wine lists, and we settle in for a couple of hours of good food and relaxation. We need it. Tomorrow will be the most stressful day of our lives. We have a direct, late morning flight from Venice directly to JFK in New York. What happens at customs in New York will determine our future. And it will affect the future of everyone in our family.

CHAPTER 85

Today is the day. I gave Luciano's business card to Paolo yesterday and asked him to call and arrange a ten o'clock pickup for our trip to Venice's Marco Polo Airport.

At seven thirty, we call down for porters to take our luggage to the front desk. We'll follow our luggage down and have a light breakfast before we check out. We're all too jittery for a big meal.

Two porters arrive for our stuff. Mike and I hang on to our newly purchased valises. Mine is filled with odds and ends we'll need for the trip. Mike's has the costume jewelry with the Red Diamonds.

The plan is simple in concept, but may be difficult in practice. Mike will be the custodian of the Red Diamonds. He will guard them with his life. I can't think of anyone I would trust more.

He will give the jewelry to Lauri to wear each time we go through a customs checkpoint. Sounds simple enough.

* * *

Just as we are finishing the checkout process, Luciano comes bouncing up the stairs and into the lobby with a two-wheel cart. Well, the cart is bouncing, not Luciano.

"*Ciao, I miei amici!*

"*Buongiorno, Luciano.*"

"I am happy to see you again, but I am sad to see you leave."

"We are sad to be leaving."

Luciano needs a little help from a hotel porter to get us and our luggage to his boat. He is parked at the San Zaccaria vaporetto station. When all of our luggage is loaded, I tip the porter and board the water taxi for our last ride. I ask Luciano if we can take one last ride along the Canale Grande.

"*Certo.*"

We have to go slower along the Grand Canal, but it gives us a chance to say goodbye to Venice. A little before we reach the train station, Luciano takes a narrow canal through Cannaregio, the original ghetto. In ten minutes, we come out of the canal and into the open lagoon. From here, it's a straight shot to the airport docks, and we're there in less time than it took us to traverse the Grand Canal.

We're amazed to discover that there are no porters waiting to take our bags. And our euros. They must all be up at the airport waiting for a new influx of tourists. We get all of our luggage off of the water taxi. Kate looks up the grade toward the airport.

Luciano offers to help us make the two hundred meter trip up to the airport, but we decline. "It is not that far. We can manage. It looks like you will be first in line to pick up newly arriving tourists."

"Si. Si. Signore Peter. I will be."

I pay him for the trip and add a nice tip. After lots of handshakes and hugs all around, we part company. We head up the grade toward the airport as Luciano moves his boat to the departure area. The path makes a bend, and we say goodbye to Luciano with a final wave.

We get to the top of the grade and the terminal entrance. There are about eight porters milling around and chatting amongst themselves. There must be a big crowd of tourists due to arrive. We go into the small terminal, and immediately spot the Alitalia counter. Alitalia has a direct flight from Venice to JFK in New York City. I have all of our passports and tickets. I set them on the counter and put the first suitcase on the scale. An agent comes over to check us in. She sees the American Passports.

"Good morning. I hope you had a pleasant stay in Venice."

"Yes, we did. Venezia is one of my favorite cities in the whole world."

She has taken our tickets and is typing as we talk. "Then you must come back again soon. Your flight to New York City is on time. It appears that your flight from New York City to Cleveland is on time as well."

"Very good. Thank you for the information."

"And how many checked bags do you have?"

"The four of us have four bags to check." For each of us, the first checked bag is free; the second one would cost $100. We decided that the bags we bought in Venice for our trips to Paris and Ukraine were not worth the $100 it would cost to take them home, so we left them with Paolo to dispose of.

"Perfect." My fellow smugglers each put their checked bags on the scale. The agent put destination tags on each bag. "May I see your carry on pieces, please?"

We hold them up. "Again, perfect. You are all checked in. You may proceed through customs to the departure waiting area."

She hands me back our tickets and passports. "Thank you. And the restrooms?"

She points to the far end of the line of counters. "There. There are more in the departure waiting area."

"*Grazie. Arrivederci.*"

CHAPTER 86

I don't think Mike has let go of his valise since he left their hotel room. He motions for all of us to come closer. "Let's head for the restrooms." Then *sotto voce*: "Time for a jewelry change."

Actually, Lauri is not wearing any jewelry. Only her wristwatch. She's ready to put on the Red Diamonds for her trip through Italian Security. As we walk to the restrooms, we pass right by Airport Security. It looks the same as any American TSA facility. There are three roller conveyors on which to place carry-on luggage. In the middle of each conveyor is a box-like x-ray machine with a conveyor belt through it, and a monitor on top of it. Standing at each monitor is a Security Guard. Between the conveyors are three walk through metal detectors. Each is manned by another Security Guard. Italy has not modernized to full body scanners yet. It looks like there will be no surprises.

When we get to the restrooms, Mike and Lauri huddle for a minute; Mike drops the Red Diamonds into Lauri's purse. Lauri and Kate head for the lady's room. "Meet you right here."

We go into the men's room, and come back out before the girls. I look around for a drinking fountain, and then remember that we're in Italy. We won't see a drinking fountain until New York.

Kate comes out first, then Lauri. Lauri glows. Literally. The Red Diamonds are way too noticeable. Maybe it's just me. Maybe no one else will see what I see. I'm afraid to ask.

"Are we ready ladies?" They nod and we head for security.

We put our carry-ons onto a roller conveyer, and empty our pockets into plastic containers. Lauri and Kate have a lot more stuff to put into their containers than Mike and I. Their purses take up half of the container. Phones, watches, books, jackets, fill up the other half. There is barely room for Lauri's jewelry. She crams everything in, though; that's probably good; it makes the Red Diamonds less visible.

Lauri goes through the metal detector first. No alarm. She stands at the exit of the x-ray machine waiting for her stuff. Her carry-on comes out and she grabs it. Then the Security Guard stops the conveyor with Lauri's plastic container still inside. He looks at Lauri, then at the monitor -- for at least a minute -- then shrugs and turns the belt back on. Lauri grabs her container as soon as it comes out and walks quickly to a nearby row of chairs to wait for us. We all try very hard not to breathe a huge sigh of relief. Kate, Mike, and I go through the process without incident. We join Lauri, and sit to get our belongings organized.

Lauri looks pale. Mike sits beside her and gives her a hug. "Step one done."

From here, we go to Passport Control. There are two doorways, with another Security Guard standing between them at a small high table. There are signs above each doorway. The one on the left says European Union Residents in about five languages; the one on the right says Non-European Union Residents in even more languages. The Security Guard is checking identity documents and directing passengers through the appropriate door.

We are directed through the door on the right. When we go through the door, we see three small booths, each with a window on the side toward us. There is a short line at each window. Lauri and Mike get into one line, Kate and I into another. At each window is another Security Guard sitting at a computer. In our line, I go first, then Kate. In their adjoining line, Mike lets Lauri go before him. As each of us gets to the window, we hand our passports to the official in the booth. He compares the passport photo to the person, scans the passport RFID chip, looks at his monitor, nods, and stamps the passport. And that's it. The official says nothing to any of us. We leave the booths and see another door with USCITA. EXIT, SORTIE, AUSGANG, SALIDA painted on it. We go through the door – and we're in the departure lounge.

We expected Italian Customs to be easy, but not that easy. Apparently, they figure that if you're leaving with lots of stuff, that means you left lots of Euros in Italy.

Marco Polo Airport is not very large. We have no trouble finding the departure gate for Alitalia flight 7616.

We're right on schedule. Our flight should board in about thirty minutes. Mike and I sit down on a row of chairs facing the windows and our Boeing 767. Lauri and Kate head for the restroom. They're back out very quickly, but now Lauri has on a green pendant and matching bracelet. She sits next to Mike and puts her rather large purse between them. He casually looks around, then reaches into Lauri's purse, pulls out a zip lock bag, and quickly drops it into his valise.

"Dad, I'm going to hit the restroom before we board. Want to join me?"

"Good idea." I leave my valise with Kate. Mike takes his.

There is nobody else in the restroom. "I want to pack the jewelry a little more securely." He goes into one of the stalls. I pee, then wash and dry my hands. I move slowly so that if anybody comes in, it doesn't look like I'm loitering. Mike comes out of the stall, and hands me his valise.

"Done."

"I'll wait outside."

In about three minutes, Mike comes out, I hand him his valise, and we walk back to where the girls are seated.

We sit in silence. In about ten minutes, the agent announces that we are going to board. As usual, she starts with first class, then business class, and then us peasants: tourist class. We have seats 19A and B, and 20A and B. The girls stash their carry-ons overhead. I do the same. Mike keeps his. The girls take the window seats. Mike and I take the aisle seats.

A flight attendant comes by. She spots Mike's valise. "*Signore, deve mettere la vostra valigia in scomparto superiore.*"

Before I can attempt to translate, Mike smiles at her. "I want to keep it with me."

She switches to somewhat accented English. "Then it must go beneath the seat in front of you."

"Okay." He slides it in between his feet and sits up. Almost immediately, another attendant uses the PA system to announce our imminent departure in four languages.

And we're on our way home.

CHAPTER 87

The big Boeing taxis out toward the runway. As we approach the runway, the pilot comes on the PA system, introduces himself as Captain Fabio Giordano, thanks us for flying with Alitalia, and tells the cabin crew to prepare for immediate takeoff. There is no wait. Captain Giordano turns us onto the runway and pushes the throttles forward. The aircraft is full, but we accelerate rapidly. The nose comes up. In about ten seconds, the wheels are off the ground and we're climbing steeply. We hear the clunk of the landing gear doors closing, and we start accelerating even more quickly.

We're banking and turning to the right. I look across the aircraft to the window on the far side. I can see the flat farm land of the Po valley. The pilot levels off and heads northwest. Now I can see the Alps out of Kate's window. We're on our way.

We left at one thirty, Venice time and we're scheduled to arrive at about four thirty, New York time. But the flight is ten hours long. The first couple of hours pass quietly and uneventfully. Kate reads a Debbie Macomber novel on her iPad. I turn on my Nook, and start to read the latest Stephen King novel. I may be old fashioned, but I still prefer my books in paper form. When I'm traveling though, a Nook is a lot easier to carry than paper.

After a while, Kate sets her iPad in her lap, and naps with her head on my shoulder. I close my Nook and start to think about the next step in our journey. This step is the big one. This one determines our future. This one happens when we land in New York.

The number of the government agencies involved in "protecting" our borders is amazing: U.S. Transportation Security Administration; U.S. Customs and Border Protection; U.S. Immigration and Customs Enforcement; U.S. Border Patrol; U. S. Customs Service; U.S. Citizenship and Immigration Services; Drug Enforcement Agency; Bureau of Alcohol, Tobacco, Firearms and Explosives, and on and on.

The U.S. Department of Homeland Security employs over two hundred forty thousand people; it's Organizational Chart has over twenty-five boxes. And yet there are millions of illegal aliens living and working in America. Not reassuring, to say the least.

But we get to face them in New York. Mike recommended re-entering the United States through JFK Airport in New York City. It is the busiest entry point in the U.S. It is understaffed. Its staff is known for their surliness and impatience. It is here that we stand the smallest chance of being thoroughly questioned and searched.

We are, after all, smuggling unimaginable millions of dollars' worth of diamonds into the United States. Diamonds entrusted to my great-grandfather Metodyj by Tsar Nicholas. Diamonds once held by Tsarina Alexandria. Diamonds that were once part of Russia's Crown Jewels. Diamonds we took from Ukraine.

* * *

As we leave Europe and head out over the ocean, the weather deteriorates rapidly. Captain Giordano turns on the Fasten Seatbelts signs when it starts to get bumpy. He comes on the PA system and apologizes for the rough ride. He explains in Italian and in English that there are major storms over most of the North Atlantic. The Captain tells us that he is going to attempt to climb above the storms; he does not sound like he believes that he is going to be able to do so.

We spend most of the rest of the flight bouncing and jostling, flying through rain and lightning, and listening to crying babies and sick adults. All in all, it is not a good experience, but at least it takes my mind off of what is coming in New York.

The Alitalia flight crew makes the best of an unpleasant situation. Though it works better if you take it before getting air sick, they offer Dramamine to those who are sick. And they offer everybody free snacks and soft drinks. It is kind of hard to put into words, but the whole flight crew just acts like – they care.

* * *

After what seems like forever, we touch down at JFK. And the passengers start applauding. I'm not sure if they applauding the flight crew or the fact that we have landed safely. Maybe a little of both. Kate and Lauri, and Mike and I join in the applause.

People start gathering up their belongings as we taxi to our gate. The pilot stops, shuts down the engines, and turns on the cabin lights. We have arrived. Mike and I join about three hundred other passengers trying to stand in the aisles and get our bags out of the overhead. Mike is a little bigger than the average passenger, and a little more forceful. He runs interference for me. I notice that his valise is setting on his seat, and that Lauri has her hand on it.

We get our other bags down, and wait for people to start to move. We're fairly near the door so it doesn't take long. We walk up the jet way and emerge into the terminal – and chaos!

Terminal 4, the new International Arrivals Building was built in 2001. It was designed to handle seven million international passengers a year; last year it handled nearly twice that number. The corridors are packed with people; people who have arrived from all over the world; people who are tired; people who are a little lost; people who are trying to figure out where they should go next; people who are trying to figure out what they should do next. We're more fortunate than most; we can read the signs; we can ask questions; we can understand the answers.

We follow the crowd; everyone is going to the same place: Passport Control. This is step one in the entry process. As we approach the Passport Control room, we encounter our first line. We take our place at the end of the line. This line is moving fairly quickly -- at about a baby's crawling speed. But at least, it's moving.

In a few minutes, we pass through the door and into the room itself. It looks kind of like a grocery store checkout area. There are about ten checkout lines in operation. Each has a waist high counter; but no conveyor belt. In the middle of each counter, and across from the public is a Customs Officer. Rather than standing at a cash register, he is standing at a computer terminal. There is a sign at the beginning of each counter – WAIT HERE UNTIL CALLED – ESPERAR AQUI HASTA QUE FUE LLAMADO. Typical of the United States these days: signs in English and Spanish.

At the head of the line, there is another Customs Officer directing people into what he thinks is the shortest line. Mike is first; he is holding his maroon Official U. S. Passport so that the officer can't miss seeing it. When Mike gets to the head of the line, the officer looks at the passport, then at him. "Are you traveling alone sir?"

"No. We are a group of four."

"All with Official Passports?"

"No. the others are my family. They all have regular blue passports."

"You can all go to Line 1."

Mike nods. "Thank you."

Line 1 is the furthest away, but the shortest line, by far. We're happy to walk the short distance.

By the time we get there, there is no line. Mike walks directly across from the Customs Officer. He hands over his passport and customs declaration form. The officer scans his passport's RFID chip, and waits while looking at his computer screen. It's turned away from us so that we can't see what he is seeing. In a minute he stamps Mike's passport and his form, hands then back, and looks at Lauri. "Next."

We all go through the same process. The only thing the officer says to any of us is "Next."

When all four of us are finished, we follow the crowd out of the room and down a featureless hallway.

CHAPTER 88

We come to a pair of down escalators with a staircase in between. Some ambitious souls are using the stairs. We opt for an escalator. At the bottom is the baggage claim area. I check the digital display that shows flight numbers and baggage carousel numbers. Our flight is not listed.

Mike spots a uniformed worker with a clipboard. The girls guard the carry-ons and we chase the clipboard lady. We catch up with her just before she disappears through an unmarked door. Mike flashes his badge and explains that our flight is not listed on the displays.

She nods. "How long ago did you land?"

"We just walked here from Gate 10 and through Passport Control. Maybe a half hour?"

"Right now, the baggage handlers are running about an hour behind. You might as well find a place to camp and relax for a while."

Mike flashes her a big smile. "Thanks, dear."

Mike finds a bench; I lay claim to it while Mike goes after the girls and our carry-ons. It only takes a couple of minutes for them to join me on the bench.

Mike has explained to Kate and Lauri that we've got a half hour wait. We try small talk; that doesn't work. We try guessing what will happen when we get to customs; that doesn't work. We try planning our next steps after customs; that doesn't work. We sit and stare off into space, each lost in our own thoughts; that doesn't work either.

Kate and I announce that we're going for a walk. We walk to the end of the baggage claim area. There is a set of double doors. The sign above the doors says United States Immigration and Customs Enforcement. There is a small but steady stream of passengers dragging their belongings through the doors. Some are obviously Americans returning from business or vacation trips. Others are just as obviously foreigners trying to figure out how to enter America.

We stand there for a minute watching the stream of people pass by. Just then the monitor mounted on the ceiling nearby updates. Our flight's luggage will be arriving at Baggage Carousel Five. We head for the bench where we left Lauri and Mike.

When we get to the bench, Mike is standing and holding on to a four wheeled luggage cart similar to what hotels use. I've seen a few being pushed around by uniformed baggage agents and porters, but none piloted by civilians. Then again, Mike isn't exactly a civilian.

We head for Baggage Carousel Five. I am surprised to see that Lauri is wearing the Red Diamonds. "Nice pendant, Lauri."

I'm not sure why she feels the need to explain – especially to me. "I decided that I like this one better than the green one I had on before. I got lots of great costume jewelry in Venice and Paris…"

We get to Baggage Carousel Five about the same time as two hundred fifty other passengers. It's a mad house. Everyone is tired. Everyone is in a hurry. Two hundred fifty passengers try to position themselves next to the moving belt, and in a position where they can see the suitcases entering the baggage area from the little tunnel. It doesn't work. There is lots of bumping and jostling.

Mike parks the luggage cart about teen feet from the belt. "Lauri, you and Kate guard the cart and carry-ons. Dad, you get ready to grab suitcases as I pull them off the belt."

He positions himself at the first curve in the belt; he has an excellent view of what's coming down the line. A twenty-something male squeezes in front of him. Mike taps him on the shoulder. "Sir, please don't stand in front of me."

The somewhat scruffy guy looks over his shoulder. "I'll stand where I want."

Mike can be imposing; very imposing. His face darkens, and he seems to grow a few inches. He taps the guy a little harder. The guy looks over his shoulder again. Mike puts on his best First Sergeant voice. "I said please *do not* get in front of me."

The guy spins around, opens his mouth to attack Mike verbally, then looks up at Mike and closes his mouth again. He moves from between Mike and the belt. Several other people move away just a little bit and watch.

Finally, scruffy guy sulks away and gets in front of an elderly woman about twenty feet down the belt.

Mike shakes his head and smiles at me.

After what seems like two hundred suitcases, Mike spots my green one coming down the belt. He grabs it and swings it over to me. I put it on the cart and go back, just in time to take Kate's pink suitcase. Next comes Lauri's bright print Vera Bradley suitcase. And finally, Mike's olive drab one.

We gently push through the clump of people around the carousel, and join the crowd heading for customs.

* * *

I go through the double doors first, and hold them open for the girls, and then for Mike. He's pushing the cart and still holding his passport in plain view. We immediately encounter another Customs Officer – the gatekeeper. He stops the four of us. He points to Lauri then Mike. "You two that way." He points down a hall to his right. He nods to me and Kate. "You two this way." He uses his left thumb to point over his shoulder to the customs inspection room behind him.

Mike holds up his maroon Official U.S. Passport. "But we're traveling together, sir."

"Then you can meet on the other side." And he repeats his directions.

Mike looks at him for a full fifteen seconds. The Customs Officer looks back. People start to stack up behind us.

Then Mike breaks the impasse and turns to me. "You guys take the cart. We'll meet you in a few minutes."

He and Lauri get their suitcases off of the cart, pull out the handles, and put their carry-ons on top. They waive and head down the hallway to the gatekeeper's right.

I look at Customs Officer. "May I ask why they are going that way?"

"Different Customs Hall."

It is obvious that he is not going to say anything else. Kate and I go around him and move into the large room. The process is pretty clear. We wait until we see an empty spot on the line of low tables in front of us. We almost run to get there before anybody else. We put our suitcases and carry-ons on the table, and open them. We stand behind our stuff and hold our passports and customs declarations forms in front of us.

In a few minutes, a middle-aged Customs Officer with bright red hair comes over to us. She takes our customs forms and smiles. "Welcome home. Vacation?"

Kate answers. "Yes. Two really great weeks."

"Where were you?"

"I was in Venice and Paris. My husband was in Venice and Ukraine."

She looks at me. "Ukraine?"

"'My son and I spent a week in western Ukraine looking for my family's roots."

"You're traveling with your son?"

Kate answers. "And with his wife. She went to Paris with me while the guys were in Ukraine."

"And where are they now?"

Kate points toward the entrance to the room. "The gatekeeper made them go to the other room.

"Figures."

She flips the lids of our suitcases closed. "You're done."

"Huh?"

"You're done. Get out of here. Go find your son and daughter-in-law."

We thank her. We thank her several times, as we close up our suitcases and put them back on the cart. She smiles and walks away, looking for her next customers.

CHAPTER 89

As before, like sheep, we follow the crowd to the exit door. On the other side is another hallway; people are visibly happier as they move down this hallway. Their encounter with customs is over. Welcome home. Welcome to America. Another hallway comes in from the left and merges with our hallway. A small stream of people is coming down this hallway and merging with our people. This must come from where Mike and Lauri went. We step off to the side and wait. And wait.

And wait. Kate can't stand waiting any more. "I'm going to walk down the hall a little way; they might be down there waiting for us."

"Okay."

And wait. I periodically look one way for Mike and Lauri; then the other way for Kate. A Customs Officer comes up the hallway that Kate went down. "Are you waiting for someone?"

"My son and his wife went to the other customs hall."

"You can't wait here. Wait at the end of this hall." He points the way Kate went.

I start to push the cart. "Dad!"

Lauri looks a little rattled, but they are smiling. "Hi guys."

Lauri hugs me. While she's hugging me, she almost whispers. "Our search was *very* thorough."

"Let's go catch up with Kate."

Mike puts their luggage on the cart and takes over driving. The officer moves on. I stand beside Mike for a minute. "Few things shake me, Dad. *That* did."

"Let's go find Kate. And a place to sit and have coffee. And talk."

* * *

The hallway opens to a fairly large common area. Kate is standing at the hallway's exit, kind of swaying from foot to foot. She spots us, then the Red Diamonds on Lauri. She breaks into a huge smile. "What took you so long?"

"We got searched. Let's find a place to sit, and maybe have some coffee."

"There's a Starbuck's this way"

"Welcome to America!"

CHAPTER 90

We find a table. Mike parks the luggage cart next to it. Lauri and Kate head for the counter; they know what we want. Mike and I sit silently for a while. I break the silence. "Are we okay?"

Mike almost shudders. "Yes."

They are back in a few minutes with four coffees and a small assortment of pastries – scones and coffee cake.

After they get settled, I start. "I will go first; we were a lot quicker; we obviously have less to tell."

Kate interrupts. "But your story is much more important. Tell us."

Mike takes over, talking softly. We all lean in toward him. "I've been here before. The back room is smaller; it's for more thorough searches. It's the gatekeepers job to decide who looks 'worthy' of a more thorough search."

"So what did they do?"

"Two officers worked on us together. They took everything out of our suitcases and carry-ons. They searched for stuff hidden in the linings."

"They even went through our toiletries, and my little cloth bag of jewelry."

"They disassembled all of the matryoshkas."

"They compared our pile of souvenirs to what we listed on the declaration forms."

"One guard asked me about the hunting knives. I told him that I got them in the Ukraine; that they were for me and my two brothers. He just nodded."

"The scariest part was when one guard said, 'Nice pendant, may I see it?' I about peed my pants. I asked him if he wanted me to take it off."

"He said, 'Not if you'll allow me to handle it.' I didn't know what Mike was going to do."

Mike shakes his head. "*I* didn't know what I was going to do... I didn't know if he was trying to antagonize us or what."

Lauri continues. "I nodded. He held the stone in the palm of his hand and looked at it closely. He turned it over, and looked at it some more. 'Did you get this in Europe?'"

I told him I got it in Paris. That I liked it and it was cheap. But that I didn't like the point on the back; that it was uncomfortable. "He said, 'Cheap and quality rarely go together.' And he let it go. It hit my breastbone fairly hard. It was creepy."

"I think his partner thought so, too. He looked at his coworker, then said, "Okay, you can repack your suitcases and go. We're done. Come on, Steve."

"Wow!"

Kate gets up, walks around the table and hugs Laurie. "I agree with my husband. Wow!"

She sits back down. She looks at me, then Mike. "So this is it? We are through customs? We are now in the United States? With a gazillion dollars' worth of Russian Crown Jewels?"

Mike and I say it almost in unison. "Yes."

Lauri looks like she is going to jump up and do a dance. "I don't think that really sunk in until just now. The Red Diamonds are ours. We *did* it! Oh, shite!"

She leans over and hugs Mike. He kisses her. Very soundly.

None of us has touched the pastries. I make a suggestion. "Let's bag these pastries for later and go have a celebratory lunch. We have over two hours before our Cleveland flight."

* * *

Our flight to Cleveland will leave from Terminal 2. Terminal 2 is adjacent to Terminal 4; it's an easy walk, but we'll have to go outside, drag our luggage up a little grade, and go into Terminal 2. We'll have to re-check our suitcases, and go through TSA Security again.

Lauri opts to keep wearing the Red Diamonds until she's through security. Mike says the restaurants are better here in Terminal 4. He recommends the Stadium Club upstairs. We head for an elevator.

At the Stadium Club, Mike checks the hostess's nametag. He flips his wallet open to show her his badge. "Keesha, is there somewhere that we can stash our luggage cart while we have lunch?"

She points to an alcove. "Right over there, sir. I'll keep an eye on it."

She checks out Lauri's Red Diamonds. "I love your pendant and bracelet."

"Thank you."

"Where did you find them?"

"Paris."

"Oh. Well. That's further than I can go on my lunch break."

They laugh a little as Keesha walks us to our table. "Enjoy."

"Thank you, Keesha."

Our first American food in two weeks. It's airport food, but it's American. Mike and I opt for burgers, mine a "Black and Blue Burger," his a "Mushroom and Swiss Burger." The girls order steak salads.

As soon as our waitress leaves, I start the conversation. "Why do you think the 'gatekeeper' sent you to the more thorough search room?"

"It's entirely at his discretion. Could have been completely random. Could have been that he was pissed that we had a luggage cart. Maybe he doesn't like people with Official Passports. I seriously doubt it, but he might have been suspicious. I just don't know."

"Has that happened to you before?"

"Once in a while. Especially here at JFK. They're real hard asses."

"Our experience was just the opposite."

Kate takes over. "We chatted with a female Customs Officer for a few minutes. She never even looked into our suitcases."

"When Kate told her that the gatekeeper split us up, she said, "Figures." She flipped our suitcase lids down and told us we were done; to go find you guys."

"Cool."

Lauri's turn. "I'm so glad that's over. As somebody once said, I'm getting too old for this. One more TSA check and we're done!"

"And homeward bound!"

Just then, our lunch arrives.

CHAPTER 91

The last leg of our adventure is anticlimactic.

After lunch, we make the trek from Terminal 4 to Terminal 2,

We check our luggage at the Delta counter. I booked our flights through Travelocity. All of the trans-Atlantic flights were European flag carriers, but the domestic flights were a mishmash of other carriers; the JFK to Cleveland flight is Delta.

After we get our boarding passes, we head for Security. It's busy, but not horribly so. The TSA people here are even more surly than the customs people. They herd us through the full body scanners as our carry-ons go through the x-ray machines. They don't look at anything closely. It makes me wonder how secure our security really is.

Almost before we know what has happened, we're standing on the other side of the TSA area, carry-ons and shoes still in hand.

There are no benches. We lean on each other and put our shoes back on.

Lauri looks frazzled. "I need to go to the restroom. Kate?"

"Good idea. Mike, do you know where they are?"

"Straight ahead fifty feet, and on your left."

"Go ahead, girls. Give us your carry-ons. We will catch up and wait for you there."

They do and we do.

When we get to the restrooms, I look at Mike. "I might as well go, too."

"Go ahead. I'll wait 'til you're done."

* * *

When we're all rest roomed, we walk the two hundred yards to Gate C68. I notice that Lauri is not wearing the Red Diamonds. I assume that Mike has them in his carry-on valise.

We get to the gate just as they are starting to board First Class. In not very long, we are seated in our usual seats: windows for the girls and aisles for us boys. We buckle in for the two-hour flight. Mike has his valise under the seat in front of him; that tells me all I need to know about the location of the Red Diamonds.

* * *

Two hours later, we're over Lake Erie and approaching Cleveland Hopkins from the northeast. We land on runway 24L and taxi to Gate B1. Home!

We deplane and go downstairs to baggage claim. As we were taxiing to the gate, the flight attendant announced that our luggage would be on Carousel C. The airport is not busy at this time of day. Almost as soon as we get to the carousel, the bell rings and the belt starts moving. It doesn't take us very long to gather up our luggage. Right out the door is the shuttle to the Car Rental Facility. A few years ago, Cleveland Hopkins moved all rental car agencies to an off-site facility. The free shuttle takes about twenty minutes. In another twenty minutes, we are on Interstate 480 heading west to the Lakehouse.

Mike is driving. I decide to call Gabe.

"Hi, guy. We made it!"

"Any trouble?"

"We will be talking about the trip home for the rest of our lives."

"That bad?"

"Some scary times. Some really scary times. But we made it. We have lots of souvenirs."

"We'll be there tomorrow afternoon."

"We?"

"Karen is coming with me. I hope that's okay."

"Of course it is okay. Are you bringing the girls, too?"

"No. We're just coming for an overnighter. They're staying with friends."

"Too bad. I would love to see them. Email me your flight info and we'll pick you up at the airport."

"Dad, there is one other thing. I know you have some high end stuff from Uncle John's estate that you might want to appraise and/or auction."

"Yeah?"

"Can you take some pictures and email them to asmcbride@christies.com?"

"When?"

"She'll be expecting them tomorrow morning."

"I'll try. See you tomorrow afternoon, Gabe."

"Okay, Dad. Bye."

"Bye."

As we drive home I fill everybody in on the details of the conversation.

Mike looks skeptical. "Is it safe to email photos of the Red Diamonds?

"I don't know what is safe and what is not safe anymore, Mike. I really don't."

"To tell the truth, Dad, I don't know either. And I'm in the business so to speak."

"I have a bogus email account that I set up a couple of years ago to see how easy it is to establish an email account using a fictitious name and address. I will use that; it is not traceable back to me."

"I take it that setting up a bogus account was pretty easy."

"Amazingly so."

We stop at the dog sitter's place and pick up Daisy. After two weeks, she is frantic. She howls at us; it is her way of giving us hell for leaving her. She moves from lap to lap, and licks everybody. She finally settles down and curls up in Kate's lap about the time we get to the Lakehouse.

* * *

After we get the car unpacked and get Lauri and Mike installed in the loft guest room, we settle into our favorite chairs downstairs in the family/TV room. I think it is everyone's intent to just veg for the evening. Except Mike. He plops a Zip Lock bag containing the Red Diamonds onto the coffee table, and looks at me. "If we're going to take photos, we need to take these out of the mounts and clean them up.

He is right. "I will go get my jewelry tools. Any ideas for cleaning?"

Kate offers her suggestions. "Soap and water for the hairspray. Then alcohol?"

"Sounds good. Let's move out to the big table."

In a half hour, all of the diamonds are liberated from the costume jewelry mounts, and cleaned and drying on a towel.

I go upstairs to get my digital Nikon. I set up a small halogen floodlight to illuminate the diamonds. Might as well take good pictures.

I position the large Peruzzi cut diamond on a white towel next to a six-inch rule to indicate size. I take front, side, and perspective shots. The photos are incredible. The diamond is on fire with the light it captures. It is truly amazing.

I do the same thing with one of the smaller Mazarin cut diamonds. And I take one last photo of all six of them together.

Because I took high resolution photos, the JPGs are quite large. I send two emails: one with the photos of the Peruzzi, and one with the photos of the Mazarins. The photos should get Christie's attention.

CHAPTER 92

It's nine am; everyone is up, and in various stages of grumpiness. I'm working on my second cup of coffee and trying to adjust to the time change. I am one of the grumpier ones. My cell phone rings; it's Gabe. "Hello?"

"Good morning, Dad. I didn't wake you?"

I take my coffee into the library. It's quieter than the kitchen. And the cell phone signal is stronger. I go from two bars to four. "No. I'm working on my second cup of coffee and trying to adjust to the time change."

"Good. That I didn't wake you up, I mean. We still plan to be in Cleveland at one pm."

"And you called because?"

"I just got off the phone with Christie's. Your photos impressed them. A lot. A whole lot."

"And?"

"Dad, I think they know the history of the diamonds. I think they know that the Red Diamonds once belonged to Alexandra. My contact, Smith McBride kept talking about how amazing it is that these 'very old' diamonds have come to light in America. And she kept asking for information on how we came to possess them. I told her that she would have to ask you."

"Gee. Thanks. Did you give her my contact info?"

"No, but she might get to ask you in person."

"Oh?"

"Smith stressed over and over how discrete they can be with a private sale. She was almost giddy with excitement. She wants you to take the diamonds to New York City."

"Oh really? When?"

"Tomorrow."

"*That* can't happen."

"Yes it can. If we're willing to go to New York City, they will have their Gulfstream at Cleveland's Burke Lakefront Airport at nine am tomorrow."

"Oh. Wow. When do we have to let them know?"

"Any time today."

"I will discuss it with the gang. We will decide when you get here."

"Sounds good."

"Call my cell phone when you hit the ground in Cleveland. I don't know who will be picking you up, but whoever it is will have my cell phone."

"That works, Dad. See you soon."

"Bye, son.

* * *

I gather up the gang. "Do you guys want to go out to breakfast? There's a good place a few miles west of here."

I get universal assent. "Before we leave, I need to tell you about the conversation I just had with Gabe."

That gets everyone's attention. I repeat what Gabe said to me as nearly verbatim as I can.

They all look more than a little shocked. Lauri speaks first. "Their Gulfstream. Shite."

Mike is next. "Who goes?"

"From the way Gabe talked, all of us."

We head out into the chilly morning and breakfast at the International.

* * *

After breakfast, we return to the Lakehouse. Lauri asks Kate if she can do some laundry. "Sure. I'll help."

As they start sorting two weeks' worth of dirty clothes, Mike and I get another cup of coffee and head for the library. "I love this room, Dad."

"I always wanted a library with floor to ceiling bookshelves and a rolling ladder. I finally got it."

Mike gently closes the door. "The ten-foot ceiling really makes it impressive."

"What's up?"

"It is vitally important that we all tell the same story of exactly how and where you found the Red Diamonds. And we all have to agree on the purpose of our trip to Italy and Ukraine. Any major deviation will raise questions. Questions we don't want to answer."

"I agree. To change the subject only slightly, there is one loose end that bothers me: Father Pataki."

"Actually, that is not too loose of an end. You found the maps in the safe along with the diamonds. You asked for help in translating the maps to help you understand where the Red Diamonds came from."

"You are right. That does work."

"I thought so. What you need to do is sit down and write a narrative that starts with you finding the safe at Uncle John's place, and ends with us going to Christie's."

"When?"

"I'd say today. We all need to go over it together before we go to New York City."

"I guess I can do that."

CHAPTER 93

Kate and I decide to go pick up Gabe and Karen. We know the airport, and we know the way there.

We decide to take Daisy along for the ride. Daisy is our Maltese; Daisy is eight pounds of attitude. We're curious as to how she'll react.

Daisy knows the Cleveland Hopkins terminal. When I come to pick Kate up, or Kate comes to pick me up, as soon as Daisy sees the terminal building, she goes nuts. She barks and yips and whines until she sees the missing person. Then she howls at the missing person to let them know she's mad at them. Finally, after she licks them to claim them as hers, she settles into their lap for the ride home.

We get to the airport just before one. We've heard nothing from Gabe, so I park in the cell phone lot. Almost as soon as I park, I get a text. "on the ground."

I text back. "at airport. when you have your luggage, text the door #."

"no checked bags. will text door #."

We settle in to wait. Soon I get another text. "deplaned at c5. heading for baggage area exits."

I start the Envoy, hand my cell phone to Kate, and head for Arrivals. Just as we get to Arrivals, Kate reads another text. "at door 2."

Daisy is confused. She recognizes the terminal, but none of her humans are missing. She looks worried; maybe she thinks one of us is going to leave. I spot Karen, then Gabe. So does Daisy. She goes into her routine. We laugh as I pull up to the curb. Gabe opens the back and puts their carry-ons in. Kate and I get out while Daisy barks happily. After hugs and kisses all around, Kate says, "Karen and I will sit in the back. You guys can have the front."

Once everyone is in and Daisy has said hello and picked her spot – Karen's lap -- we head for the Lakehouse.

"So what's the consensus, Dad? Are we going to New York tomorrow?"

"I think we all agree that we should go. We are hoping to get some idea of the worth of the Red Diamonds."

"From the way Smith McBride talked, they are worth a bunch. The big diamond could sell for over a hundred million dollars; it could break the record for the most ever paid at auction for a single diamond. The six matching smaller ones could bring in another hundred million. It was pretty obvious that she was seeing dollar signs; their commission will be huge."

"Why them instead of Sotheby's"

"I just got the sense that they were more interested. When I described the Red Diamonds and told them that the previous owner, Uncle John, was the son of Russian immigrants who came here during World War One, they assigned Smith to our account. She is their 'Historical Jewels' curator. As soon as she saw the pictures, she called and offered their Gulfstream."

"And Sotheby's didn't show that same interest?"

"No. Not so much. I'm not sure that they believed that we had anything worth their time and trouble."

"Then Christie's makes sense."

"Do you want to discuss this with the rest of the family?"

"Yeah, we probably should, but I suspect that we're all going for a Gulfstream ride tomorrow."

* * *

We order several Papa Joe's Pizzas for dinner. Mike brings up the subject of our cover story. "I asked Dad to put together a brief statement outlining how we got from Uncle John's death to Christie's. It's important that we all tell the same story."

Gabe has a question. "How exact do we need to be? I think we all know the general story, but not a lot of the details."

"That's okay. Criminologists expect to hear different stories from different individuals who witness the same event. In fact, when two or more people tell exactly the same story, that raises red flags. It usually means that the story is rehearsed."

"Okay. That helps. Dad, you're on."

"Well. The story line I have come up with is really pretty simple. Too simple, perhaps."

"What do you mean?"

"I don't think that *I* would believe that somebody just found a huge stash of diamonds worth millions of dollars, and then decided to go to Italy and Ukraine to try to find out their history. I *would* believe 'Peddle the diamonds first, and then try to find out where they came from.'"

"I agree, but that doesn't fit the facts."

"Tell us your story. Then maybe we can modify it."

"The story line is pretty simple:

- One – As Uncle John's executor, I had to organize his house and possessions for the upcoming auction.
- Two – I knew about his gun room, but not the safe.
- Three -- I found the safe and had it peeled.
- Four – I found the letters and maps.
- Five – I asked Father Pataki for help in translating old Ukrainian.
- Six – I started to plan a trip to Italy and Ukraine to try to retrieve the Red Diamonds.
- Seven -- Two days later, I found that the safe has a false button; the Red Diamonds were hidden underneath.

- Eight -- We went to Italy and then to Ukraine to try to find out how the Red Diamonds got to America.
- Nine – We found our ancestor's home village and some distant relatives, but no info on the Red Diamonds. We even retraced the map's directions. Nothing.
- Ten – While we were gone, Gabe contacted Sotheby's and Christie's.
- Eleven – We decide to go to Christie's."

Kate shakes her head. "I see what you mean. The order seems wrong."

I defend my story. "But that's my story and I'm stickin' to it. Wasn't that a song?"

Gabe offers his opinion. "Yes. But that's the key. 'I'm stickin' to it.' Nobody can prove that the diamonds were not in the safe. Nobody can prove that they haven't been here for a very long time. The authorities may *suspect* that we found the diamonds in Ukraine and smuggled them into the United States, but they can't prove it."

Lauri continues. "They were an un-itemized part of John's estate. You are auctioning them off so that you can divide up the proceeds according to Uncle John's will."

Gabe asks a big question. "What *does* his will say?"

"It's simple. I am to sell everything and divide the proceeds three ways: Beth, George, and me. Nobody, including John I think, really expected that there would be much to divide. Everybody was wrong. Very wrong."

"I guess."

"Beth and George have no heirs; I don't know what they'll do with their share. Obviously you guys will get my share."

Gabe asks the question we have all been studiously avoiding. "Well. Are we going to New York tomorrow?"

Several hands go up. Several heads nod yes. I hear several affirmative mumbles. "Does anybody think we should NOT go?"

There is silence. "Okay. Gabe, call Christie's. Tell Smith that we will be at Burke Lakefront at ten."

CHAPTER 94

So what do you wear to meet with the Auction House that is going to make you very, very wealthy? Mornings are still a little chilly, so I opt for a light sweater over an oxford cloth shirt and Ralph Lauren dress khakis. Karen has on a light weight Chico's pants suit. The rest of the gang dresses pretty much the same. Kate and I had to loan them a few things because of their limited supply of traveling clothes. I suspect that today, our life style changes.

It's about a forty-five-minute drive to Burke Lakefront Airport. Rather than drive two cars to the airport, I scrambled around last night and found us a limo and driver. At nine am, our doorbell rings. I answer; it is our driver. She introduces herself as Wanda; I ask her to give us a few minutes to get organized. "Will there be much luggage, sir?"

"None. This is a day trip. And call me Peter, please."

"Yes, sir. Peter."

I let Daisy out for one last potty break. Wanda fusses with her. "You said daytrip. Do you have transportation home?"

"No, we don't. But I don't know what time we'll be returning."

She hands me a business card. "The time doesn't matter. Text me when you know your arrival time back in Cleveland. I should be free, but if I'm not, I'll have dispatch send another car and driver."

"That's great, Wanda. Thank you."

"No. Thank you for the business. Just out of curiosity, where are you going?"

"New York City."

"For a day trip? That's rather unique."

"I had an uncle who died recently; four days short of his hundredth birthday. We have some family business to take care of."

"I'm sorry for your loss. You have my condolences."

As we have been talking, the rest of the gang has piled up behind me. I look over my shoulder. "Are we all ready?"

Kate answers. "Yes. Come Daisy, let's get you a treat."

The gang moves to the limo and gets in while Kate says goodbye to Daisy.

And, "We're off to see the wizard."

* * *

I've been past Burke Lakefront many times, but never flown in or out. It's a general aviation airport on the Lake Erie shore right in the middle of downtown Cleveland. It's mainly used for corporate aircraft serving Cleveland businesses. I don't know where to go.

I don't have to know; Wanda knows. She drives up to the terminal entrance, and comes around to open the limo door and let us out. We have no luggage. The girls have big purses with a few spare items of clothing. Mike has my black leather attaché case. Gabe and I have nothing.

Gabe does a lot of corporate jet travel as part of his job, so I ask him to take over. He goes up to the small counter while the rest of us take seats in upholstered arm chairs surrounding a low round table.

In a few minutes, Gabe comes over to us. He is accompanied by an attractive thirty something woman with short blond, almost white hair. "Gang, this is Smith McBride. Smith, this is the gang. I'll let them introduce themselves."

We all stand. Each of us shakes hands introduce ourselves. Kate comments on Smith's pant suit. "Thank you. Chico's."

"Mine, too."

I'm last to introduce myself. "Peter Bradovich. First of all, I didn't expect you to be here to meet us."

"I took it as an opportunity to ride in our new jet. And perhaps to be the first at Christie's to see the diamonds." Her eyes lock on mine for a minute.

I look around. There is nobody in the terminal building except a few employees behind the counter. Mike is watching me. I nod.

Mike puts the attaché case on the table and pops the latches. He takes out a pair of white cotton gloves and puts on the left one; he hands Smith the right one. He takes a small cloth pouch out of the attaché case. I don't know when or where he got the gloves and the pouch, but they're a nice touch.

Smith puts on the right glove; Mike slides the fifty caret, Peruzzi-cut blood red diamond out of the pouch into the palm of his left hand: Smith gasps. "Oh my God."

Mike holds it up to Smith. "Here. Take it."

She does. "It is real. – It is amazing. -- I didn't really believe that you had it. -- Do you know who owned this? -- Do you have any idea of what this is worth? -- Where did you get it?"

While she is talking, Mike opens another pouch and slides out one of the smaller dark pink Mazarin-cut diamonds. "There are five more just like this one."

Smith looks at the Mazarin-cut diamond. She looks a little faint. She holds the diamond out to Mike. "Please put them back in your case... This place is too public… We should have guards… Armed guards…"

Mike puts the diamonds back in their pouches and puts the pouches back in the attaché case. He closes the case and stands up. He flips open his wallet with his left hand and hold his jacket open with his right hand. Smith can see his badge and ID, and his gun. "We do. Have an armed guard, I mean."

"But I thought you were Peter's son."

"I am. I am also a U.S. Marshal. A happy coincidence."

"A happy coincidence. Oh, wow."

Smith's cell phone rings. She answers it. "McBride."

She listens for a minute, says "Okay," then hangs up. "We can board whenever we wish."

"Let's do it then." We follow Smith out a door labelled Gate 1, across the tarmac, and into a Gulfstream G150. Discretely lettered on the fuselage aft of the door and on the tail is the name CHRISTIE'S.

We all settle in to the luxurious beige leather seats. Smith stands forward near the door and introduces our Flight Attendant. "After we're airborne and at cruising altitude, Susan will be serving brunch. She has several choices for you. She'll be around to take your drink orders and to give you a menu in a bit. It's a little over an hour flying time. Enjoy the trip."

And we do.

* * *

In a little over an hour, we touch down at LaGuardia Airport. We're fed and rested and ready to go.

Smith has been on her phone almost the entire trip. I haven't heard much of her conversation, but I have caught a few phrases: "This is huge."; "Well, get him there."; "Just do it."; "We're a half hour out, so you have time."; "The offer has to come from the top."

As we taxi to the terminal, Smith stands up. "Our limo will meet us planeside. We have about a fifteen-minute ride to the office. If you want to freshen up, this might be a good time."

Lauri has a question. "Where is your office?"

"Mid-town Manhattan. Twenty Rockefeller Plaza."

CHAPTER 95

The ride from LaGuardia to Christie's is uneventful. Traffic is heavy; it's more like a half hour than fifteen minutes.

Our limo stops in front of 20 Rockefeller Plaza. It is impressive. At one time or another, everybody has seen pictures of Rockefeller Plaza. This is it. It earns an "Oh shite" from Lauri.

Our driver opens our door and we all get out and stretch. My first impression is that we are way underdressed, but a look around indicates otherwise. I see everything from Armani and haute coterie to Levis and homeless.

The entrance to Christie's is as it should be: in a word, ostentatious. Smith gives us a moment to take it all in, then takes charge. "This way please."

We go in to the lobby, and up a long flight of marble stairs. We stop at a reception desk while Smith leans over and says something to the receptionist. We go through a set of glass doors, down a short hall, and into a lavishly appointed conference room.

Smith opens a drawer in a very old sideboard along one wall. She takes out a rolled up black felt. She unrolls the two-foot square at the head of the table. "There are three people coming that I want you to meet. Please sit anywhere except in these three seats." She points to the three chairs closest to the felt.

Mike and I take the two seats closest to the reserved ones. As the others are getting seated, Smith goes over to Mike. "Mike, while we are waiting, will you please put the diamonds out on the felt?"

"Be happy to." He puts the attaché case on the table next to the felt, opens it, puts on the cotton gloves, and one by one, arranges the diamonds on the felt. He places the big diamond nearest the head of the table, and arranges the smaller ones in two rows above it. As he is doing that, Smith gets a small high intensity desk light from the sideboard and arranges it to illuminate the diamonds.

Seen under these conditions, the diamonds are absolutely awesome. Even Mike, who has lived with them for a week, stops to admire them. Lauri stands up and walks over to Smith. "Mind if I get a couple of pictures?"

"They are still your diamonds. Of course I don't mind."

Lauri takes several photos with her iPhone. Kate gets up and does the same. Gabe and Karen just stare.

The conference room door opens, and three people walk in. The first is a sixty-something, white haired gentleman in a very expensive black pinstriped three-piece suit. He sports a neatly trimmed goatee. He reminds me of Colonel Sanders of fried chicken fame. Next is a fifty something, completely bald gentleman in a dark blue lightweight wool suit. He has the look of the stereotypical attorney. Last through the door is woman wearing a simple but elegant red dress. As they stand at their reserved seats, Smith introduces them. But they are not looking at us; they are looking at the Red Diamonds. "The gentleman at the head of the table [Colonel Sanders] is the manager of Christie's American operations, Senior Vice President Bradley Poole. The gentleman to his right is our Director of Private Sales, John Swaden. Across from him is Melissa Cohanson, our Chief Jewelry Appraiser."

Smith continues. "John, next to you is the family patriarch, Peter Bradovich. Next to him is his younger son, Gabe..."

They all look away from the Red Diamonds only briefly as Smith names each of us. She gives up. "We'll do introductions later. The Red Diamonds are why we are all here."

Bradley sits down. His underlings follow suit. "I see why Amy is excited. This is a monumental find. I like the term Red Diamonds.

The Red Diamonds are truly amazing. Easily the most valuable collection that has ever been in our Auction House."

Melissa takes a pair of latex gloves and an eye loupe from her purse. "May I handle them?"

Mike answers. "Of course."

I look at Bradley Poole. "So you are interested in selling them for us? Private or public auction?"

"Yes, we are interested. Very interested. We can talk about the details later. Right now, let's talk about the Red Diamonds themselves. There is the question of provenance."

"Okay. Let's talk."

"I shall ask the obvious question. Where did you get them?"

"Before I answer that, I need some assurance that what I say will remain with those currently in this room. But before that, who is Amy?"

Smith chuckles. "Me. Smith is my middle name; my given name is Amy. In college, just as a joke, my sorority sisters started calling me 'Smitty.' And it stuck. Somewhere along the line 'Smitty' became Smith."

Poole continues. "Maybe I'm old fashioned, but I refuse to call a very attractive young woman 'Smith.'"

I smile. "I agree. 'Smith' just doesn't sound right."

"To answer your other question, John, in addition to being Director of Private Sales, is one of our attorneys. Assuming that we represent you in this sale, anything you say will be protected by attorney-client confidentiality."

"Okay. Good enough. I had an uncle who died a few weeks ago. He died four days short of his hundredth birthday."

"I'm sorry…"

"He had a good life. He was a blue collar worker and avid sportsman who also had a side business as a gunsmith. He hunted and fished all over North America. I am executer of his will. While I was organizing his belongs for auction, I discovered that he had a safe. The Red Diamonds were in the safe."

"That brings up two more questions. What are the instructions in his will? Did you know of the Red Diamonds before you opened the safe?"

"The will is simple. I am to sell everything he owned at auction and divide the proceeds equally between me and my two siblings. I honestly do not believe that he thought of the Red Diamonds at all when he wrote his will."

"I would have to agree. He was very old. But where did *he* get them?""

"I never heard any mention of the Red Diamonds by anyone in my family. I am the oldest living Bradovich in our branch of the family. Any knowledge of the Red Diamonds died with my ancestors."

I pause. Then. "Except…"

CHAPTER 96

"Except what?"

I hesitate. "This must remain absolutely confidential."

"You have my word. And the word of Christie's."

"Uncle John's safe was a floor safe. The Red Diamonds were concealed under a false bottom. I didn't find them until several days after I opened the safe. But also in the safe was a packet of very old documents. Mike, may I have the folder?"

He hands me the folder. I take out a copy of the cover letter and hand it to Bradley. This is the letter that details the story of my great grandfather, Metodyj. It is the letter that talks of Metodyj being summoned to the Hermitage, of meeting Alexandra, of the Russian Revolution, and of hiding the jewels. As Bradley finishes each page, he gives it to John. John reads each page and passes it on to Melissa.

When Melissa has finished the last page, Bradley clears his throat. "That settles the issue of provenance. The letter does not say how the Red Diamonds got to the United States?"

"That is the missing piece of the puzzle. We simply don't know. We went to Velykyi Bereznyi to try to find the answer. We found nothing."

"When your son described the Red Diamonds to us, Amy immediately thought of the Imperial Russian Crown Jewels. The Red Diamonds are described in some of the old inventories, but nobody knows what happened to them. When we saw the photos, we were virtually certain that the Red Diamonds had re-appeared. The letter makes it a certainty."

John joins the conversation. "Our concern is that if we announce that we are going to sell the Red Diamonds at auction, the Russians will demand that they be repatriated."

"Can they do that?"

"In a word, yes. The precedent was set after World War Two when many works of art and other valuable artifacts confiscated by the Nazis were returned to their rightful owners.

"What if there was no letter? What if the diamonds were just found in Uncle John's safe?"

"The Russians might not be able to prove their claim, but it is very unlikely that there are two sets of Red Diamonds: one that disappeared with the Tsarina and one that reappeared with Uncle John, the son of Russian immigrants. The Russians will go to great lengths to get them back. They can be very unpleasant."

"So we are looking at a private sale?"

"At this point, we are undecided. We must consider all of our options. As for the diamonds themselves, they are truly remarkable."

John continues. "I have been with Christie's for twenty-five years. Never have I seen anything like the Red Diamonds. They are -- breathtaking."

During this discussion, Melissa has been carefully examining the Red Diamonds. She sets down the last diamond and removes her eye loupe. "These diamonds are absolutely flawless. And I mean Grade Flawless. They are as perfect as anything I have ever seen. And the colors are phenomenal. The six Mazarin-cut stones are exact matches. It is almost as if they were cut from the same stone. And the Peruzzi – I have never seen a red diamond of any size that is as vibrantly red as this one."

Bradley nods to her. "Your initial thoughts?"

"They are African or maybe Indian. They were cut in Venice around 1680. They are almost certainly Alexandra's diamonds. They will easily bring two million dollars a caret. Probably more if we find a buyer who wants to keep them together."

Bradley looks at me. "Christie's will waive the Seller's Premium. We will reduce the Buyer's Premium to 12.5%. We will, of course store and exhibit the Red Diamonds. We will also consider conducting the sale offshore. If we do conduct the sale offshore, we will deposit your proceeds into an offshore account of your choosing. Whether you bring the proceeds into the United States or not is entirely your decision. Whether you report the proceeds to the American IRS is also your decision. Whether or not you are liable for American taxes is between you and the IRS. That said, Christie's does have several tax experts on our payroll. We will make them available to you if you wish."

"That is a lot to decide. It is something I will have to discuss with my siblings. We will reach a decision within the week."

"Excellent. When we are informed of your decision, we will discuss our next steps."

"In the meantime, will you store the Red Diamonds here? Now that you have confirmed their value, I realize that we have no safe place to store them."

"Most assuredly. Melissa will have the documents drawn up."

The Christie's contingent stands up. So does the Bradovich contingent. Now we do introductions all around. Now that Christie's knows what we have and we know what Christie's is going to do, the atmosphere is much more relaxed. We have formed several small groups and we are chatting amongst ourselves.

Smith (Amy?) claps her hands to get our attention. "Do we have any more business to conduct? No? Good. I have made reservations for a late lunch at SixtyFive. But we have over an hour to kill. May I suggest a tour of Christie's and a walk around Rockefeller Plaza?"

Kate is the one to ask. "The tour and walk sound great, but what is SixtyFive?"

"It's a restaurant on the sixty-fifth floor of the building next door. It has some of the best views of Manhattan at any price."

Kate is not wild about high places. Her comment is a very tepid "Oh."

Smith picks up on it. "Is that a problem, Kate?"

"I'm not wild about high places."

"Neither am I. We'll stay away from the windows."

She turns to Melissa. "You'll take care of the diamonds?"

"Absolutely."

* * *

The tour of Christie's is impressive. And the walk around Rockefeller Plaza is great. We Bradoviches have travelled extensively; we appreciate the opportunity to play tourist.

Eventually Smith leads us to the building next to Christie's. Thirty Rockefeller Plaza. There are a dozen elevators, but one has a sign above the door that reads simply "SixtyFive."

We take the non-stop elevator up to the sixty-fifth floor. The elevator door open. In front of us is the hostess lectern – and Manhattan. The windows behind the hostess are floor to ceiling. The view is amazing. Heights do not bother me. But for a moment, I feel a little vertigo. I look at Kate. She is transfixed. I put my arm around her. "Are you okay?"

She nods yes, but she is clearly not. "We'll get you seated with your back to the windows."

Smith is on Kate's other side. "Me too. As many times as I've been here, I still don't feel at ease."

The menu selection at SixtyFive is huge, and the prices are huge. I suspect that Christie's can afford it. After all, 12.5% of a couple hundred million dollars is a *lot* of money.

* * *

In another hour and a half, we are relaxing in the limo as it takes us back to LaGuardia. Smith is still with us. "I'm sorry that I can't accompany you back to Cleveland. I have another engagement this evening. I just can't squeeze in another three hours of flying time."

Kate answers for all of us. "We appreciate that you have been with us all day. It really helped make a very stressful day more palatable. Thank you."

I add my thanks. "From all of us, thank you. Kate said it very well."

"It was not a chore at all. I enjoyed getting to know you all. I enjoyed spending the day with you."

Mike takes care of business. "When we make our decision, who do we contact?"

"Contact me. I have been assigned as liaison throughout the project. You have my phone numbers and email address."

The limo pulls into LaGuardia's Terminal A. Smith has one more task before she leaves us. "I'll take you to the aircraft. General Aviation is a little different than commercial airlines. The process is actually simpler, but it is not as obvious. Follow me."

CHAPTER 97

During the flight from LaGuardia to Burke Lakefront, we find that we have very little to discuss. We all pretty much agree that we should let Christie's sell the Red Diamonds. I think a lot of that agreement comes from the fact that we don't know of any other good alternatives.

I know that as executer of Uncle John's will, how I deal with the Red Diamonds is my decision, but I feel that I need to involve George and Beth. I also need to get Devin working on finding us a good tax attorney; one who has worked with offshore accounts.

I pull out my cell phone. As I expected, no bars. We're thirty thousand feet above the cell towers. But I wonder.

I get out of my seat, and walk forward to talk to our flight attendant. "Hi Susan. I have a question."

"Yes, sir?"

"Peter, please. I need to make some phone calls. As I expected, my cell phone has no signal. But I have been on a few commercial flights that had telephones built into the seatbacks. Do you have anything like that?"

"We do. See the lounge aft of the standard seating area?"

"I do."

"If you go back and have a seat, I'll bring you a phone."

I stop to tell Kate what I'm doing and invite her to join me. She declines; I go aft to the lounge. The lounge is four beige leather seats surrounding a low circular coffee table. The seats and table are all bolted to the floor. I sit in the seat facing the front of the aircraft. Susan comes back, sets a standard desk phone on the table and plugs it into one of the assortment of jacks located in a small depression in the center of the coffee table. "Thank you. How do I pay for the calls?"

"You don't. Christie's provides the phone as a courtesy to their customers."

"Thank you."

I look up Devin's cell phone number on my cell phone, lift the handset on the desk phone from its cradle and dial his number. It's supper time in Florida; Devin answers with a mouth full of food. "Hello?"

"Hi Devin, it's your dear old dad. Sorry for the call at supper time."

"No problem. Always glad to hear from you. My caller ID says 'Christie's'?"

"I am calling from Christie's Gulfstream somewhere between New York and Cleveland. They flew us all to New York City today to talk to them."

"What is Christie's? Who is all?"

"Christie's Auction House. Your mom, me, Mike, Lauri, Gabe, and Karen."

"Really? Why?"

"Really. I don't want to go into a lot of detail over the phone, but as you know, I'm executer of Uncle John's will. It turns out that he had a safe mounted in the floor of his gun room. There were some very old papers in his safe, and some jewels that Christie's is going to auction off for us."

"I thought they did big stuff like Old Masters and Crown Jewels."

"They do. This *is* big stuff. Over a hundred million dollars' worth of big stuff."

"Huh? We're talking about Uncle John's estate?"

"Yes we are."

"A hundred million dollars?"

"Yes."

"You're not kidding, are you?"

"No, Devin, I am not kidding. I have never been more serious."

"Where did Uncle John get the jewels?"

"I do not want to discuss it over the phone. Do you remember when I called you a few days ago and asked you to recommend a good inheritance attorney?"

"Yeah?"

"Well, now I have a few more requirements for that attorney. He has to be used to dealing with very large inheritances, and he has to be familiar with dealing with money in offshore accounts."

"You're not going to tell me where these jewels came from, or how they came to be in Uncle John's safe, are you?"

"I can't. Not over the phone."

"I get it. I'll work on an attorney."

"Thanks, Devin."

"When do I get the whole story?"

"Just as soon as we're face to face."

* * *

I go through the same conversation with my brother, George. Except I don't ask him to recommend an attorney. I just want to tell him that he stands to inherit one third of over a hundred million dollars and that some of it may be in offshore accounts.

He wants to call his lawyer immediately. "Don't."

"But we've got to start planning. We…"

"George, stop. You don't know the details. Before you talk to anybody, you have to know the whole story."

"So tell me the whole story."

"I can't. Not on the phone. Can you drive up tomorrow?"

"If I have to, yes. I guess so."

"You have to. As soon as I get off the phone with you, I am going to call Beth. She will want to drive up from Columbus. If you can both get here in the early afternoon, we can all sit down together."

"Okay, Pete; I'll be there. Can I bring Carol?"

"Sure. I will call you back after I talk to Beth."

* * *

I go through it one more time with Beth. She is an attorney for the State of Ohio. Her reaction is as I expected. "I need to know the whole story. I'll take tomorrow off. Expect me at your place a little after noon."

I call George back to tell him Beth's plans. He agrees to be at the Lakehouse shortly after noon tomorrow.

* * *

I go back to my seat next to Kate. I explain that I talked to Devin, George, and Beth. Devin will be finding us a good inheritance/tax/offshore attorney; just in case we want a second opinion. And George and Beth will be at the Lakehouse early tomorrow afternoon.

"Are they staying?"

"I doubt it. Let me go fill the gang in on what is happening."

We're in Row 2. Mike and Lauri are in Row 3, and Gabe and Karen are in Row 4. I scrunch down in the aisle between Rows 3 and 4. "Hey guys, I have an update."

They all lean toward me so they can hear me better. "I talked to Devin. I didn't tell him much beyond the fact that Uncle John's estate is going to probably be over a hundred million dollars. He's going to look for a good inheritance/tax/offshore attorney just in case we don't like Christie's."

They all nod. "I also talked to my brother and my sister. They are both going to be at the Lakehouse tomorrow afternoon."

More nods. "Remind me. When are you guys leaving?"

Gabe answers first. "We have reservations for noon tomorrow. I'm hoping to leave for the airport about nine am. Can somebody take us to the airport?"

Mike answers. "We can. Our return tickets are open ended. We can leave anytime, but we're thinking day after tomorrow."

My turn. "I didn't think you could buy a ticket with an open return anymore."

Mike smiles. "*You* can't."

CHAPTER 98

The gang is up at seven and finishing their breakfast at eight thirty. Somewhat begrudgingly, I'm up and having breakfast with them. I'm glad that Mike and Lauri are taking Gabe and Karen to the airport.

At nine o'clock, Gabe and Karen are all packed and ready to go. As we say our goodbyes, I grab a moment with Gabe. "I wish I could say it's been fun. Interesting, maybe. Exciting, definitely. Fun, not so much. Thanks for coming. I am glad that you are involved."

"I wouldn't have missed it for anything. Not even a hundred million dollars..."

I smile and nod. "Call or text when you get in."

"Will do."

"Safe travels."

* * *

Beth pulls in about eleven thirty. Needless to say, she wants to know everything. Immediately. She is in lawyer mode.

She declines coffee. I show her the photos of the Red Diamonds that Kate took.

She is silent. And that takes a lot. After a good two minutes of just looking at the photos, she looks at me. "These are diamonds? Red diamonds?"

"Yes and yes. Red diamonds are very rare."

"It's hard to get a feel for how big they are. They are unusual cuts."

"They are very old – late seventeenth century. The big one is called a Peruzzi cut; it weighs in at fifty carats. The six smaller ones are Mazarin cut; they weigh about ten carats each."

"Am I right in thinking that that is large?"

"The Hope Diamond is forty-five carats. So yes, that is large. As I told you on the phone, we took them to Christie's yesterday. Christie's expects them to bring about two million dollars a carat at auction."

She turns a little pale as she does the math. "Oh my God."

Then she asks the question that I knew was coming. "Where did Uncle John get them? Where did they come from?"

"I'll answer that when George gets here. In the meantime, you need to read this letter. I found it and some other old documents in Uncle John's safe." I give her a copy of what I have started to call the cover letter.

"He had a safe?"

"Yes. A floor safe in his gun room."

"His gun room?"

"He had a secret room in his basement. It housed his collection of guns. Only Kate and I knew about it. Please read the letter."

She's not happy, but she starts to read.

* * *

She's about halfway through the letter when the doorbell rings. It's George and his wife, Carol.

"Hi guys, glad you could come. Gabe and Karen had to leave, but Mike and Lauri and Beth are here. Come on downstairs."

After hellos all around, George comes over to the desk where I'm sitting. "What is this all about?"

I show him and Carol the photos that Kate took. And I repeat almost exactly the conversation I had with Beth.

By the time we get to the "Where did Uncle John get them?" question, Beth has finished the cover letter. "Beth, can you please let George and Carol read the letter?"

While they are reading, I get the folder with the other old documents. And a diet Pepsi.

When they have finished reading, I ask everyone to gather round our large downstairs dining table. I sit at the head of the table. I ask if anybody wants pop or water or coffee.

"Some of you know all of this tale; some of you only a little. It's important that you all know the entire story. The truth about the Red Diamonds"

I read them Oleksandr's letter. I lay a copy of his original map on the table, and I place the English version on top of it. "We got help from a Ukrainian Orthodox Priest and some of his old parishioners; they translated old Ukrainian into English for us."

I read Mitri's letter to them. "Mike and Lauri and Kate and I went to Venice. We found Mitri's map. We had Father Pataki's old parishioners translate the notes for us."

Beth interrupts. "So that's why you guys went to Europe."

Mike answers her. "Yep."

I continue. "Mike and I went to Ukraine. We went west to Velykyi Bereznyi. We followed the maps and found the Red Diamonds."

George just shakes his head. "This sounds like an Indiana Jones movie."

"Doesn't it though? Next comes one of the scarier parts: we smuggled the Red Diamonds out of Ukraine and into Italy hidden in matryoshka dolls. And we almost got caught. For a while we didn't know if we were going to get imprisoned or shot.

Anyway, in Italy, we mounted the Red Diamonds in a costume jewelry pendant and bracelet; Lauri wore them through customs in Italy and the United States."

Kate sums it up. "And so here we sit."

Beth is first to react. "Christie's is going to auction them off? What happens to the proceeds? You said something about offshore accounts?"

"Christie's is thinking about a private offshore auction. They are afraid that if we go public, the Russians may try to repatriate the Red Diamonds. They *were* part of the Imperial Russian Crown Jewels after all."

Beth continues. "That makes sense. And it is also a little scary. The Russians don't play nice sometimes."

Everybody is listening intently to our conversation. "Uncle John's will says that all of his possessions are to be auctioned off within ninety days of his death. The proceeds are to be split three ways: Beth, George, and me. I figure that he had the maps; without the maps we wouldn't have the Red Diamonds; the proceeds from their auction should be split as the will states."

"I don't know that that is fair to Mike and Lauri. They took a huge chance going after the diamonds."

"I kind of agree, but I don't know how else to do it."

"Had you gotten caught, the four of you could sitting in jail right now. In the US, or in Italy, or worse yet, in Ukraine."

"Believe me, we thought of that constantly as we smuggled the diamonds from Ukraine to here."

There are murmurs of agreement. "We have time to figure that out. Now that you all know the real story, there is one part of it that we must hide from everybody – forever. We cannot admit smuggling the diamonds into the United States, or we could still wind up in jail."

Beth interjects a comment. "I agree with *that*."

"I told Christie's that I found the diamonds under a false bottom in Uncle John's safe. I told them that we went to Italy and Ukraine to try to figure out how the diamonds got here. It is a little weak, but it is our story."

Kate can't resist. "And we're stickin' to it."

"And that's all I have to say about that."

That breaks the mood of seriousness and impending doom that talking about jail fostered. The meeting is over. People start talking to each other about details of the story.

CHAPTER 99

About two thirty, our home landline phone rings. The phone's Caller ID says PRIVATE NUMBER. Probably a telemarketer. I lift the handset from the cradle and set it back down. This is not a good time for telemarketers. Almost immediately the landline starts to ring again. I lift the handset from the cradle and set it back down again. My cell phone dings; incoming text. It's Gabe; the text reads, "Dad, answer your landline."

The landline phone rings again. This is weird. I answer it. "Hello?"

"It's Gabe."

"Are you guys home already?"

"No. We are in a TSA office at BWI – Baltimore Washington International. Put me on speaker; everyone needs to hear what I have to say."

I call everybody over. "It is Gabe."

Then hit the Speaker button. "What's wrong?"

"They know, Dad. They know."

"Who knows? What do they know?"

"The feds know all about the Red Diamonds. I'm sitting here with Leonard Greer, Undersecretary of State for Eastern European Affairs, Wesley Harper, FBI Assistant Director for Europe, John

Walker, CIA Agent in Charge for Russia, and last but not least Arkady Vasiliev, Rezident at the Russian Embassy in Washington."

I feel the blood drain from my face. I feel a little dizzy. "What do they know? What do they want?"

"They have been tracking you and Mike since you contacted Father Pataki. Something one of you did or said or texted or emailed tripped a red flag in some NSA supercomputer buried somewhere underground."

"Are you sure?"

His voice has a tinge of panic in it. "They have played us recordings of your conversations. They have shown us photos of you in Venice, in Kiev, and in Velykyi Bereznyi. They told me how you smuggled the Red Diamonds out of Ukraine and into the United States. Dad, they've got us."

I've never heard Gabe sound scared before. But he is scared. I look around at my family. They are all badly shaken. And me? I'm sure Gabe can hear the fear in my voice. "Now what? What do they want?"

"The diamonds."

"What? What about…"

"Russia demands that they have the Red Diamonds back. They consider them to be part of the Imperial Russian Crown Jewels. They want to repatriate them. Our government agrees with the Russian demand."

"But…"

"*Listen* to me! They want to do this quietly and quickly. They want no publicity. They don't want an incident with the Ukrainian Government."

"If we went public…"

"No, Dad. Don't even *think* about it. Do you have any idea of how many laws you have broken in how many countries? They do. They read us the list. We could all go to prison."

"I see."

"This group of gentlemen is going to visit you tomorrow afternoon. They're going to make you an offer. I hate to sound like a cliché, but it is 'an offer you can't refuse.' I know the offer, but they won't let me tell you. Listen to them."

"Do I have any choice?"

"No. Not really. Oh, Dad, one other thing. They know who is at the Lakehouse. You have been under constant surveillance. They've asked that all of your 'visitors' stay until tomorrow afternoon."

"Are you and Karen okay, Gabe?"

"Shaken, but okay, Dad."

"Tell them we'll be waiting for them."

"They can all hear. You're on speaker."

"Call me when you're out of there."

"Okay, Dad. 'Bye."

I hang up. Everyone is looking at me. "Don't look at me. I am out of ideas. All of our work just became a gigantic waste of time."

Kate comes over to me. I stand. We hug. I look at her. "I'm sorry."

"For what?"

"For wasting a year on a folly."

"You didn't waste a year. It was a wonderful adventure."

"Yeah. Right."

CHAPTER 100

Last night was hard for all of us. We could do nothing but wait. There was little to talk about. We watched TV for a while. We tried playing dominos for a while, but our hearts weren't in it. Beth spent some time looking over the books in the library. George and Carol went home to take care of their cats and dogs. They promised to be back by noon today.

Karen called on her cell phone as they were driving home from the airport. She was shaken by this. I tried to ask her questions about their experience, but she wouldn't tell me anything. "Dad, I know they have my phone – all of our phones – tapped. They told me not to tell you anything. They said to tell you to wait until tomorrow. They said they will answer your questions. I'm afraid, Dad."

* * *

So we're waiting. George and Carol got back just before noon. I'm sitting in the library; from here I can monitor the street outside. We live on a dead end street in a small gated community, so there is virtually no traffic. I cannot see the gate from here, but I can see most of the street that leads up to the Lakehouse. The library is adjacent to the front door, so I can also answer the gate intercom and buzz people in from here.

Four unmarked black Chevy Suburbans come down the street and fill up our driveway. I don't know how they got past the gate. I don't think I want to ask.

The four drivers stay in their cars. The four front seat passengers get out, open the four passenger-side rear doors, and allow four gentlemen to get out. The door openers stay with the Suburbans. The four back-seat passengers walk up the sidewalk to the front door.

One of them rings the bell. I move from the library to the entrance hall and I open the door.

The bell ringer smiles and holds out his hand. "Good afternoon, I am Leonard Greer, Undersecretary of State for Eastern European Affairs. I assume that you are Peter Bradovich."

We shake hands. "Yes, I am."

"I'm glad to meet you. May we come in?"

I step aside. "Yes. Of course."

He comes in to the foyer. The next gentleman steps up to the threshold. "Wesley Harper, FBI Assistant Director for Europe."

We shake hands. "Peter Bradovich."

Next comes, "John Walker, CIA Agent in Charge for Russia."

And finally, "Arkady Vasiliev, Rezident at the Russian Embassy in Washington."

I close the door behind the Russian. "Everybody is downstairs. Follow me, please."

I walk them to the stairs going down. They stop for a moment to admire the view of Lake Erie through the twenty-five-foot-high windows in the cathedral ceilinged great room. The Russian is the only one to speak. "Your view is very beautiful." He looks up at the loft overlooking the great room. "Your home is very beautiful, as well."

"Thank you. This way please."

They follow me downstairs. Everyone is sitting at the large dining table. We have planned the seating. The chair at the head of the table is empty, and there are four empty chairs at the far end of the table.

I stand behind the chair at the head of the table. Our visitors move to stand behind the four empty chairs. "I am going to ask that everybody introduce themselves. Mike will you start, please? We will just go around the table."

Mike stands. "Mike Bradovich, Peter's oldest son."

He sits, and Lauri stands. "Lauri Bradovich, Mike's wife."

We go around the table. Kate is last.

When she is seated, I look at Leonard Greer. "You traveled here to talk to us. Who is your spokesman?"

I guessed right. Greer stands and moves to the foot of the table. "I'll keep this as brief as possible. First of all, you have our condolences on the loss of your family patriarch, John Bradovich."

I speak for the Bradoviches. "Thank you."

"We know that you found a number of very old letters, maps, and other documents in John Bradovich's floor safe. We would like to make archival quality copies of those documents, if possible."

"We can arrange that."

"We know that after you translated the map into English, four of you went to Venice, where you found the second map. We know that you, Peter, went with your son, Michael, to Velykyi Bereznyi, where you followed the maps, and found what you have been referring to as the Red Diamonds."

"May I ask how you 'know' all of this?"

"That is not important. To continue, we know that you hid the Red Diamonds in some matryoshka dolls, and smuggled them out of Ukraine and into Italy. We also know that you almost lost them at Ukrainian Customs."

Greer pauses. "Go on with your story, please."

"In Venice, you mounted the Red Diamonds in some quite inexpensive costume jewelry. You then smuggled the Red Diamonds into the United States in a rather brazen way. Lauri actually wore the jewelry through Italian and American Customs."

"That's quite a story."

"Yesterday you took the Red Diamonds to Christie's in New York. They are currently at Christie's while they plan a private auction."

"I am certain that the two attorneys in our family would tell me not to admit to anything. But assuming that these Red Diamonds exist, why are you here? What do you want?"

"Before I answer that may we take a short break. It's a long ride from the Cleveland Airport."

"Of course. There is a bathroom right on the other side of the summer kitchen. There is another upstairs by the front door."

"Thank you."

The four of them slide their chairs back and head for bathrooms."

* * *

As they come back, I offer them coffee. Three of them accept the offer. Vasiliev declines coffee, but accepts a Diet Pepsi.

When everybody is seated again, I repeat my questions. "As I asked before our little break, assuming you're your story is true, and I'm not admitting that it is, why are you here? What do you want?"

"We who represent your American government, want nothing other than to facilitate the request of the Russian government."

Vasiliev stands. "The Red Diamonds are part of the Imperial Russian Crown Jewels. They were lost during the Revolution and the World War that followed. I am here to repatriate them."

"You expect us to just give them to you?"

"No. No. You and your son worked very hard to recover the Red Diamonds. Had you not done that, they would still be buried in the Carpathian Mountains. You got them out of Ukraine. They certainly would not have allowed that if they had known. You and your family deserve to be rewarded.

"Go on."

"In exchange for the Red Diamonds, we will deposit into the account of your choosing, fifty million US dollars."

Kate gasps.

Vasiliev continues. "Though they had nothing to do with the recovery of the Red Diamonds, we will deposit into the accounts of your siblings George Bradovich and Beth Bradovich, five million US dollars. We will also deposit into the accounts of each of your children, one million US dollars."

"That is patently unfair to Mike. Without him the diamonds would still be lost. He deserves more. Much more."

Vasiliev pauses. He looks briefly at Greer. Then he continues." You are correct. He will receive twenty-five million US dollars."

Vasiliev sits down.

Another visitor stands up. "I am Assistant FBI Director Wesley Harper. The US government has decided that these payments are neither earned income nor investment income. None of you will be liable for any income tax or other taxes on these payments."

He sits down. Greer stands. "You should know that the IRS is aware of this offer. They have agreed that this is not taxable income for any of you. They have also indicated that should we not reach an agreement, every member of Bradovich family will be flagged for tax audits every year for the last ten years, and for every year in the foreseeable future."

"I see. When must we give you an answer?"

"Today."

"Guys, let's go up to the library. I'm not making this decision by myself."

* * *

"Please close the door, Kate."

Mike starts the discussion. "Dad, we're looking at almost a hundred million tax free dollars. I'm not sure we would make out that well with an auction at Christie's."

"I agree. Any other thoughts."

Lauri puts up her hand. "How do we know they'll live up to the deal?"

Beth answers. "We want this in writing. We want it signed by the four of them."

Lauri adds her two cents. "We want it signed by the President and the Premier."

George looks a Beth. "Will they do that?"

Beth ends the discussion. "For several hundred million dollars. For the Red Diamonds, You betcha!"

* * *

We go back down stairs. I look at Greer. "You've got a deal."

EPILOG

It has been six months since we accepted the deal, and gave the Red Diamonds to Russia.

So what do you do with $50,000,000? We didn't know what else to do, so we paid off the house; that left $49,900,000. Then we paid off all of our other debts: cars, boat, credit cards, etc.; that left $49,870,000. Though we have always been generous in our giving, I've never bought into the Christian concept of tithing. But giving ten percent of our wind fall to our favorite charities felt like the right thing to do. We had loads of fun presenting those checks. That leaves $44,870,000.

Now what? We just don't know. Our lifestyle hasn't really changed much. We've both kept our jobs until we figure out what we want to do with the rest of our lives.

Both Kate and I work out of home offices. She works for a Fortune 100 industrial distributer; I work for a small engineering consulting company. The Lakehouse works perfectly for us. My desk is up in the loft and Kate's is down on the lower level. We meet in the middle for lunch. We both have views of Lake Erie from our desks. It's getting to be near Christmas. The lake is not frozen yet, but it looks like it will start to freeze soon. There is snow on the beach and the small waves hitting the breakwater are leaving icicles.

It's about two in the afternoon and I'm only halfheartedly working. My mind keeps wandering back to the events of six months ago.

Our home phone rings. I usually check the Caller ID and wait for Kate to answer it. She is the more social of us, and most of the calls are for her. The Caller ID says PRIVATE NUMBER. Telemarketer? I answer. "Merry Christmas." A slightly accented female voice responds. "Hello. Please wait for a call from Vadim Vadimovich Lazarev, Chief of Station of the Embassy of the Russian Federation."

I buzz Kate on our intercom. "Pick up the home phone. I'm on hold for a call from the Chief of Station of the Russian Embassy."

We wait.

"Mr. Bradovich, this is Vadim Lazarev. How are you this afternoon?"

"Good?"

"I want to thank you again for returning the Red Diamonds to their home."

"You are welcome?"

"We are building a special place in the Armory Museum in the Kremlin for the Red Diamonds."

"Oh?"

"The display will be opened to the public in the spring."

"Why are you telling me all of this?"

"It is because of you that the Red Diamonds are back where they belong. We would like you and your wife to be present for the Grand Opening."